A Fashionably FRENCH MURDER

Kensington Books by Colleen Cambridge

The Phyllida Bright mystery series

Murder at Mallowan Hall

A Trace of Poison

Murder by Invitation Only

Murder Takes the Stage

Two Truths & A Murder

An American in Paris mystery series

Mastering the Art of French Murder

A Murder Most French

A Fashionably French Murder

A Fashionably
FRENCH
MURDER

Colleen Cambridge

KENSINGTON
PUBLISHING CORP.

kensingtonbooks.com

KENSINGTON BOOKS are published by

Kensington Publishing Corp.
900 Third Avenue
New York, NY 10022

Copyright © 2025 by Colleen Gleason

All Kensington titles, imprints and distributed lines are available at special quantity discounts for bulk purchases for sales promotion, premiums, fund-raising, educational or institutional use. Special book excerpts or customized printings can also be created to fit specific needs. For details, write or phone the office of the Kensington Special Sales Manager: Kensington Publishing Corp., 900 Third Avenue, New York, NY, 10022. Attn. Special Sales Department. Phone: 1-800-221-2647.

KENSINGTON and the K with book logo Reg. US Pat & TM Off.

Library of Congress Control Number: 2024951807

ISBN: 978-1-4967-5119-5

First Kensington Hardcover Edition: May 2025

ISBN: 978-1-4967-5121-8 (ebook)

10 9 8 7 6 5 4 3 2 1

Printed in the United States of America

The authorized representative in the EU for product safety and compliance
is eucomply OU, Parnu mnt 139b-14, Apt 123
Tallinn, Berlin 11317, hello@eucompliancepartner.com

A Note from the Author

Although Julia Child lived at 81 rue de l'Université in Paris in 1950, and she did attend at least one fashion show, she never witnessed or was involved in a murder at any haute couture house . . . or anywhere. Nor was Christian Dior ever accused of murder (as far as the author knows!).

Thus, Tabitha Knight, her "messieurs," and the deadly occurrences in this book are complete figments of the author's imagination.

CHAPTER 1

Paris
February 1950

"*I*T'S THE *EASIEST* THING YOU'LL EVER MAKE," JULIA ASSURED ME gaily. "Just plop it all in a pot and let it cook."

I eyed her suspiciously. Something that was easy for Julia Child to cook was not necessarily easy for *me* to cook.

"I swear it!" she said, laughing, her eyes dancing as she wiped her hands on her apron, then reached for an onion.

"So you're telling me that to make this soup, all I have to do is boil everything?" I looked up from my second to last bite of potato leek soup, still highly suspicious. There was no way something this creamy and aromatic could be that easy to make.

Julia winced visibly. "Now, Tabitha, I didn't say a *thing* about boiling. You're going to peel and cut up the potatoes into chunks—and it doesn't matter if they look like wrinkly old men, as they tend to do this time of year—then slice the leeks and add all of it to the pot. A little salt and pepper, too, of course. Just barely cover it all with water and then you're just going to let it *simmer.* You need to be *delicate* but firm with those little lovelies."

"Delicate but firm? I'm not disciplining them, Julia."

She laughed heartily. "You just let those chunks and slices mingle nicely in a gentle, *quiet* bubble bath. They'll sort of dance together—not like the bunny hop," she added quickly with a laugh, "but more like a waltz. We want our potatoes and leeks to be *genteel* and *proper* when they're simmering—*simmering*, Tabs, not boiling and hopping about—and then when they're nice and soft, you blend them together."

"Wait." I held up a hand . . . and then reached for a piece of baguette to drag through the last bit of soup in my bowl. "I have to blend them? In a blender?"

"Of course, dearie. How else do you think it gets all smooth and creamy?" She patted me on the arm. "You can't mess it up, Tabs. I promise. And it's so *versatile*! Why, you can serve it cold—which of course we're not going to do in the dead of *winter*—and you can add chicken to it. Or cream—which makes it even *more* delectable. And chives, of course. It's really quite the simplest thing you'll *ever* make."

I rolled my eyes and stuffed the last bite of soup-drenched bread into my mouth. "If you say so." Did my *grand-père*'s kitchen even have a blender?

We were sitting in the tiny kitchen at Roo de Loo—the nickname Julia and her husband Paul had given their apartment on rue de l'Université, located on the Left Bank in Paris. It was early February and the sun was shining brightly through the window, even though it was crisp and cold outside.

I was anxious for winter to end, to get back to a warmer, more pleasant season . . . although winter here had its charms too. After all, it was *Paris*. How could it not be charming even on cold, bitter, spitting-weather days? Even when you had to hold your breath against the fumes and smoke that seemed to linger near the walks, and when the ear-splitting honks of the heavy traffic broke into your day, it was still *Paris*.

"What time do we have to leave today?" I asked, wondering if there was any soup left in the pot. It was still sitting on the stove, so there was hope.

I could get up and look, but the kitchen was tiny and Julia was in a constant state of movement in the small space. If she wasn't checking inside the oven, she was peeling or chopping or grating something, or stirring or measuring or tasting. She was like a whirling dervish, and I didn't want to get into her path—especially when she was holding a knife.

"Oh, goodness, I'd almost lost track of time," Julia said, pausing from the rat-a-tat-tat chopping of the onion as she stood at the counter. "We're meeting Charmaine at Maison Lannet at four thirty."

"It's almost three thirty now," I pointed out. "I should go home and change. And put my things in the icebox." I looked at my market bag, filled with turnips, parsnips, beets, eggs. I also had a filet of sole at home, which I had no real idea what I was going to do with, but this morning when we were at the market, Julia had raved over how sweet and fresh the sole smelled, and I'd been inspired to buy it.

Julia sighed. "I wish we had an icebox. I don't know *what* I'm going to do when the weather gets warm again—although I'll certainly enjoy the options at the market better." She gave a jaundiced glance at the sad-looking onion she was preparing. "I simply *can't wait* for spring peas, and tomatoes, and strawberries, and asparagus, and, oh, *everything* to come back in! And lettuce! My kingdom for some fresh lettuce or a delicate raspberry!" She clutched the remaining half of the onion to her chest and looked as if she were onstage, singing for her supper.

She was, of course, exaggerating. There were places to buy some of those items even in February—such as the huge market Les Halles in Le Marais—but that required a special trip much farther than we had time for most days. Besides, although they might be available, the fresh raspberries and baby lettuce shipped in from Algeria were expensive in February.

Smiling at Julia's antics, I rose, giving the soup pot a look of reluctant goodbye. It wasn't as if I hadn't eaten enough. It was just that it was so good.

Even though I was only going across the street, I pulled on a hat and buttoned my coat. Riding down in the elevator from the second floor of Julia and Paul's flat—where her kitchen was located—I couldn't help but remember back in December when I had ridden down in the same elevator with a woman who was later found dead in the cellar of this very building.

That incident had propelled me into a fascination with crime solving and murder investigations—to Julia's delight, and the dismay of one Inspecteur Étienne Merveille.

It wasn't that I was *looking* for opportunities to investigate murders. They just seemed to find me—rather like Agatha Christie's Miss Marple (although I was *far, far* too young to be compared with Jane Marple). And since my father is a police detective back home in the suburb of Detroit where I'd grown up and bugged him for stories about his work, it seemed a natural development. I'd even asked him to send me books or industry publications that would help me to learn more about the process—without actually telling him why, of course.

I might have given him the impression I was going to try writing my own murder mystery.

Not long after the first incident with the dead woman at Julia's apartment building I'd become involved with a second set of murders . . . ones that had hit a little too close to home. I still had nightmares over how close I'd come to losing my wonderful life with Grand-père and Oncle Rafe.

I let myself into the house on rue de l'Université where I lived with them—my two messieurs, Grand-père and Oncle Rafe—and their pair of pets.

House is really a misnomer, for the edifice in which we lived was more like a mansion. It was made from the distinctive Lutetian limestone found throughout Paris, with ornate wrought iron grilles in front of every one of the many windows and gabled dormers in the Mansard-style roof. There were three spacious floors, each with a full bathroom on its level, a large *cuisine* that made Julia moan with envy, and a private courtyard in the back. The ceiling of the front foyer was three stories high and its floor was white-and-black marble with rose-pink decorative touches. The rest of the house was just as fancy and well-appointed.

It was truly a *grande maison*, and I could hardly believe I lived there, rent-free, with two of the most interesting, loving, and mysterious men I've ever known.

My arrival was heralded by the ecstatic yipping and bouncing from Oncle Rafe's little dog, Oscar Wilde, who'd raced to the top of the first-floor stairs at the sound of my entrance. I was still getting used to the fact that in Paris, as throughout Europe, what we Americans think of as the second floor is known as the first floor. I had entered on the ground floor and Monsieur Wilde was looking down at me, yapping and yipping for all he was worth.

He had no intention of running down the stairs to greet me—that would take too much energy, and he might have to make his way back up, which would require even more exertion on his part. He merely wanted to inform me that he would graciously accept a treat, and would I please give it to him as soon as possible.

As M. Wilde yipped down at me, his nemesis and partner in crime, Madame X, made her appearance. She was a sleek black cat outfitted in a collar of real diamonds. She was far too lady-like to join M. Wilde in creating a ruckus, but she certainly would deign to accept a tiny catnip biscuit as my tax for entering her domain.

I pulled off my boots, sniffing the air hopefully. No, no one had magically decided to cook something for dinner yet. Ugh.

"Tabi! Is that you?" called Grand-père.

"I certainly hope so," I called back, tossing my coat and hat on a chair in the foyer. There was no need to hang them, as I'd be leaving soon enough. "Who else has a key? I'll be right there after I put away the things from the market."

When I dashed up the stairs a few minutes later, M. Wilde greeted me with the same alacrity as before. I reached down to pat his little head, crooning at him as he sproinged up and down on two back feet to make sure I noticed him. He had the softest, silkiest fur and ears that were far too big for his little noggin. They were broad and perked up, with long hair that flowed almost to the floor. Oncle Rafe combed him thoroughly each day to keep the mats at bay.

"All right you little beastie," I said, plucking a biscuit the size of my pinkie nail from the jar next to Oncle Rafe's chair. Oscar Wilde took it eagerly, nearly nipping off the tip of my fingers with his teeny teeth. He bolted off to eat it in peace.

"Well, and how is Madame Child today?" asked Grand-père as I bent to kiss Oncle Rafe on his warm cheek, just above the beard.

I rolled my eyes affectionately and navigated over to my grandfather's armchair to kiss him as well. He smelled of some sort of spicy male aftershave mingled with tobacco smoke.

My messieurs had been the recipients of delicious meals from Julia many times, especially over the last few months when I'd been embroiled in those murder investigations, and I knew Grand-père was angling to see whether Julia had sent anything home for them today.

I didn't really blame him. I was not very good in the kitchen, and Grand-père and Oncle Rafe (and I) had suffered through too many meals that I'd prepared since their housekeeper and cook had left to take care of her ailing mother several months ago.

"Julia is just fine. She's going to show me how to make potato leek soup," I said. "I had hers today and it was delicious."

"Ah," said Oncle Rafe, visibly disappointed that I hadn't schlepped some of the soup home for them. Then, always the gentleman, he rallied. "I'm certain it will be very delicious, *ma petite*."

"What's all this?" I asked, just noticing papers—which looked like blueprints—and other drawings all over the table.

The first floor salon was where Grand-père and Oncle Rafe spent most of their days. I wasn't certain of their exact ages, but they had to be somewhere around eighty, give or take, and in the winter they preferred to sit wrapped up in blankets between the fireplace and a radiator. They each had a cozy armchair with a table next to it, and a large table in between the pair and a small sofa.

The salon was comfortable and had everything they needed: a full stock of wine and spirits at the bar cabinet, treats for their respective pets, comfortable chairs, large windows, and a doorway that led into Grand-père's greenhouse, which was built on top of the portico in the courtyard. There were also a bathroom and bedrooms just down the hall, so neither of them had to use the stairs unless they wanted to. I preferred that they didn't, especially my *grand-père*, who sometimes appeared more frail than I liked.

Even so, he still had a full head of thick, white hair, which he combed neatly every day after adding the slightest bit of vetiver-scented oil. His face was very handsome and always clean-shaven, with smooth, taut, fair skin that gave me hope for a family tendency to age well. He was tall and slender and, I imagined, had been very rakish in his younger years.

Oncle Rafe, who was not any sort of blood relation to me at all, was a study in contrasts to my grandfather. He was either naturally bald or kept his head shaved to appear that way, but he grew a full, neat mustache and beard. They were still surprisingly dark but grizzled, with the white beginning to take over near the corners of his mouth. More solid than Grand-père but shorter, Rafe had olive skin, thick, slashing brows, and deep brown eyes that seemed to miss nothing.

"But these are the plans for Maison de Verre, of course," said Grand-père.

"You're really doing it?" I asked, feeling a spark of excitement. "Reopening the restaurant?"

Maison de Verre had been a favorite eatery of theirs until the German Occupation when the Nazis came in and took over the establishment. The place eventually closed during the war. I'd learned about—and, let's be honest, broken into—the restaurant during the incidents of the poisoned wine last month. I'd heard my messieurs talk about buying the building and reopening it, but I hadn't realized it was actually going to happen.

"*Oui.*" Oncle Rafe smiled as he lit a cigarette. It was the small brown variety that he preferred, with a spicy scent that lingered in the smoke. "We are meeting with the interior designer tomorrow—Monsieur Grandpierre, who has done so much of the work for Monsieur Dior at his atelier, you see, that we must have him and his people. And so of course your *grand-père* and I must debate over the decor. Of course *he* would like all of the soft paisleys and the pastel silks—"

"And *he* would like the dark and gloomy," retorted Grand-père, stabbing into the air with his own cigarette, his eyes flashing.

"I see," I said.

"But it *must* be the colors of night, Maurice, don't you see? It is Maison de *Verre*. The glass is *everything*! And so it is like the night sky with the glittering stars and the chandeliers lit up—"

"But then one cannot see one's *food*," Grand-père argued. "*Ah*—or *le vin*, if it is dark like the night sky. And how will you see the color of the Bordeaux or that the pink of the steak is perfect if it is like night?"

"I am not suggesting it would be *dark*," Oncle Rafe said. "Only that it not be like the fuss and frill of a woman's boudoir!"

I struggled not to giggle. They both appeared so intensely self-righteous about their divergent ideas. Even their respective pets were taking notice, watching them carefully as if prepared to jump out of the way should a more physical altercation occur. "I'm certain you'll figure it out with the help of the decorators and find a happy medium."

"*Oui, oui,* of course," said Grand-père, but he continued to give his companion a dark look, and Oncle Rafe sneered right back at him.

"Well, I'll leave you to your . . . er . . . discussions," I said. "I've got to change into something a little more respectable."

"And where is it you are off to now, *ma mie?*" asked Grand-père, eyeing my long skirt and the ugly, heavy woolen stockings I'd worn under it.

Since I wasn't riding my bicycle through the snow and slush now that I had a snappy little Renault, I didn't dare don the trousers I'd become used to wearing back home during my work at the bomber plant. For, as I'd discovered, trousers were technically only legal for women to wear in Paris if they were riding a bike or a horse.

Thus, for my trip to the market with Julia, I'd bundled up in thick, ungainly stockings, a too-long skirt, and heavy boots—which clearly offended my very Parisian grandfather. However, a woman in trousers tended to offend him even more, which I found amusing since he and Oncle Rafe—by their own admissions—had skirted the law more than once during their lives. And it wasn't as if a police agent was going to arrest me for wearing pants!

"An American friend of Julia and Paul's was looking for a translator for a visit to a fashion atelier. Her daughter is getting married in Paris this summer and she wants to wear haute couture for the wedding, but her French isn't very good. And so I am going as a translator to make certain there aren't any misunderstandings."

Although I'd been born and raised in Michigan, my Parisian mother and grandmother had made certain I was fluent in their native language. Thus, I'd started up a small service since coming here, teaching French to wives and children of some of the expats who worked with Paul Child at the embassy. I'd once almost been hired to tutor a French woman in English, but my services had ultimately been declined because my accent was "too American."

"Ah, yes, that is an excellent idea," said Oncle Rafe as his attention skimmed over my attire. "But you will be there only to translate, *non?*"

I gave him a narrow look. "Are you suggesting I don't have very good fashion sense?"

"Ah, well, Tabi, of course I am not saying such a thing," Oncle Rafe replied, looking a little as if I'd caught him with his hand in the cookie jar.

I continued to look at him severely, even though my lips twitched. "Maybe the restaurant *would* be better off with paisleys and pastels."

My grandfather guffawed and waved his cigarette. "You see, there, Rafe? The girl knows."

"Are you going to Maison Dior, then?" asked Oncle Rafe, likely to distract from the direction the conversation had taken.

"No. I don't think she was able to get an appointment there. But I don't think this will be the only atelier we visit," I said. "There may be other appointments in the future."

"But Monsieur Dior . . . he has completely revitalized the haute couture!" Grand-père spoke with such energy that Oscar Wilde was jolted awake from where he'd settled in Oncle Rafe's lap for a snooze once the argument had waned. "He is brilliant! He has been the revolutionary, for the entire world of haute couture—something Paris has sadly needed since the war."

"I think Madame Lannet was a protégé of Christian Dior," I said. "She has only just opened her own atelier a year ago."

"Hmph." Grand-père didn't seem the least bit satisfied by this information, and I exchanged glances with Oncle Rafe. "But I suppose if her atelier has been accepted by the Chambre Syndicale . . ." His voice trailed off as if to suggest that such an approval might not be enough, in his mind anyway.

I could only shrug. Grand-père scoffed under his breath, exchanging glances with Rafe.

"Well, I must get changed so I don't embarrass my messieurs by entering a fancy atelier in outmoded clothing," I said, giving them both a level look.

"But what is it you'll be making for dinner?" asked Grand-père as I started up the stairs to the second floor.

"I haven't figured that out yet," I called back as I bounded up the steps. "I'll ask Julia for some ideas."

That at least should comfort them.

I grew up in a small suburb of Detroit in the Midwest United States, in a household that, while we were never hand-to-mouth, didn't have a lot of extra money. Even though my mother and grandmother had come to America from Paris after the Great War when my parents got married, they didn't have the time or resources—perhaps not even the interest—to expend on high fashion.

Detroit was a big city, but it wasn't New York or London or Paris, and so exclusive and bespoke fashion was something that was a distant concept for me and everyone I knew. We saw pictures in magazines like *Harper's Bazaar* and *Vogue*, of course, and appreciated them, but most of those frocks and gowns and coats were much more exclusive and certainly far more expensive than anything I or any of my friends could afford.

I bought most of my clothes at Crowley's or Hudson's in Detroit, and they were what the French called *prêt-à-porter*: ready to wear. During the war, no one bought clothes. There were hardly any options because of shortages of fabric and also rationing.

I loved gorgeous gowns and pretty frocks as much as any female, but it wasn't until I arrived in Paris and I was exposed to haute couture that I begin to understand what it actually was: an utterly French entity—not unlike champagne or Roquefort—that was closely regulated by an entity of the government called the Chambre Syndicale de la Haute Couture Parisienne.

An atelier, or workshop, that wanted to be considered haute couture had to meet certain, specific requirements identified by the Chambre Syndicale, including how many employees and workers the designer had. The atelier also had to be located in Paris, and was required to have at least two collections per year with a minimum of pieces in each collection.

I had known Paris was the fashion center of the world—a distinction which Christian Dior had helped to wrest back to the City of Light after the Occupation, during which London and New York had tried to seize the title. I certainly had seen pictures of fancy dresses in magazines and on signs around the city, but never even considered that I would see one in real life, let alone own or even wear one.

Everything I knew about the haute couture houses—or *maisons*—suggested they were exclusive and highbrow. I was glad I was only going along as a translator, not as a potential client.

"Charmaine!" Julia called, waving at a woman walking toward us along the sidewalk of avenue Montaigne.

Charmaine Bauer was an attractive and elegant woman with a beautiful smile. She was tall and slender—not quite as tall as Julia's six feet two or three, but certainly taller than my five feet five. Even beneath her bulky winter coat—fur; possibly mink, trimmed with something else at the collar—I could see that she had a willowy physique and knew any style of gown would look flattering on her. She wore a fantastic matching fur hat that framed a perfectly made-up face with patrician features. Since she had a grown daughter who was getting married, she had to be older than both Julia and me; probably in her fifties, but she appeared much younger.

"Bonjour!" said Charmaine as she approached us. She enfolded Julia in a boisterous hug complete with kisses on each cheek, then turned to me with a smile. The tip of her rounded nose was pink from the chill. "And you are Tabitha. Thank you very much for coming with me today. I just don't want to make a mistake and get the wrong *dress*! The French speak so fast I can't keep up. And I certainly don't know all their words for clothing and trims and details."

"I'm more than happy to help, Mrs. Bauer," I told her with a smile. "It will be a pleasure."

"Please call me Charmaine," she replied, patting me on the arm. "Mrs. Bauer is what I call my husband's mother and I don't really care to be reminded of her. But I suppose she'll somehow make her way over here for the wedding. That was one of the reasons I encouraged Louise to get married over here, in the hopes that my mother-in-law wouldn't be able to make it." Her genteel laugh created a little puff of mist in the cold air. Then she gave a little shiver and said, "I'm nervous. I don't know why, but I'm *nervous* about buying a *dress*!" There was a lot of Southern in her voice, and I remembered Julia telling me she and her husband were from Richmond, Virginia.

"Oh, it'll be just fine," Julia said, linking arms with Charmaine and then with me. "I went to a fashion show once at one of these places. It was quite a thing. All these people crowded into a room, some of them were sitting but some weren't . . . and then a model just walks in and around and sort of through everyone. You could reach out and *touch* her frock—if you wanted to. There were plenty of people who did, but I didn't *dare!*" She laughed.

"She was a mannequin, not a model," I corrected her with a smile. "Here in Paris, the women who walk around displaying the clothing are called mannequins. And they *wear* the *model* of the design. Like a sample."

"Why, that's completely opposite of back home," Charmaine said, her eyes wide.

"Right. *And* if you use the term *modèle* to refer to an actual person, not the sample of the design . . . well, that actually refers to a someone who poses naked for an artist like a painter," I said. "So that's not the same at all."

We all laughed and Charmaine said, "Now I'm *really* glad you're here, Tabitha. I'd surely make some sort of silly mistake and they'd all laugh at me. And they'd create some ugly, terrible frock but tell me that it's spectacular . . . Oh, I'm being silly, aren't I? Still, I'm glad you're going with me, Tabitha." She still looked a little nervous. "Anyhow, did you buy anything from the fashion show, Julie?"

Julia laughed and shook her head. "I can't fit into anything they make, and even if I could, I'd look like a giraffe in whatever it was. I did find it interesting to watch and there were some *beautiful* clothes. But they'd be absolutely *appalled* if a giantess like me came in to Christian Dior and asked for a frock!" She laughed heartily and easily, for Julia was a woman confident in her own body. Part of that had to do with the strong love and attraction between her and Paul.

"Honestly, the closest I've ever come to haute couture is when I took a hat-making class when I first got to Paris! I was *so bored* . . . but *that* was *tedious!* I'm so glad I've found cooking, otherwise I'd be relegated to *hat-making* and playing *bridge*." Julia gave a little shudder. "Shall we be off, then, ladies?"

"Yes," said Charmaine with a grin. "We don't want to be late to the snooty-too!"

Maison Lannet was located on avenue Montaigne, just down the street from no. 30, where Maison Dior was located, and among most of the other haute couture houses.

We were greeted effusively by an elegant and attractive woman in her forties as we came inside—the lead vendeuse, who introduced herself as Madame Pineau—and we all exchanged equally energetic bonjours. A younger woman appeared to take our coats, and I quickly stuffed my gloves into a pocket as I handed over mine. Fortunately, our hats could remain in place, for whenever I removed any head covering during the winter months, my hair was revealed as a staticky mess that looked like a nimbus around my head.

"Madame Bauer," said Madame Pineau, leading us up the stairs to the first floor, where the salon was located, "if you and your companions would make yourselves comfortable in those chairs. Dorothy will bring *vin,* or *café* if you prefer, for your refreshment. The mannequins will be out shortly to show you some pieces from Madame's collection which might be suitable for a mother-of-the-bride wedding gown."

"Yes, thank you," said Charmaine with a Southern flair to her French. "And will Madame Lannet be joining us soon?" Her grammar was fair but her pronunciation was slightly better.

"Madame Lannet? But, no, of course not, madame." Madame Pineau seemed appalled at the idea. "No, no. She is far too busy to meet with every client, madame. Please accept my apologies. She is the couturier." Her slender eyebrows had risen so high her eyelids lifted as well. "I will be at your service, madame."

Charmaine glanced at me, her cheeks a bit pinker than they had been.

I launched into a smooth explanation about how Madame Bauer had only wished to congratulate Madame Lannet on the success of her recent collection should the couturier have the time to spare, and that we were all looking forward to seeing the models of evening gowns . . . and as many other niceties as I could think of to smooth over the awkward moment.

My flawless French and, likely, the fact that I looked like a Parisian in features and the clothing I'd changed into, with Grand-père's approval (albeit not haute couture), assisted in circumventing any possibility of Madame Pineau treating Charmaine Bauer as if she were an ignorant American. Not that she would be rude—certainly not—but an ignorant American could be taken advantage of in a number of different ways. And, perhaps more likely, snickered about in the back rooms.

Charmaine cast me a grateful look as the vendeuse's initial horror faded and Madame Pineau returned to her warm and charming demeanor. We settled for *le vin* instead of coffee— after all, we were in Paris—and arranged ourselves in the simple white-painted bamboo chairs that had been arranged in a short row in the room. Two dozen or more other chairs were pushed against the wall in neat rows.

I had the opportunity to admire the salon as we sipped our wine. The ceiling was high and lit with chandeliers of blue sea glass and translucent shells. Glazed glass sconces mounted on walls hung with creamy, rippled silk offered more lighting. The floor was a serviceable but highly polished wood, and there were several tables covered by the same silk coverings as the walls. Large vases spilled with silk peonies in pink, cream, and red-tipped white. The faint scent of some delicate, floral perfume lingered in the air. It must have cost a fortune to decorate this place . . . and the taxes must be out of this world.

I had recently learned, to my surprise, that property taxes in Paris were calculated not by the size or location of the property, but by how well and expensively furnished it was. Apparently, in order to circumvent as much taxation as possible, many French people outfitted their public rooms like the salons and parlors beautifully in an effort to impress their visitors, but kept their private areas—bedrooms and personal sitting rooms—quite spare.

Across from the chairs where we sat was the sweep of a staircase with a heavy, gilt balustrade. It was at the top that the first mannequin appeared.

"The Deep," said Madame Pineau, which, I explained to Charmaine in an undertone, was the name of the design.

The Deep was an evening gown of taffeta that shined from cobalt to emerald hues. It flowed and gleamed with every movement. Flowerlike frills danced on the shoulders, and a single wavelike ruffle running down the back of the long skirt evoked the churning sea.

As gorgeous as the gown was, my attention drifted from the dress to the mannequin's personal features—specifically, her hair. It was cropped very short in the back, leaving her nape tantalizingly exposed with the hair cutting sharply across the back of her neck. The front was longer and was arranged in a full, tousled cap around her forehead and temples.

I found myself examining not the details of the gown, but the cut of the young woman's hair. I had been thinking about hacking off all of my wild, unruly mess in hopes of finding a style that looked less girlish and more chic—and was easier to manage. Looking at the woman in the green-blue dress, I was certain I'd found it.

Seeing the mannequin displaying a stunning gown with such panache, working for one of the leading designers in Paris, sporting a short, boyish hairstyle gave me the confidence I needed to want to try it myself. If it was good enough for one of Madame Lannet's mannequins, surely it was good enough for Tabitha Knight.

I elbowed Julia and murmured, "I want to cut my hair like hers."

Her eyes widened and she looked from me to the mannequin and back again as the young woman walked directly in front of us. The mannequin paused, then slowly turned so we could see all the details of the dress were we so inclined to look.

"Yes!" Julia muttered back to me, her eyes dancing as she grasped my wrist in emphatic agreement. "Yes!"

I glanced at Charmaine, sitting on my other side. She seemed to be as entranced by the gown as I was by the mannequin's hair, leaning forward to see every detail.

After another moment, the young woman turned and walked away, for another had appeared at the top of the stairs.

"The Glow," said Madame Pineau.

This gown was a shimmery confection of gold silk fashioned into tiny pleats at the waist, then flowing into a full, rippling skirt. The material was an ethereal sort of fabric, light and airy, and it seemed to have its very own energy.

The front was a low-cut narrow vee, also pleated up and over the shoulders, where it was gathered at the seams. It reminded me a little of a toga, but far more fashionable and elegant. The arms were completely bare, but the mannequin wore black gloves that ended halfway between wrist and elbow. An interesting bit of black sequined detail was sewn onto the top of one shoulder and at the lowest part of the vee in the back. The gown was simple but elegant, and very eye-catching.

There were several other gowns in the collection, but these first two were the ones Charmaine seemed most interested in.

I earned my keep, so to speak, in assisting in a conversation between her and Madame Pineau. Charmaine ultimately decided on The Glow, and arrangements were made for her to come for her first of three fittings.

And then the snag occurred.

"But you are American," said Madame Pineau when Charmaine commented that she was very pleased to be wearing the gown for her daughter's wedding in Paris. The vendeuse seemed appalled and horrified by this realization.

"Yes, of course," Charmaine said, glancing at me for direction. "And what difference does that make?"

"But Madame Lannet has already an agreement for The Glow to be sold to Madame Outhier here in Paris. I'm afraid . . . I am so very sorry, madame, but we cannot proceed."

That was when I understood the situation. I turned to Charmaine to explain in rapid English. "When haute couture pieces are sold, they're exclusive to the buyer. So no one else can buy the same piece and potentially be seen in it. Each designer has their own rules, but there is a definite exclusivity to all of them.

"Madame Pineau assumed since you're American that you would be wearing the gown in America, and that wouldn't conflict with the madame here in Paris. But since you're planning to wear it for your daughter's wedding here, madame cannot sell it to you."

Charmaine gaped at me for a moment. "But that's . . . do you mean they will only make one of these dresses for all of Paris?"

"In all of Europe—including England," I said. "In the case of Madame Lannet's designs, anyway. That's part of what makes it haute couture."

Charmaine stared at me for a moment, then blinked once. "I see. And The Deep?" she said, turning to Madame Pineau. "Is that available for sale here in Paris?"

"I regret to say, madame, that it is not," replied Madame Pineau. She seemed as dismayed as Charmaine. "You see, the collection has been shown for three weeks already, madame. Many orders have already been placed. We have been doing showings every day."

"Is there anything from this collection available for sale here in Paris?" I asked, anticipating Charmaine's next question.

Madame Pineau shook her head sadly. "For America, yes. For Paris, no. I am very sorry, madame."

Charmaine was gracious about the misunderstanding; mostly, I think, because she was still trying to comprehend the idea that only one dress of each style could be sold in a particular geographic area.

There was nothing to do but to take our leave, and now that she realized a sale would not be made, Madame Pineau gently but firmly made it clear that the boutique was past closing time. "It is time to turn off the lights, you see," she said, gesturing to the exit.

"Well, that was a fine mess," Julia said as we walked away from Maison Lannet a few minutes later.

A bit of snow was drifting down and I felt a flake land on my nose. It was after six o'clock and the sun had slipped down behind the city. Streetlamps glowed and cars filled the *rue*. Pedestrians strode along the sidewalk, some with dogs, some in pairs, some simply in a hurry to get somewhere else.

We walked along together, crossing to the other side of avenue Montaigne to a little cafe. We found a table tucked close to the building and under an awning and ordered coffee.

"I simply can't believe it," Charmaine said after the server had brought our *cafés*. "Now what am I going to do?" She looked at me.

"You can try to attend a showing at another atelier and see whether any of their collections have pieces available," I told her, adding a couple of sugar cubes to my drink. "Or you can find a reputable couturier to make you a dress that isn't haute couture. There are plenty of seamstresses in the city who are very skilled and can make something fashionable and beautiful."

"I suppose," Charmaine said unhappily. "But I so wanted something from Madame Lannet. She seems to be the hot new thing, if you know what I mean. People are saying she might even overshadow Dior!"

"I highly doubt that," I said with a smile. "But if she does, it would be wonderful, wouldn't it?"

"You can still have something, as long as you don't wear it in Paris, Charmy," said Julia, patting her on the shoulder.

We laughed at this and I was relieved to see that, although disappointed, Charmaine wasn't going to sulk over the setback.

Protected from the sprinkling of snow by the cafe's awning, we sat and finished our hot beverages and discussed when I would be available to accompany Charmaine to a different appointment. At last, Charmaine bid us bonsoir and gave each of us a friendly hug.

As I rose, I stuck my hands in my pockets to pull out my gloves, but only one was there.

"One of my gloves must have fallen out of my pocket back at the boutique," I said to Julia as we turned to head toward the street where she'd parked. "I'm going to dash back to Maison Lannet and grab it."

"While you're there, you should ask that model—I mean mannequin—where she gets her hair cut," Julia suggested as she began to walk with me back toward Maison Lannet.

I liked that idea, and we picked up our pace. Madame Pineau

had made it clear the boutique was closing and I wanted to get there before everyone was gone.

"I'll wait here," Julia said when we got to the shop and strode up the little walkway that led to the front door. The entrance, flanked by two huge potted boxwoods, was covered by a curved awning that would protect her from the flurries. "No need for both of us to disrupt Madame Pineau."

I cautiously tried the door, and to my surprise, it opened. The foyer was quiet and empty but the lights were still on. The charming little sign hanging discreetly by the door had not yet been turned to CLOSED.

"Bonjour!" I called, stepping inside and expecting Madame Pineau or maybe Dorothy to make an appearance.

I didn't hear any sign of life, so I called again as I walked in. I had seen the direction Dorothy had taken our coats earlier and started off that way, down a short corridor.

"Bonjour!" I called again, just as I noticed a dark blob on the ground a few feet in front of me. It was my missing glove, and I scooped it up.

I felt a little strange poking around inside Maison Lannet without anyone around, but I'd retrieved my glove and that was what I'd come to do.

I'd wanted to see if I could find the mannequin and ask her about her hair stylist, so when I came back out of the back hall, I glanced toward the grand stairway that led upstairs to the salon.

Although it was quiet, there was still a light on at the top of the stairs. I hesitated and called, "Bonjour! Is anyone there?"

Silence.

I stood there, feeling a strange prickle down my spine. Everything was eerily quiet, and yet the lights were still on, as if someone was still here. The front door was unlocked. The sign still read OPEN.

But it felt *wrong*.

Something prodded at me to go upstairs and survey the situation. Maybe it was because of my recent experience with murder. Maybe it was because of my impertinent internal imp, who was a little nosy and curious and impetuous. Maybe it was just because I really wanted the name of the mannequin's hair stylist.

It didn't matter why, but I started climbing up the stairs.

As I ascended, the feeling that something was wrong continued to grow.

And, boy, was I *right.*

CHAPTER 2

I WAS QUICK BUT SILENT GOING UP THE STAIRS. THE URGE TO CALL out had faded away as my sense of foreboding grew.

At the top of the grand, curving stairway was the salon, but it was quiet and empty. My skin still prickled, and I'd come this far, so I climbed up the steps to the second floor.

This time I found myself on a small landing that branched out into an abbreviated hall. Another set of stairs—not nearly as grand and definitely more utilitarian—continued on to the third floor and beyond, where I guessed the workshops were located for the creation of the frocks and gowns.

There were three doors off the small, foyerlike hallway. One to the right and two more to the left. Something drew my attention to the first door on the left, which was ajar. I took a step toward it, surprised by how hesitant I felt.

I'd like to point out that most all of the lights in the boutique were still on. It wasn't as if I was sneaking around in the dark, or even poking into things that had been closed down or locked up for the night. I could see everything; it wasn't as if there were shadows where someone could hide.

But the hair on the back of my neck lifted, and I was compelled to move toward the door that was ajar. I didn't call out anymore.

The very strong smell of some lovely perfume—but far too much of it—wafted to my nose. Now I could see into a wedge of the room. The chamber's walls were mirrored, reflecting the rows of vanity tables and their matching chairs lined up in front of the reflective glass. This must be the *cabine*, where the mannequins dressed, did their hair, and waited before donning and showing the pieces in the collection.

I gingerly pushed the door open a little more, still uncertain why I had such an overwhelming feeling of apprehension . . . and then I saw that one of the chairs had been knocked over from its position in front of a vanity. There were several bottles glinting on the floor. One was smashed—the perfume I smelled.

My heart thumped harder as I peered around the edge of the door, stepping into the room at last.

I immediately spotted the crumpled figure of a woman on the floor. With a little cry, I rushed over and crouched by her side, letting my handbag slide off my arm and onto the floor. At my touch, she gave no sign of life, and it was immediately clear as to why.

A long piece of cream-colored lace had been wrapped around her neck and pulled long and tightly enough to strangle her.

I fell back onto my butt, not so much from surprise as from losing my balance when I tried to bolt to my feet too quickly. My hand landed on something hard. I felt the sharpness of pain from the broken bottle, but I ignored it as I pulled to my feet.

My heart was racing even faster now because it occurred to me that whoever this woman was—I didn't recognize her, but I could see she was too mature to be a mannequin—she hadn't been dead very long. She wasn't cold to the touch, and Julia and Charmaine and I hadn't left the boutique more than twenty minutes ago.

That meant whoever had done this could still be around.

My palms were damp and my senses were on high alert as I fumbled beneath my coat to a dress pocket for my ever-present Swiss Army knife. It would be a small, relatively ineffective weapon, but it was something and it had previously saved my life. Twice.

I stood there for a moment, holding the knife with its largest blade extended. My palm was slick with blood; I'd cut myself on a shard from the perfume bottle. The only sounds were the ramming heartbeat in my ears and the distant call of car horns with the rumble of a bus from the street below.

Silence. Absolute silence in the building around me.

I breathed a little easier and, positioning myself so I faced the doorway, crouched next to the woman again. It wasn't Madame Pineau, although the dead woman might have been around her age. She was dressed in a well-cut dark blue suit and simple but elegant white silk blouse. Large rings glittered on her fingers, and a sparkling brooch was still pinned to her lapel. She was only wearing one shoe; the other was next to the broken perfume bottle. Her hair had come loose during the attack, straggling around her neck. Mindful of possible fingerprints, I pulled on my gloves and carefully pushed some of the hair away. . . .

There were scratch marks on her throat where she'd tried to pull the strangulating lace free, but the strong fabric had cut resolutely into her skin. The lace was so tight that I used the tip of my knife blade to gently lift the noose, revealing that its pattern had been imprinted on her flesh. I shuddered and my throat burned. The poor woman.

It was obvious what had happened—she'd been sitting at one of the vanities and someone had come up behind her, slipped the lace around her neck, and pulled. The ensuing struggle had knocked over the chair and beauty aids.

I closed my eyes and wished her Godspeed to wherever she was going, along with a little prayer that whoever had done this would be found and given justice.

As I pulled to my feet, my eyes were drawn from the room out into the hallway, where a large painting hung directly opposite the door.

It was the portrait of a severe-looking woman in her early fifties. She had light hair and a long, slender, haughty nose with a pointed chin. A beauty mark hovered next to the bridge of her nose. I looked back down at the dead woman to confirm the same features.

It was Madame Lannet, the woman in the portrait.

I spewed out a long breath and looked around the room. Nothing seemed disturbed other than the vanity where she'd been attacked. All the other chairs and beauty aids were neatly arranged.

I needed to call the authorities, and that most assuredly meant seeing and talking to Inspecteur Merveille again. I grimaced. He was not going to be pleased to see me in the presence of another dead body. On the bright side, this time he probably wouldn't suspect me of murder.

Unsurprisingly, there was no telephone in the *cabine*, but I did find a tissue to wipe the blood off my palm. I removed my coat and used it to cover Madame Lannet. I left my handbag on the floor and my gloves on my hands.

Silent, with prickling over my shoulders and still brandishing the little knife, I went out into the hall. No telephone there, so I carefully opened the door to the room at the right of the stairs.

It was instantly clear that this was Madame Lannet's office. The majestic wooden desk, the swatches of fabric, the drawings on onionskin paper tacked up willy-nilly, the dressmaker's form for fitting models before the pieces went on a live person . . . and a telephone.

I headed quickly to the desk, so I missed the figure behind the door.

Whoever it was, they shoved me *hard* from behind. I flew forward, my arms spiraling helplessly, the tool knife flying from my hand. My forehead hit the front edge of the desk as I went down.

I quite literally saw stars as I dropped to the floor. Everything wavered and went dim and brown, and then really dark. . . .

I didn't pass out, thank goodness, and I could vaguely hear noises from far away—thudding footsteps, maybe the slam of a door—but I was so stunned that I couldn't pull myself to my feet in time to pursue. Not that I really wanted to.

My stomach heaved with nausea and for a moment, I thought I might lose what was left of my lunch there on the floor. My head hurt, but I had the presence of mind to be grateful I hadn't hit the corner of the desk—or even the sharp edge—for that might have been a serious injury. Even, if murder mystery writers were to be believed, instant death.

When I finally got to my feet, my knees were shaking and my stomach still roiled. I did not go in pursuit of my assailant; the telephone was a far more attractive option.

The operator put me through to the *police judiciaire* and I calmly and succinctly reported the situation through the pounding in my head. I did not ask for Merveille.

As soon as I hung up, I felt a smattering of relief. Help was on the way. Whoever had been lurking in this office was surely long gone, rushing out and into the night—

Julia.

My breath caught. I bolted from the room and hurried down the stairs with still-wobbly knees and throbbing forehead. If the killer—it had to have been the killer who'd pushed me—had run out through the front entrance, had he or she seen Julia? She'd be a lot more difficult to shove over than I was, but that didn't mean it hadn't happened. Or something worse.

There was still no sign of life downstairs in the gallery where we'd seen the collection, nor in the foyer where we'd entered. I flung open the front door and burst outside. Julia shrieked and stumbled backward, bumping into the railing and dropping her handbag.

"Are you all right?" I asked.

"I am now," she said, looking at me with her hand clapped to her chest. Her eyes were wide. "What the heck happened to you? Did Madame Pineau chase you out of there?"

I caught my breath. My knees were still a little weak. "Did anyone come out this way?"

"No. What's wrong, Tabitha? You look as if you've seen a ghost. Don't *tell* me you've found another dead body," she said with a warbling laugh as she stooped to pick up her purse. "Even for you, dearie, that would be—*no!*"

I had been nodding in grim affirmation, which she saw as she rose. "Someone strangled Madame Lannet with a couple yards of fine lace," I told her. "And whoever it was attacked me."

Julia's eyes had gone so wide they looked as if they were going to pop out of her head. I told her the details. "No one else seems to be around," I finished, touching my forehead. There was definitely a squishy spot, but no blood came away on my glove.

"What was the killer doing in Madame Lannet's office?" said Julia as she opened the door. She marched inside and I followed.

"I don't think he was calling the police," I said grimly.

"If I strangled someone, I wouldn't stick around, that's for sure," Julia said. She headed for the stairs, and I followed.

"Where are you going?" Of course I followed her.

"Someone ought to stay with Madame Lannet, and someone else ought to poke around in her office before the cops get here and see if they can find anything interesting," Julia said, giving me a sly look over her shoulder. "I'll do the first, you do the second."

"I don't—"

"Oh yes you do," she said firmly as she stepped onto the landing. "If you hadn't been worried about me at the hands of the strangler, you'd have already done it. Better do it before *l'inspecteur* Merveille with the gorgeous ocean-blue eyes arrives," she added with a sly grin.

"I didn't ask for him," I told her with great complacency. I didn't bother to point out that Merveille's eyes were more gray than blue. A very dark, churning ocean gray. "I'm sure there are other homicide detectives at the 36." The 36 was the nickname for the *police judiciaire*, referring to its location on 36 quai des Orfèvres—similar to how Scotland Yard had gotten its name.

Julia just gave me a look and went into the *cabine*, leaving me to stand in the corridor and debate whether I should snoop around or wait to direct *les flics* when they arrived.

Who was I kidding? Of course I was going to snoop. Besides, I needed to retrieve my Swiss Army knife.

That was an excellent excuse to go back into Madame Lannet's office. Even Merveille couldn't argue that.

I was still wearing my gloves, so I felt confident I could poke around without leaving a trace of my nosiness. If the killer had strangled Madame Lannet and then came in here instead of hightailing it away, surely they were looking for something.

Nothing was obviously out of order in her office; not knowing what sort of state her work area was normally in, I couldn't tell whether the papers strewn all over were normally like that or if they'd been left by the killer. And of course, I had no idea what I was looking for.

Still . . . I snooped, ignoring the insistent pounding in my head.

There were lots of pages of fashion drawings, many on onionskin paper that had obviously been traced from others. I picked one up and admired the long, flowing lines of an evening gown. This must be for Madame Lannet's winter collection, which would be—or would have been, I reminded myself, for the couturier was gone now—unveiled in June or July.

That made me wonder what would happen to the current collection—frocks and gowns and feminine suits in the process of being made for spring and summer wear. Would the seamstresses continue with the projects without their couturier to finalize and approve?

And that in turn made me wonder whether someone didn't want Madame Lannet to continue designing clothing. Could the strangulation have been due to some kind of professional jealousy?

As I poked around, using a pencil to shift papers on her desk and my gloved hands to open drawers and peek inside (there was a bottle of whisky tucked in one of them), I thought about her murder. She'd been strangled with lace. Had that simply been a handy weapon—after all, we were in a fashion house—or had someone used lace purposely *because* we were in a fashion house? And if so, had they brought the length of lace with them?

If so, that made the murder premeditated. If they didn't bring the lace, then it might have been a crime of passion, so to speak, where someone grabbed a convenient method to silence Madame Lannet.

I heard voices in the corridor—a strident female one, surprised and demanding then horrified—and Julia's calmer one.

I slipped back out of Madame Lannet's office in time to see Madame Pineau shove past Julia into the *cabine*. I heard the choked-back cry followed by a moan of pain or grief.

"*Non, non, non!*" Madame Pineau was crouched next to Madame Lannet, sobbing. The designer's face had been uncovered as if the vendeuse needed to confirm her identity, and Madame Pineau stroked the woman's cheek. She looked up as my feet came into view. "What is this? What have you *done!*" She struggled to her feet less gracefully than I had done—although she didn't fall on her butt—and rounded on me. "What have you *done?*"

"Madame Pineau, I'm so very sorry for your loss," I said, standing firm in the face of her fury. "I called—"

"But what are you doing here? What have you *done? Merde!*" She launched herself at me, fingers curled into talons with well-tended nails that would leave deep marks.

I dodged her and grabbed a chair to place it between us as she whirled around, preparing to attack again. "Madame Pineau," I said in a sharp voice. "I didn't do anything but find Madame Lannet like this, here on the floor. Whoever did it also attacked me as they ran away. I called the *police judiciaire* and someone should be arriving soon."

Madame Pineau's face was streaked with tears, her careful makeup making tracks down her cheeks. Her lipstick was smudged around her mouth. "But what has happened to my Rose?" she said, her fury dissipating into a keening tone. "Who would have done this?" Her hand shook as she gestured to the inert body.

"I'm so sorry," I told her again, and noticed Julia had disappeared. The sounds of voices from below told me she'd gone down to meet *les flics*. I spoke quickly, "Do you have any idea who might have done this, Madame Pineau?"

The vendeuse's expression shriveled. "But . . . no, no one would do such a thing."

"Not a rival or someone who was jealous of Madame's work?" I asked urgently, for the sounds of several pairs of footsteps were coming closer on the stairs.

Madame Pineau's eyes went wide and her mouth opened in a shocked O. But before she could speak, a man walked into the *cabine* exuding pompous authority.

It was not Inspecteur Merveille.

I didn't feel the slightest stab of disappointment that he was not the investigator who'd arrived in the company of two police agents. It was far better that I didn't have to explain why, once again, I was at the scene of a violent death.

And I completely avoided looking at Julia, who was trying desperately to give me what she probably thought was a consoling look. *I* didn't need consoling, but Madame Pineau clearly did.

"I am Inspecteur Allard," said the man. He was quite the opposite from Merveille in nearly every way except for the stern expression on his face. I supposed that was something that came with a job steeped in murder.

Inspecteur Allard, who looked as if he were in his late forties, was shorter than me by about an inch, and far rounder. He had light pink skin with a slender mustache that looked like someone had taken a thick brown felt tip marker and drawn a line across his upper lip. His eyebrows were exactly the same: two straight brown slashes over his dark eyes.

He wore an overcoat, suit, and tie, and carried a hat . . . but his ensemble seemed like a hodgepodge of items that had been shoved in the bottom of a closet and blindly extracted. They were creased in the wrong places and didn't quite match, being random shades of brown and blue. Evidently, Inspecteur Allard was not a connoisseur of fashion. He was wearing a wedding ring, and I wondered how he'd managed to get out of the house dressed in such a way without his wife stopping him.

"What has happened here, mademoiselle?"

He was looking at me.

I explained that I'd been the one to call the 36 but left out the part that I knew his colleague. "I lost my glove here after a meeting with Madame Pineau." I gestured to the vendeuse. "When I came back to find it, there was no one here. The door was unlocked and the lights were on," I went on as Madame Pineau began to object. "I only wanted my glove. It was very quiet and . . . well, something felt wrong about the place—"

"*Ah, l'intuition féminine!* But of course."

I ignored Allard's comment and went on, embellishing a little because I didn't want to have to admit I'd sneaked upstairs just to get the name of a hair stylist. "I thought I heard something strange from above, and so I went up to investigate. I found Madame Lannet here on the floor. She was already dead, but her body was not cold or stiff."

"Did you move the body?"

"No. I only touched her hand. She was lying on the floor on her back, just as she is now, and so I could see her face. I did move some of the hair away from her neck when I saw the—the lace."

Inspecteur Allard was eyeing me carefully as he extracted a notebook from his overcoat pocket. "And then what next, mademoiselle? You did not scream or faint, or cry for help from your friend here, eh?"

"No, I didn't scream and I certainly didn't faint."

"But most women, if they were to come upon such a scene, would surely scream or cry out," Allard pressed.

I didn't like the way he was looking at me, so I gave him a steady, cool look. "It was a terrible, shocking scene, but I didn't scream. I went in search of a telephone to call for help instead. I found a room that turned out to be Madame Lannet's office and as I went to the desk, someone came out from behind the door and pushed me. They ran away, and I acquired this," I said, gesturing to the bump on my forehead. I'd been too busy and distracted to think about ice for it, but I was going to need some soon.

The *inspecteur* clicked his tongue in sympathy over my injury, then asked, "And this person who injured you so—did you see who it was?"

I shook my head. "Unfortunately, I did not. He or she was hiding behind the door and I walked past them to the desk for the telephone. They came up behind and pushed me. By the time I recovered, they were gone. I heard them run away."

"Did you notice anything about them, mademoiselle? Could it have been a man or a woman? What about their shoes? Did you perhaps see them behind you when you stumbled?" He'd retrieved a pencil from his pocket as well and was poised to make notes.

I didn't respond immediately. Instead, I closed my eyes. If I was going to continue my . . . shall we say interest? . . . in police investigation, I would have to learn to be observant. I pictured myself hurrying toward the desk in Madame Lannet's office, then I felt sudden movement behind me and the forceful shove . . . the sound of the person turning and leaving . . . the thuds of their feet as they ran off. . . .

"It's more likely the person was a man than a woman," I said when I opened my eyes and found Inspecteur Allard watching me with interest instead of suspicion.

"And why is that, mademoiselle?"

"Because the person was not wearing heels," I replied. "The footsteps sounded different from the way they sound when a woman is wearing heels." I measured two inches with my fingers in order to show him what I meant. "High heels make a sort of clicking sound; the flatter ones thud. Besides, the person was strong enough to give me a good push."

Allard clicked his tongue again, and made an up-and-down gesture with his pencil, acknowledging my figure. "But you are not much of a mountain, mademoiselle. It would not take so much effort to fell you." He glanced at Julia meaningfully, then back at me. "*Non?*"

I shrugged. He was probably right.

"Is there anything else, mademoiselle?"

"No," I said.

He turned to Julia. "And you, mademoiselle?"

"I was outside the entire time until Tabitha came down to tell me what had happened. No one came out the door where I was standing—at the front entrance."

"Tabitha?" Allard's expression sharpened and he looked at me again. "Excuse me, mademoiselle, but your name is Tabitha?"

I don't know why, but my cheeks grew hot. "*Oui, Inspecteur.* Tabitha Knight."

He made a sound that could have been one of surprise or satisfaction, or merely interest. I realized I didn't want to know.

"And you, mademoiselle?" asked Allard after a few scratchings on his notepad. He looked at Julia this time.

"*Madame* Julia Child," she replied with a little smile. "Is it possible that our reputations have preceded us?" At least, that was what she meant to say, but the question in her still labored French came out more like "have we preceded our reputations."

Allard gave the sort of noncommittal shrug the French are famous for. "Niakaté, if you will take the pertinent information of these ladies," he said to one of the agents standing there.

"You know they already *have* our information," Julia muttered, giving me a knowing look. But she readily rattled off her full name and address, along with the information that her husband Paul worked for the embassy.

Meanwhile, I was trying to hear the details of the conversation with Madame Pineau and the *inspecteur.* Julia must have caught on, because I noticed she drew the police agent aside and engaged him in intense conversation. I have no idea what it was about, but I appreciated her efforts.

"Now, madame, if you please, tell to me what happened here tonight," Allard was saying to Madame Pineau.

By now, the older woman had regained her composure and even wiped away some of the mess of makeup on her face. Her hand trembled as she brought a handkerchief to her eyes to drag away the last trickle of a tear.

"It was time to close up for the day and the mannequins and the others had all gone. Madame Lannet—"

"Pardon me, madame, but what is her full name?"

"Rose-Marie Lannet," replied Madame Pineau.

"And does she have family? A husband? A sister? Children?" he asked.

Madame Pineau shook her head, her face pale. "*Non*, monsieur. There is no husband or children. Only me, and—and her work here."

"*Très bien*, madame. And what is your name?"

"Gabrielle Pineau."

Allard nodded and jotted a note. "Now, please continue."

"Everyone had gone for the day except Rose-Marie and I. We were to have dinner, and so I went to get it from a brasserie around the corner. W-we often order from there. W-when I left, she was looking through some f-fabric swatches in her office." Madame Pineau swallowed, then collected herself and went on. "And then I came back, and . . ." She flapped her hands out in an expression of disbelief and confusion.

"And you saw no one who might have just left the boutique?" said Allard.

"No. I used the front door where she was standing"—she indicated Julia—"because that is the closest way to Le Bistro Mignon."

I had been hovering out of Allard's eyesight, hoping he wouldn't notice my presence. So far, I was successful.

"Very well. And everyone had gone—the workers?—before you left for the *bistro?*"

"As far as I am aware," replied Madame. She had a wry smile. "The mannequins, they are always ready to leave as soon as possible, for they must wait around all day long for the showings. They cry over the boredom."

"And *les petites mains? Les premières* as well? They were all gone?" Allard said, surprising me with his knowledge of the inner workings of a fashion house. Although, I supposed I shouldn't be surprised that he knew those terms. After all, haute couture was a uniquely Parisian entity.

"Yes, yes, all of the workers and *les premières* had gone," Madame replied. Her eyes, shiny with unshed tears, flashed. "You must find out who did this, instead of asking me all of these questions! It was no one here at Maison Lannet. *No one* here would have hurt Rose."

"*Oui,* madame, please do not overset yourself. I must ask these questions in order to do only that. Now, can you think of anyone who might have wanted to hurt Madame Lannet?"

Madame Pineau's expression hardened. "Oh, *oui, Inspecteur,* I know exactly who did such a thing. It was Christian Dior!"

CHAPTER 3

ALLARD'S FACE MIRRORED MY SHOCK. "CHRISTIAN DIOR? DO YOU mean to say, Christian Dior—the couturier—killed Madame Lannet?"

Madame Pineau nodded sharply, throwing her shoulders back. "*Bien sûr*. It was him. Of *course* it was him! He was jealous of Madame Lannet's success, you see! She was about to become the most celebrated couturier in Paris."

Allard continued to look at her with astonishment. "Madame, do you truly suggest that Christian Dior sneaked into this boutique and strangled Madame Lannet?"

"It is not a suggestion, Inspecteur. It is a *fact*."

At that moment, Allard glanced in my direction. His eyes—which had been filled with disbelief—widened with surprise and irritation, but I wasn't completely sure whether it was directed at me or at Madame Pineau's absurd accusation.

"*Eh, bien,*" he said to the vendeuse. "But is there anyone else who might have had it in for Madame Lannet?"

"No! I tell you, it was Dior! Now, you go and arrest that man! Throw him into the jail and leave him to rot. My poor, poor Rose . . ." She dissolved into heartbroken sobs.

I decided it was time to make my exit before Allard turned his frustrated attention onto me. I caught Julia's eye and she extracted herself from the poor police agent with whom she'd been chatting energetically.

Just as we turned to go, I remembered I hadn't retrieved my tool knife from where it had fallen in Madame Lannet's office. I told Julia and ducked inside just as three men appeared at the top of the steps carrying a stretcher.

I slipped into the office as Allard was giving instructions to the men from the coroner's office. I had to stifle my opinion that the *inspecteur* hadn't spent enough time examining the body and crime scene—he'd been talking to us instead of giving the body a close look—and searched for my knife. I found it on the floor under a chair and scooped it up, sliding it back into my dress pocket.

As Julia and I came down the stairs into the salon, I automatically glanced down the hall where I'd dropped my glove. The lights were still on, and I noticed something glinting on the ground about halfway along the hall.

Taking Julia by the arm, I pulled her with me down the corridor. "This wasn't here when I was looking for my glove," I said, pouncing on the object.

It was a small metal tube, no more than three inches long and about the diameter of the straw they give you with shakes and malts. It was hollow inside and there was a narrow opening along part of it. I couldn't imagine what it was for.

"The killer could have dropped it on his way out," Julia said, looking at it with a frown. "Whatever it is. *Is* there a way out down here?"

"Let's find out." With a glance back toward the salon, I confirmed that no one was there to see us, and tucked the metal tube object into my dress pocket.

There was a large coatroom along the hall, along with two more doors. One led into an area that appeared to be a break room, for there were tables and chairs, ashtrays, a sink, and a small hot plate for, I assumed, coffee. It made sense to keep any food and beverage far away from the fine fabrics and elegant trimmings that were being assembled into gorgeous, one-of-a-kind fashion pieces on the floors above.

The second door did lead to the outside, and I cast Julia a

smug look when I opened it to fresh air and a brick alley. I looked down, but there weren't any footprints that might give a clue to the culprit, for the top of the ground was frozen and we hadn't had any snow for a while.

Even so, I stepped outside to look around. There was a street-light at one end that cast a stingy glow in the narrow alley, and the place smelled like urine and other unpleasant things. No one was in sight, and there wasn't any activity except a few pedestrians walking past the end of the alley.

As I came back inside, chilled from the cold, I realized I'd left my coat covering Madame Lannet. Julia traipsed back with me to the salon and upstairs, only to find that Madame Lannet's body—along with my coat—had already been removed. In-specteur Allard didn't seem the least bit apologetic or con-cerned. However, he was, I was pleased to see, poking around the room like a real detective. He even had an agent taking pho-tographs.

"Well, that's a fine kettle," Julia said grumpily as we clumped down the stairs. "You'd have thought they'd remove the coat when they wrapped her up. You've got so little meat on your bones, you're going to freeze without it! And besides, you're hurt. Take this."

She was about to take off her coat, but I said, "No, just your scarf will be fine, Julia. It's not a long walk to the car." She handed me her scarf, which I wrapped around my neck.

"I'm sure I'll get my coat back," I said, trying to remember if I'd left anything important in the pockets. Fortunately, I had my house and car keys in my pocketbook, which I still possessed. And my gloves were on my hands because I'd been taking care not to leave fingerprints as I mucked about the crime scene.

As Julia drove us back to the Left Bank with the car's heat blasting, I was no longer able to put off deciding what I was going to make for my messieurs for dinner. It was after seven o'clock—more than an hour later than I'd anticipated arriving home—and I'd done absolutely nothing to plan for a meal.

I was determined not to ask Julia for help this time. I relied on her far too much, and even though cooking was the thing she was most passionate about and she loved doing it, I often felt as if I were taking advantage of her knowledge.

"Your messieurs are going to be thrilled you've become involved in another murder," Julia trilled as we meandered along the curve of Place du Palais-Bourbon toward rue de Bourgogne.

"I wouldn't say I'm *involved*," I replied. "I just happened to find the body."

"And a clue," she reminded me.

"I didn't give that little metal thing to Inspecteur Allard," I said, clapping a hand to my side pocket. "I forgot when I found out my coat was gone."

Julia cast me a knowing look. "Then you'll just have to deliver it to the 36 yourself." I rolled my eyes because her tone suggested I'd forgotten on purpose, and she continued, "I wonder why Merveille wasn't there tonight."

"I'm sure there's more than one homicide detective in a city the size of Paris," I retorted. Julia, who was wonderfully happy in her own marriage, was determined that I, too, should find a husband and be as ecstatically content as she was and for some reason, she'd fixated on Inspecteur Merveille. "Besides, I don't know why you keep poking me about Merveille. He's got a picture of his *fiancée* on his desk! The man isn't available even if I was interested."

"Appearances can be deceiving, Tabs." I scoffed, and she went on, "Anyway, what are you making for your gentlemen for dinner tonight?"

"Oh, I thought I'd roast a chicken, and maybe do a parsnip and potato mash," I lied, conveniently ignoring the fact that I had two nice fillets of sole in the refrigerator. If I'd mentioned that, she'd have asked what I was going to make with the fish, and I'd have had to admit I had no idea and then I'd be right where I'd been trying to avoid: relying on her for help.

I'd become so good at roasting chicken since Julia's tutelage that we had the dish at least once a week. It was delicious, but I sensed that Grand-père and Oncle Rafe might be getting a little tired of it, succulent and juicy as it was.

It struck me then . . . was that why they were so determined to reopen Maison de Verre? So they had a place to eat instead of settling for my rudimentary cooking?

The thought should have pleased me, and alleviated some of my anxiety over having to cook on a regular basis, but instead it made me feel guilty. Here I was, living in a gorgeous mansion—rent-free—in the most beautiful city in the world with two of the most lovely men I'd ever known, and I couldn't manage to hold up my end of the bargain of cooking them dinner most nights.

Ugh.

"What's wrong, Tabs?" Julia—who was such a font of energy and enthusiasm—was also empathetic enough to sense when something was bothering someone. "Is it your head? Should I take you to the hospital? You might have a concussion."

"No, it's not my head. I just wish I could cook even half as well as you can. I think Grand-père and Oncle Rafe are getting tired of omelettes and roasted chicken and veal roast," I said, naming the other dishes Julia had tutored me through and that I'd become fairly adept at making. I'd never be able to make them as easily as she did, but at least I wasn't setting chicken feathers on fire or making rubbery eggs anymore.

"*Tabitha!* Don't you *dare* be so hard on yourself. I've been seriously studying cooking for over a year now, and besides, you've made some great progress! Your messieurs absolutely *adore* you, and they know you're doing your best," she went on, reaching over to pat my gloved hand. "Why, you've come a long way from opening a jar of Ragú and pouring it over noodles."

I laughed along with her and that made my forehead pound harder. I needed some ice. What she said was true, and it was also something I'd never do again. The horrified expressions on the faces of my grandfather and honorary uncle when I served them jarred spaghetti sauce—not Ragú here in Paris, but close enough—over pasta was forever etched in my mind.

"I have a better idea," Julia said. "I've got some delectable tomatoey-fish broth made up that should be used. I can give it to you and you can make bouillabaisse with it and that sole you bought earlier. With a loaf of crusty bread and a bottle of Monsieur Fautrier's wine, it'll be *divine*, Tabs."

I hesitated. I really hadn't been angling for help from her this time, but it would certainly solve my problem. I steeled myself. "Oh, Julia, I really appreciate the offer, but I've got those parsnips and turnips I bought today."

"Good *heavens*, Tabs, it's not like they'll go bad tomorrow—or even next week!" Her laugh was loud and jolly. "There's *plenty* of broth—all you need is to add in the seafood. Some mussels and shrimp would be just *gorgeous* in it, too," she said, her eyes lighting up and her voice lilting and dancing as it always did when she talked food. "You really need to have four or five different kinds of seafood in *bouillabaisse* to make it perfect. We can stop at the fishmonger and you can dash in and get some. Then you just dump it all in the broth and *voilà!* The most delectable fish stew you've ever had in your *life.* I *promise.*"

My hesitation vanished. At least in this case, I would actually be doing some of the cooking. "Julia, you're a lifesaver. That sounds so much better than roasted chicken and turnip mash *again.* Are you certain all I have to do is add the seafood?"

"That's all I was going to do," she said with a laugh. "But then I decided to make *galantine de poulet* because Paul will be late tonight and it is served cold. So my *delicious* broth needs a *home!*"

I had no idea what a *galantine* was, but I gathered it was some sort of cold chicken. But the idea of being the recipient of some of Julia's broth . . . "Oh, thank you, Julia! That sounds perfect."

So we stopped at the fishmonger and I zipped inside to get some mussels and shrimp, and also a bit of cod to make up the fourth type of fish. I didn't think there was a house in Paris that didn't have a loaf of crusty bread on hand—our day maids, Bet and Blythe, brought one or two fresh from the bakery each morning—and so I was feeling quite pleased with myself a short while later when I finally returned home with Julia's broth and the rest of the ingredients.

"I'm home!" I called up over the cacophony of Oscar Wilde's frantic yip-yapping. "I'll bring dinner up in a few minutes."

But in the kitchen, I had a moment of anxiety as I held a bottle of cold milk to the wound on my forehead. The bottle felt good against the cut on my palm too.

Could this dish really be as easy as Julia had said?

Heat the broth to a little simmer. A simmer, Tabs. Not a rollicking boil! Then dump in the shrimp and the mussels, and chunks of the fish. You can splash in a bit of white wine or vermouth if you want. I would, she'd added with a grin. *And just let it cook nice and easy until the shrimp is white and opaque. Ten minutes, maybe twelve. Oh, and chop up some dill and parsley from your grandfather's herb garden and sprinkle that on top. And, here, this little bit of dried orange peel—drop this in too.*

I couldn't believe it when everything went just as she said. Not only that, but the broth smelled like heaven. And then I scooped up a spoonful to taste. . . .

I snatched the telephone receiver off its perch and dialed her number. "You have to teach me how to make this," I exclaimed when she answered. "Julia, it tastes like *heaven.*"

Her hearty laugh filled my ears. "It's so easy, you'll cry, Tabitha, I swear it! Now go and enjoy—don't forget to put the herbs on top!—and tell your messieurs all about your new murder case."

I didn't bother to deny that it was my murder case. It wasn't, but I'd be lying if I claimed I wasn't interested and intrigued. There was no reason for me to be involved, but that didn't mean I wasn't going to be thinking about it and, possibly, trying to find a way to keep tabs on it.

I loaded up the very convenient dumbwaiter with the crock of stew, large, shallow bowls, ladle, spoons, butter, and bread, then dashed upstairs.

To my surprise, when I came into the salon, I discovered my two messieurs sitting there silently. There was no fond greeting, no gesturing for me to come over and offer a kiss on the cheek.

Not even a "but what is it that smells so good, *ma mie?*" or exclamations over my wound.

Neither of them were talking, looking at each other, or even reading the newspaper or a magazine, although the pages of designs and notes for the restaurant were still spilled all over the table.

Oscar Wilde sat curled up in Oncle Rafe's lap, and Madame X was overseeing the scene from her cozy perch on the fireplace mantel. The mood in the room was stiff, cold, and fraught with tension.

I felt a little stab of apprehension. Were they angry at me for being late and not calling to let them know? They'd never seemed to worry about my comings and goings before, but there had been times during my involvement with those murder cases where I'd been in danger.

But then, so had they. . . .

"Bonsoir, messieurs," I said brightly, my attention bouncing from Grand-père—who sat smoking with flat, unsmiling lips—to Oncle Rafe, whose arms were folded over his chest, his brows in the same angry line as Grand-père's lips.

"Ah, Tabi," said Grand-père, as if he'd just noticed me. "There you are."

"Here I am," I said, still brightly, still looking from one to the other.

"Bonsoir, *petite*." Oncle Rafe gave me a warm smile, but as his attention slid from me and skimmed over Grand-père, the smile turned to a sneer.

"Uh . . . I have something delicious for dinner," I said, making my way over to where the dumbwaiter opened up in the wall. "I hope you're hungry. Julia helped me make it," I added, hoping to tease some sort of response from them.

"Ah, yes, of course," said Oncle Rafe. "Let me move these papers out of the way." He rose to gather up the messy pile of drawings on the table and Oscar Wilde landed on the floor.

"Ah, so *that* is your plan!" To my shock, Grand-père bolted from his chair and lunged for some of the papers. (Bolted and lunged are exaggerations, but for a man with his creaky and unsteady sort of mobility, in comparison to his normal movements, it was fast.) "The moment my head is turned, you will *toss* them into the fire!" Grand-père scrabbled for some of the pages as Monsieur Wilde began barking and bounding around with excitement. "And then my ideas will be gone—lost—nowhere to be found!"

Oncle Rafe gave a contemptuous laugh and shoved a few papers at Grand-père while holding others protectively to his chest. "But of course I would do no such thing—although I do not put it past you to *'lose'* only the papers of *my* designs, eh, Maurice? Just as you did once before!" He gestured to the room at large, his mouth still twisted in a sneer. "Do not think I didn't know it was you who *lost* my drawings for the gardens!" He flung his arm toward the window which overlooked the winter-barren courtyard. "And now look at them!"

"But of course I did not!" Grand-père responded furiously, his cigarette waving from a gesticulating hand as he sank back into his chair. "The gardener did not like the plans, of course, and so *he* put them away. And the mess that is down there now is due to Joseph's laziness and not *me*."

"You'll never admit it, you old goat, but I know better," Rafe said furiously. "Ah, I *know* you, Maurice! Have I not known you for fifty long years?"

"Peh, you stubborn old crow," Grand-père snarled back. "You wouldn't know a beautiful design if it came up and bit you on the nose! Instead, you insist on the gloom and the *dark*!"

"*Beh,*" scoffed Rafe, then turned and shoved the papers into a drawer. "You and your *frills*. If you want the look of a boudoir, then you shall have it—and no one will darken the door of Maison de Verre!"

Oscar Wilde continued to bark. Madame X, who'd jumped lazily to the sideboard, surveyed the chaos with a supercilious expression that indicated she was above all of it.

"What is going on?" I put my hands on my hips like a teacher dealing with recalcitrant students.

"Eh! Your *grand-père* . . . he will not listen to reason," snapped Oncle Rafe as he settled into his seat, picking up the wild Oscar Wilde from the floor.

"*I*? *I* will not listen to reason?" Grand-père hauled himself up half out of the chair once more, then sank back down. "There has never been a more stubborn *ass* in all of history than *him!*"

Oncle Rafe laughed mirthlessly as he stroked Oscar Wilde with maybe a little too much vigor. The poor pooch's head bounced under the effort. "Stubborn? He calls *me* stubborn? Do you hear the old goat, Tabitha? And who is it who *insists* that it is only his ideas that are worthwhile? *Eh!*" He made a scoffing sound of disgust.

"How about some dinner," I said, loudly and firmly when Grand-père threatened to shout back. "And you ought to calm down a little or it will affect your digestion. You'd hate to miss Madame Child's bouillabaisse."

To my relief, the two men subsided from their fiery exchange. But that didn't stop the grumbling and sidelong glowers.

For my part, I was glad I was facing the dumbwaiter so they couldn't see me fighting off laughter. Their spat, while obviously very serious to them, was hilarious to me. I'd never seen the two of them be anything but affectionate and warm to each other—and to me—and this was another side of their relationship I found fascinating.

I'd only been living with Grand-père and Oncle Rafe for three weeks when I realized that not only was Oncle Rafe no blood relation to me whatsoever, but that he and Grand-père were in a long-term, loving relationship. As close to a marriage as one could get with someone of the same sex.

At first, I'd been a little surprised and, to be honest, a little uncomfortable. Even though I knew there were men who preferred men and women who preferred women, I hadn't been exposed to those sorts of relationships until I went to work at the Willow Run Bomber Plant—near Detroit—during the war.

It was while living in the dormitories on-site at the plant that I witnessed intimate interactions between some of the women I worked with—including one who'd become a good friend of mine. Her name was Lizzy, and she was surprisingly open—with me, anyway—about her preference for women over men.

"It's just the way I am," she told me with a shrug. But there was a little sadness in her eyes. "If I could have it any other way, I would—it would be a lot easier, wouldn't it? But it's who I am."

With that in mind, the initial strangeness I felt about the depth of Grand-père and Oncle Rafe's relationship was very brief. Now I was rabidly protective of them, even though they'd probably laugh if they knew I felt like I'd slay dragons—or fight off killers—to protect them.

I'd only once broached the subject with Grand-père, and it was when we were alone. I didn't want Oncle Rafe to feel as if I didn't accept him. And I only brought it up because I wondered about my *grand-mère*, who'd come to live in America when my parents got married. She and Grand-père had been separated for over thirty years.

"Do you miss her?" I asked. "Did you ask her to leave, or did she want to go?"

Grand-père's face softened, although there was a bit of worry lurking behind his eyes. "We were—and are—very good friends, Tabi. I miss her terribly. We wrote each other every week from the time she left and until she died. But . . . both of us are—were—much happier no longer living such a lie, you see?"

He gave me Grand-mère's letters, and I asked my mother to send me the ones he'd sent to her.

When I read them, I realized he was right. They missed each other, they even loved each other, but were much happier living separate lives.

And I was thinking about all of this when it occurred to me that maybe Madame Pineau and Madame Lannet had been in the same sort of relationship. Madame Pineau's grief over the death of the couturier had seemed deep and serious—like one would have over someone very close, like a child or a lover. Since the women were close in age, I wondered if they had been lovers. When Inspecteur Allard had asked about family, Madame Pineau had said, "There is only me."

"And how was your visit to Maison Lannet?" asked Grand-père when I'd taken my seat on the sofa. Although he and Oncle Rafe hadn't spoken another word to each other, they had expressed their delight with the bouillabaisse.

"Well," I said, looking at them both, "I found a dead body."

CHAPTER 4

*T*HE NEXT MORNING, I TOOK MY COFFEE AND A CROISSANT INTO Grand-père's greenhouse.

The greenhouse, where Grand-père puttered over his *bébés-délicieux*, was situated on the roof of the portico in the recently maligned courtyard where I parked my cherry-red Renault and where my messieurs had their Bentley Mark VI. A door led into the greenhouse from the salon, making it convenient for my grandfather to visit it whenever he liked.

It was a bright and clear February morning, which made the glass-walled and ceilinged space even warmer and more humid than usual. Although it was many weeks until spring, this sunny area was as close as I was going to get to it for now. Condensation trailed down the windows and fogged up part of the view. It smelled loamy and fresh, with a bit of floral from some lavender. I sat at a little wrought iron table near the small pond with its happy, trickling fountain and the bright orange fish swimming within.

Madame X had slipped in with me before I closed the door, and I reminded her that the fish were off-limits. She gave me a disgusted look and proceeded to wander away, presumably to locate the patch of catnip Grand-père grew for her in the midst of parsley, chervil, tarragon, sorrel, and more.

A waist-high terra-cotta pot with numerous pockets held strawberry plants tumbling from some of the little openings, their runners reaching for other pockets in which to root. Even in February, a few berries were growing and ripe, thanks to my *grand-père*'s assistance in hand-pollinating them (he would bring in bees when it got warmer). I snagged the reddest berry, its juice staining my fingers. It was sweet and fresh and I felt another burst of wishing for spring.

Paris in spring was perfect.

I'd just finished buttering my croissant, which had flaked all over the plate, when the door from the salon opened.

"Ah, and here you are on this glorious morning," said Oncle Rafe. He made his way in carrying a cup of coffee in one hand and one of those dark cigarettes in the other. Over his pajamas was a dark blue dressing coat of quilted velvet with black satin trim. Heavy slippers covered his feet but his bald head was bare. "And how is your head this morning, *chérie?*"

Monsieur Wilde trotted in with him, but immediately transferred his attention to me because I had food.

"Good morning, Oncle," I said, ignoring the little paw that came to rest politely on my leg. "I'm feeling much better. The ice and the aspirin helped with the pain. But I'll have a nice bruise for a while."

"It makes you look very serious," Oncle Rafe said with a grin. "A woman not to be trifled with."

I laughed, and there was only a little twinge of pain. Progress. "Shall I make room for Grand-père as well?" There were only two chairs at the small round table, but I could pull up a stool.

"Ah, no, the stubborn old goat is still snoring abed," Oncle Rafe said. I could tell by the way he said it that the two of them were still at odds with each other. "Mmm . . . that looks good," he said, eyeing my croissant. "Bet and Blythe are here, then?"

"Yes." I pushed the plate to him and rose. "I'll get another one; you can have that. They brought plenty."

"Ah, no, no, *ma chérie*, of course I won't take your breakfast."

He made to rise but I waved him back in his seat. "I was going to get some jam for it anyhow. It's no hardship."

When I came back from the kitchen with a tray of croissants as well as strawberry jam, I found that Grand-père had joined Oncle Rafe at the table after all. They were sitting in stony silence, sipping coffee and smoking.

I did notice that Oncle Rafe had pushed the plate with my croissant on it over to Grand-père and I hid a smile.

"The old goat claims he's not hungry," Oncle Rafe said, gesturing to the croissant. "But he ate only a bit of that bouillabaisse last night." His eye roll was expressive, as if it was so much work to attend to such things as caring for his partner.

"I ate plenty," crabbed Grand-père, quite accurately, for he had eaten a healthy portion of the fish stew. Oncle Rafe wasn't the only person who kept an eye on Grand-père's appetite. "And I am perfectly capable of feeding myself. Bonjour, Tabi, *ma chère.* And your head this morning?" He squinted closely at me.

"Much better, Grand-père," I told him with a smile.

He nodded in approval. "*Très bien.* And what is it you have to do today?"

"I have two tutoring appointments, but I'm beginning to wonder if I should stay around here and play referee with the two of you," I said, putting a croissant on a plate and placing it in front of Oncle Rafe. "Especially when the designer comes for the meeting. Did you say he did some work for Christian Dior?"

"Oh, yes," said Rafe, reaching for the butter even as he kept an eagle eye on Grand-père, watching to see whether he ate. "Maison Dior was designed and decorated by Victor Grandpierre, and also Monsieur Dior's own home. Grandpierre has made the statement of a more modern design style—"

"And yet it is merely a version of the neoclassicism from before the wars," Grand-père said. "Much the same influence, yet quite pleasing."

"Do you know Monsieur Dior?" I asked, thinking of Madame Pineau's accusation last night. I hadn't told my messieurs about that ludicrous suggestion; only that I'd discovered Madame Lannet's body—and, because they'd asked—that Inspecteur Merveille had not been present.

"But of course," said Rafe. "Maurice, he knows everyone, *chérie*."

"It is a shame Dior does no collection for the menswear," said Grand-père, slathering jam on his croissant. "Only for the women, you see. He loves women, loves to see them dressed beautifully, loves to imagine them dressed."

I sipped my *café*, well sugared and strong and so much better than the Maxwell House I'd grown up on, and smiled to myself over my next statement. I well knew how they were going to react when I spoke. "Madame Pineau, the *vendeuse première*, seems to think he might have killed Madame Lannet."

They gawked, shocked, then exploded with exclamations and derisive laughter. I noted their companionable exchange of glances. The frivolity of such an accusation seemed to dissipate some of their irritation with each other—which had been my intent.

"And this woman—she thinks that Christian Dior, who has all the time of the world on his hands, sneaked into that little boutique to strangle her?" Grand-père was so amused, his piece of croissant dropped several large flakes to the floor as he gestured.

Oscar Wilde leaped upon them without hesitation, scarfing them up so quickly he was back pawing at my leg hardly before he'd swallowed.

"Ridiculous," Oncle Rafe agreed. "And why would she think such a thing, *chérie?*"

"She said it was because Monsieur Dior was jealous of Madame Lannet's success."

This was cause for more hilarity between the two men.

"The success of this little atelier of which no one has ever heard is cause for jealousy by Le Grand Dior? But this woman must be *mad* to suggest such a thing!" said Oncle Rafe.

When Grand-père had collected himself from wheezing laughter, he looked at me. "But perhaps it is time you visited Maison Dior, *ma mie*," he said, glancing at Rafe, who nodded in agreement. "And you can see for yourself."

I blanched and set down my coffee. "Me? Why would I go to Maison Dior?"

"But you will need something to wear to the opening night of our own Maison de Verre, of course," said Oncle Rafe, his eyes softening as he smiled at me. "Something very special, very grand, *non*, Maurice?"

"*Précisément*." Grand-père nodded. "The press will be there, of course—"

"And we cannot have *la petite-fille* of Maurice Saint-Léger wearing anything but Dior," finished Oncle Rafe.

"*Tout à fait vrai*. I shall make the appointment, Tabi," said Grand-père.

I blinked. I couldn't imagine myself wearing anything haute couture. It just seemed so . . . *fine* and luxurious. I knew I would feel out of my depth in a frock that would cost tens of thousands of francs. "Oh, I don't—"

"But of course you will go with us," said Oncle Rafe in a tone that brooked no further discussion.

I shrugged, then smiled. They were, after all, a stubborn goat and contrary crow. "That's very sweet of you. I look forward to it."

Despite my initial protest and hesitant reaction, I actually would look forward to it. There was no argument—Christian Dior had single-handedly revolutionized the postwar Paris fashion scene with his New Look collection. It had come out exactly three years ago, and it seemed that everything Dior did since then had the Midas touch.

The New Look had been the very first collection out of Maison Dior, and the full skirts, nipped-in waists, and layered crinolines of the dresses were in sharp contrast to the straight skirts and boxy shoulders popular during the war years.

Dior had moved from the masculine, soldierlike style made with as little material as possible due to wartime restrictions, to frothy, feminine looks with yards and yards (or meters and meters, depending on your point of view) of material and fancy trimmings. He made women look like women rather than soldiers by emphasizing waist and bust, and using soft, organic shapes and beautiful, deliberate colors. After the austerity and rationing of the war, it was no wonder the New Look had taken everyone by storm.

Not everyone approved of the New Look, however. There'd been demonstrations against Dior and his fashions in America as well as some altercations here in Paris—mainly from women who were unhappy that hemlines had gone down to midcalf from just below the knees, where they'd been during the war. They felt as if such a thing was a step backward in women's rights. I'd even attended a meeting of the so-called Just-Below-the-Knee Club in Detroit a few years ago.

"Why should a woman cover up her legs?" the founder of the group had said to cries of agreement. "They might be her best selling point!"

As the recipient of a pair of nicely turned ankles and slim calves myself, I was sympathetic to her position, even though I never thought of my legs as "selling points." I hadn't found it necessary to protest. Back home, I just wore what I wanted to wear.

Being in Paris, though, I had to admit, I had become far more fashion conscious.

"And will you go to the market today with Madame Child?" Grand-père asked. "Or do you have a tutoring appointment?"

"Yes, I have two lessons today and I do have to bring something to the 36. And I expect to hear from Madame Bauer about another appointment with an atelier, perhaps as soon as today. She didn't find anything to buy at the boutique last night."

"And perhaps that is for the better, now that Madame Lannet is dead," said Oncle Rafe soberly. "For if she had ordered something, then what?"

"Yes. I wonder what will happen to all of her clients," I said. "Will *les petites mains* still make the orders for the customers, or will they be canceled?"

"Ah, it is very likely they will be canceled. After all, with the couturier no longer able to supervise and approve, how can they move forward with confidence? And who would pay for them—especially at such a high cost?" said Grand-père.

"Could that be a motive for the murder?" I mused, breaking off a piece of croissant. I was generous and allowed some flakes to drift to the floor for Oscar Wilde, who lunged for them. "Maybe it wasn't a personal reason against Madame Lannet, but a business reason.

"I wonder who would benefit from her death and the loss of her clients. Surely not someone like Monsieur Dior or Madame Lanvin or Monsieur Fath," I said, naming the most prominent and successful of the couturiers.

"Of course those ateliers would have no need of new clients—especially castoffs like those from the Lannet, of whom no one has heard," replied Oncle Rafe.

He must have noticed my reaction to his snobbery, and he grinned. "But, Tabitha, of course the likes of Dior and Fath would consider anyone who purchases from Lannet instead of them to be castoffs. Or, perhaps it is more likely, those clients of Lannet attempted to purchase from Dior or Fath but could not afford it or could not find a design, and so had to settle for Lannet. It is the way of *la haute couture,* this protection and exclusivity. For if it isn't protected then it will lose its uniqueness and then its value, *non?*"

"I suppose," I replied. The French certainly had a thing about protecting products of their national identity, whether it was specific vintages of wine or cheese, or, in this case, fashion.

We finished our breakfast, such as it was, and I excused myself to get ready for the day. I would have time between my tutoring appointments to take the little metal tube I'd found at Maison Lannet to the 36 and leave it for Inspecteur Allard. Or I could call and leave a message for him as to whether he thought it was important to the investigation.

I didn't want to make a fuss over something that might not be important. Still, I *knew* that metal thing hadn't been in the hall before I went upstairs to the *cabine*. I would definitely have seen it. And since no one else, including Madame Pineau, by her own admission, had come through until I came down—except the killer—then it *had* to have been something left by the culprit.

I also needed to retrieve my coat. I was still surprised and irked that it had been taken away with Madame Lannet's body, and I wondered whether that meant I needed to go to the morgue—which was in the same building as the *police judiciaire*—to retrieve it or whether it would be somewhere else.

I heaved a sigh. It was looking like I was going to have to make a trip to the 36 . . . something I'd done numerous times over the last two months since I'd become embroiled in murder investigations . . . but for some reason, I felt hesitant to do so today.

The last thing I wanted was for someone—namely Inspecteur Merveille—to think I was making up excuses to be there.

Still. I needed my coat, so it seemed I had no choice.

Almost every day, I went to the market with Julia. Most Parisians made those daily trips, and usually the first thing in the morning. I found this habit so very different from back home in Michigan, where we would visit a grocery store when we needed something and do a "shopping trip," coming home with many items for many meals. Here in Paris, it was more common to buy what you needed for your meals each day. And it would be unheard of not to have a fresh baguette or loaf of bread on hand every day.

My messieurs and I were lucky that Bet and Blythe stopped at a boulangerie on their way to our house each morning to get croissants and bread. Otherwise I would have had to get up early and go myself so we would have baked goods on hand for breakfast. Although I was used to eating eggs for breakfast at home, I had discovered that an omelette was more commonly served for lunch or dinner in France.

Since Julia normally had class at Le Cordon Bleu in the mornings, we would usually visit the market on rue de Bourgogne after she returned from school, where she'd often buy the ingredients to make the same dishes she'd just learned about in class. Paul would come home for lunch from his job at the embassy and be treated to delicious food, and then he would go back to work and sometimes Julia would go to another cooking demonstration at the school.

This morning, I begged off going to the market with her before my first appointment because I wanted to retrieve my winter coat from the police. An added benefit to missing a marketing trip with Julia meant that I would also miss the questions from everyone—not only the merchants, but other people we knew who lived in the area and visited the market—about my (nonexistent) love life. And today, surely, Julia and Madame Marie—the old, wizened woman whose vegetables were the best in the market—would have plenty to say about how I'd found another body. Not only that, *but* the disappointment that Inspecteur Merveille had *not* showed up to investigate.

Julia wasn't the only person who had visions of setting me up with Merveille, even though I'd reminded her over and over that he had a photograph of his fiancée on his desk.

"Well, you'll have to come over after your meetings and tell me all about it," Julia trilled over the phone after I explained my plan for the day. "There's no cooking demonstration this afternoon because it's Wednesday and they've got one of those *scheduled blackouts*—I swear, Tabs, we are so lucky we live so close to the Chambre des Députés and don't have to *deal* with them! Anyhow, I'll be puttering *dans la cuisine* all day. Tabs, I'm making the most *delectable,* the most *gorgeous* veal stock. It's going to take *days* and it's going to be like liquid gold, I promise you! I've never made anything so careful and *perfect* as this stock is going to be! You're going to want to absolutely *roll around* in it."

"I'd rather eat it," I said, and she boomed a laugh over the line.

"Of course you will! It's going to be for our Valentine's Day dinner," she said. "I'm making a ballotine of veal and it's going to just *simmer* in that gorgeousness . . . Ye gods, my mouth is already watering! You and your messieurs will certainly get some."

"I can hardly wait!" My mouth was watering too. "I'll let you know how everything goes!" We hung up.

I'd dressed in a long, warm, wool skirt with heavy stockings and my warmest sweater, since I was without a coat. Along with a hat, a heavy muffler, and gloves, I was as prepared for the sunny winter's day as possible.

My morning tutoring appointment went smoothly, and with my payment and the added gift of a small fruitcake, I left the home of Mrs. Carver to head to the police station.

I couldn't keep a goofy smile off my face as I drove along the *haut quai* toward the bridge that would take me to the Île-de-la-Cité, the dollop of land in the middle of the Seine where the 36 was located—along with Notre-Dame and Sainte-Chappelle, a church with the most gorgeous stained glass windows I'd ever seen. I was smiling so happily because it was sunny and bright, crisp and still, and *I was in Paris.*

It never got old for me to remember where I was living. To a young woman who'd never left the Detroit area until nine months ago, living in this iconic city was a blessing—and an adventure—every day.

The traffic was surprisingly light for noon, with the shrill whistles of the traffic police less earsplitting than usual. I'd learned early on that the French were crazy drivers. As a nationality, they *loved* the automobile and they *loved* to drive fast—even in the city. The way the little Renaults and chunky Citroëns and sleek Buicks zipped around the circles and in and out and between other vehicles often made my heart leap into my throat. It seemed as if the drivers felt it was a personal challenge to get everywhere faster than the last time they'd driven. I'd heard someone once say that while Americans knew planes were faster than cars, the French seemed intent on proving exactly the opposite.

Fortunately, with the lighter traffic there were fewer close calls with cars slipping in front of mine or dodging around me, and so, as I neared the bridge, I found myself looking around for a cat.

There are about a zillion cats in Paris. They're about as quintessential as the city's creamy limestone, which was used to construct most of the buildings during the Haussmann renovations. Cats seem to inhabit every window, *rue,* alley, and park bench. They're of every color and size, hunting, sleeping, surveying, and always judging us humans.

But there was one cat in particular I'd gotten to know. He was a dingy, raggedy, tough-looking feline with a broken tail that still hung from its stump like a lifeless flag at the top of a pole. He'd saved my life—mostly accidentally, but I had the suspicion that if *he* were to tell the tale, it would have been a most courageous and definitely deliberate act on his part. He looked like a gray tiger and he had the most arrogant blue-gray eyes I'd ever seen on a cat—and that was saying something, as I was acquainted with Madame X.

I'd gotten in the habit of bringing a piece of cheese sandwich or a small bit of fish or meat for Monsieur le Chat de Gouttière when I was traveling in this area, and today was no exception. I was in no hurry to arrive at the 36, so I pulled off to the side to look for him.

There was no use in calling for him. He would absolutely ignore me if I did, even if I had a name for him. But I knew which tree he normally perched in, and which bench he often prowled about while looking for crumbs from someone's lunch.

Despite the chill and my coatlessness, I sat on that bench and put the piece of crust wrapped around a little chunk of ham—my humble offering to his godliness, as he would surely see it—at the other end. And I waited.

It took a while, but he finally made his appearance, landing lightly on the end of the bench from somewhere.

"Bonjour, monsieur," I greeted him, feeling not the least bit strange in speaking so formally to a cat. While I'd never been allowed pets when growing up, I had been living with a dog and a cat for the last ten months and it had become very obvious to me which species had the brains and which one was driven completely by creature comforts, such as food and petting.

Monsieur Alley Cat gave me a denigrating look with his cool gray eyes, then turned to sniff delicately at the crust of bread. And that was when I saw the large, oozing sore on the back of his hindquarters. There was another one on his back leg.

"Oh, no, monsieur, what happened to you?" I inched a little closer, eyeing the crusted, matted fur around the dark spots that looked like a gouge had been taken out of his flesh. It didn't look healthy. And the top of his broken tail appeared inflamed as well; it was red and shiny and swollen.

It was obvious he needed medical care. But it was just as obvious he wasn't about to let me pick him up, let alone take him anywhere. And even so . . . he was an alley cat. A wild creature who prowled the alleys and hunted in the gutters and sewers.

But I couldn't just leave him to the street. After all, he had truly saved my life.

Glad for the sunshine and lack of breeze—otherwise I'd be freezing—I inched a little nearer on the bench to see whether he'd allow me to get close. He glanced at me, but was still nibbling the treat I'd left for him. Unlike Oscar Wilde, Monsieur le Chat de Gouttière would take his time with the treat, no matter how hungry he might be.

I reached out and gently touched him on the back with my gloved hand, taking care not to brush the infectious area or his head. He gave me an affronted look, yet arched his spine a little as if to say, "Well, if you *must*."

And that was when I knew I *must*.

But the question was, how was I going to get him into my car? I couldn't just pick him up; not only would he not allow it, but I might injure him further or even get the infection on myself, not to mention get scratched by his dirty claws.

Once more, I slid my hand gently over the uninjured part of his spine. He seemed, if not receptive, at least acquiescent to my touch. "I'm going to have to make some preparations," I told him while looking him straight in the eyes. "But I'll be back.

Don't go far, all right? I'm going to get you all fixed up, monsieur."

He narrowed those arrogant eyes at me, but didn't slink away. It wasn't an approval, but it wasn't a dismissal.

I hurried back to the car, spurred by my mission. I'd be back here as soon as I could, with whatever I could think of to lure Monsieur Alley Cat into a box or cage or whatever. Would a large, heavy blanket work to wrap him up while protecting me from claws and teeth?

I parked in front of the *police judiciaire* and hurried past several police agents wearing their képi hats and carrying truncheons in their belts. One looked vaguely familiar to me, and I waved. He waved back. I'd probably seen him at at least one of the crime scenes where I'd been present.

Inside, I went straight to the front desk and absolutely did not look down the corridor that I knew led to Inspecteur Merveille's office. Even so, I remembered only a few weeks ago being in that office with him when he took my fingerprints.

Pushing away the memory of his deft, long-fingered hand holding mine as he rolled each finger in the ink and then onto the photograph paper, I explained to the police agent at the front desk why I was there: to retrieve my coat and to give Inspecteur Allard a piece of information about the murder last night.

"Ah, mademoiselle, thank you," said the man behind the desk. I had met him once before, and it was possible he remembered me. "I will need to find out the whereabouts of your coat; I'll telephone down to the morgue if you like. But I also regret to inform you that Inspecteur Allard is no longer working on the Lannet case. You can leave the information for the new *inspecteur*, mademoiselle, if you please."

I heard myself ask very faintly, "And who is the new *inspecteur* on the case, please, *monsieur l'agent?*"

"Why, it is Inspecteur Merveille," replied the agent, having absolutely no idea what sort of effect that information had on me.

Good grief. How did these things always happen to me?

"I see," I replied, still in a faint, disbelieving voice. My cheeks felt warm. "Um . . . well, I could leave this for Inspecteur Merveille. . . ." I offered an envelope in which I'd placed the metal tube for safety.

"Or you could give it to him straight away," said a deep, dry voice behind me.

My cheeks might have been warm before, but suddenly they burned hot and my stomach dropped. Ugh.

"Inspecteur Merveille," I said in as cool a voice as I could muster as I turned.

His expression was one of resignation. I could almost read his mind: *Her again?*

"Bonjour, Mademoiselle Knight," he said with a polite nod.

Merveille was in his midthirties—an age that I'd originally thought of as being young to be a seasoned homicide investigator, although he'd since proven his expertise. He had smooth, dark hair that always appeared as if he'd just combed it, even if he was taking off a hat. His olive skin was clean-shaven and he had a square jaw below a long, prominent nose. As Julia had noted, he had eyes the color of the ocean—although in my mind, it was a stormy, gray ocean, not the dark blue of the Atlantic under the sunshine that Julia imagined.

As Merveille was wearing neither a hat nor an overcoat, I assumed he'd come from his office and not from outside. What bad luck to have him passing by just as I was standing here. "Did you say you have some information about the Lannet case?" There was a sort of weary acceptance in his tone, as if he'd half been expecting me.

And maybe he had been. After all, Inspecteur Allard had interviewed me and Julia, and our information was surely in the notes he and his agents had made. Merveille was thorough enough to have reviewed them closely.

I wondered why the case had been reassigned to him. I couldn't believe Allard had messed things up so quickly—it had only been about eighteen hours since he'd been called to the scene. And he'd seemed fairly competent, even though he allowed the body to be taken away before I thought he'd done enough to examine it.

Surely he hadn't gone and arrested Christian Dior. . . .

"I'm not certain whether what I found is relevant," I told Merveille. "But I thought Inspecteur Allard would want to know anything that might help, and so I came here to give him what I found."

Merveille hesitated for a fraction of a second, then made a spare gesture to the hall that led to his office. "You certainly know the way, mademoiselle." Then he paused. "You do not have a coat, mademoiselle?"

I gave him a rueful smile and explained.

"Fenèche, if you will call down to the morgue and obtain Mademoiselle's coat," Merveille said to the agent behind the counter.

"*Bien sûr,* Inspecteur."

I have to admit, the first thing I did when I walked into Merveille's office was glance at his desk. It was, as always, terribly neat, with low stacks of folders perfectly aligned to each other and the edges of the desk. A cup with scissors, pencils, and ballpoint pens sat next to a ruler and a large, square pink eraser.

But the picture of Marguerite, his fiancée, was missing.

I swallowed my shock and kept my expression blank as I jerked my attention to the wall where Merveille usually pinned up all of the information for his cases. There was nothing tacked up there except a photograph of Rose-Marie Lannet with her name printed beneath it and one of Gabrielle Pineau next to it.

"I've only just been notified of my assignment to the case," Merveille said, obviously referencing my look at the empty wall. Normally there would be mounted maps, photographs, notes, and anything else he thought was relevant.

I found that admission surprising as well. From my experience, Merveille generally kept his cards close to his vest and never offered information or opinion unless he had to . . . and certainly not to me.

"What happened to Inspecteur Allard?" I asked, figuring I might as well try for more information. "He seemed very competent last night."

"Monsieur Allard was required to leave the city unexpectedly this morning. His wife and children were in a car crash in Alsace, and of course he went to them."

"Oh, that's *terrible*," I said, turning my attention from the crime wall to Merveille. I was reminded of the crazy speeds at which French drivers took the roads. All of my little criticisms of the absent *inspecteur* disappeared in a little mental poof. "Are . . . is everyone going to be all right?"

"We pray they will," he replied soberly. I got the sense he was personally upset about the car crash, more than one would expect than merely being a colleague of Allard. Maybe he was very close to the Allard family. "I have not heard any more information other than that he had to leave and why. He has a daughter of six and a boy of ten."

"Please . . . will you let me know any updates about their condition?" I asked, feeling as much upset about this news as that of Madame Lannet's death. "Inspecteur Allard seemed very nice and I'm sorry he's going through this." Even though he expected I should have screamed and made a fuss—or even fainted—over discovering a dead body.

Merveille gave me a spare nod, and then his implacable demeanor returned. "And so, Mademoiselle Knight, I see you have found yourself another dead person."

I gave him an exasperated look to which, of course, he remained cool and stoic. "I am certain you've already read Inspecteur Allard's notes and my statement," I said, to which he nodded again. "Of course it was an accident that I found Madame Lannet. If I had not come back for my glove, Madame Pineau would have been the one to find her."

"*Oui*, mademoiselle. It is always the accident with you, *non?*"

"Anyhow," I went on, ignoring him, "I found this in the hallway that leads to the coatroom—and the back door at the shop. It wasn't there when I retrieved my glove, which was the first thing I did when I came back to the atelier. And since the killer didn't come out the front door past Julia, then he must have gone out that way and very likely dropped it." I handed him the envelope with the metal thing.

"He? And so you've settled on the culprit's sex already, have you, Mademoiselle Knight?"

I shrugged. "A woman certainly could have done it, but, as I told Inspecteur Allard, the sound of the footprints didn't have a high heel." I gestured to my boots, which didn't have much of a heel . . . which, of course, completely deflated my premise. And then it occurred to me that many of the workers at the atelier—most of whom would be female—might have been wearing the very comfortable, thick-soled shoes that were common wear for women here in Paris. Which even further deflated my deduction. Darn.

"At the very least, whoever it was wasn't wearing high heels," I amended my statement.

"And you had no impression of height or build of the person?" he asked, looking at me closely.

I shook my head. "I'm sorry, no. I didn't see anything either. It happened very quickly."

"And you also acquired this?" He gestured to my forehead, where I'd obviously not done a very good job covering the bruise with makeup—although Mrs. Carver hadn't seemed to notice. "During the altercation with the killer?" His disapproval seemed more directed at me than at the murderer.

"I went into an office to call the police and he—or she—was hiding behind the door. They pushed me and ran away. And, yes, that is how I acquired this." I pointed to the space above my brows. "I hit the front of the desk."

"You are fortunate it wasn't anything more than a bump on the head," he said, making an obviously completely unnecessary statement.

I didn't bother to agree. Why was he being particularly testy with me? The last time I'd seen him had been a few weeks ago in Julia's kitchen, when we—my messieurs, Paul, Julia, Merveille, and I—had all been enjoying some of Julia's cooking and a bottle of some very rare wine after apprehending a murderer. Merveille had even given me a compliment in front of everyone (which certainly accounted for Julia's and my messieurs' exacerbated interest in our nonexistent relationship). And now he seemed to have lost even that little bit of fellowship with me.

"Gabrielle Pineau seems to be under the impression that Christian Dior killed Rose-Marie Lannet," I said in an effort to change the subject from my supposed good luck at not being more injured, and my bad luck at being at the scene of yet another dead body.

The ever-implacable Merveille didn't even twitch an eyelash. "So Allard has put in his notes."

I ground my teeth. Wouldn't he give me *any* sort of *anything*? Not even a little hint of humor? His impression of this accusation? A bit of information? *Anything?*

Just then, there was a knock at the door of Merveille's office—which had been left open, likely in order to keep anyone from suspecting there was even a *chance* of anything untoward happening in his office with me that might get back to Marguerite.

It was Agent Fenèche, who was carrying my coat.

I thanked him profusely and took the coat, then turned to Merveille. "Thank you for helping me retrieve this. And good luck with the case. I hope you find out who did it before someone else dies."

His eyes narrowed. "And why would you think someone else might die, mademoiselle?" His eyes pinned me like a butterfly to a lepidopterist's mount.

"In my experience, they always do," I said with a shrug.

"In your *limited* experience and in the detective novels you read," he replied flatly. "Thank you again for your assistance, Mademoiselle Knight. If you think of anything else that might be helpful, you may call the station and leave word."

Well. That made his position very clear: *Don't call me or visit me here.*

"*Bonne journée,* Inspecteur," I said stiffly, pulling on my coat. "And *bonne chance.*"

I can't say I actually *fled* the station, but I certainly didn't linger. There was nothing like being told "don't bother me ever again" in that cool, unflappable manner.

Merveille's dismissal didn't matter to me anyway. I had another appointment, and then an alley cat to catch.

CHAPTER 5

I HAD TO MAKE A PLAN TO CATCH SAID ALLEY CAT. BUT I ALSO NEEDED to go to the market so I could have some idea of what I might make for dinner.

I heaved a great sigh at the thought.

By the time I got back home after my second tutoring appointment, it was almost three o'clock. I called Julia on the off-chance that she might want to go with me to the market . . . and give me some ideas for dinner.

"Of *course* I do!" she gushed. "I need some olive oil—I can't *believe* how quickly I go through that gorgeous ingredient and anyhow, you can tell me how it went at the 36."

I winced. I'd forgotten she'd be asking about that. And I'd probably have to tell her Merveille was now in charge of the murder investigation.

Maybe I didn't.

Because it didn't matter. After all, there was no reason I'd be involved any longer. I'd turned in the clue I found and now I could think about other things—like catching a poor, sick cat so he could get medical attention.

Which is how I began my conversation with Julia when we met up in front of her apartment building.

"So you're going to try and capture him?" she said after I explained. "And then what?"

"Well, I'll take him to the vet," I said.

"Yes. And then what?" She gave me a bemused look. "Minette wouldn't even consider allowing us to take in a competitor," she said, referring to her and Paul's cat. "Surely you don't think Madame X would condone an interloper." She laughed heartily.

Right. I hadn't thought quite that far ahead. Well, yes I had, but I hadn't *dwelled* on the question of what I'd do after Monsieur le Chat de Gouttière was treated by a vet. "Maybe he'd be content to prowl around my attic room," I said.

I had the entire second floor of the house for my living space. It had originally been sleeping quarters for the maids, sectioned off into small rooms, but now it was a generous bedroom with a large salon and a full bathroom. After sharing one bathroom with my three sisters, parents, and *grand-mère* at home, the luxury of having a bathroom completely to myself was something I had gotten used to very quickly. I'd taken to soaking in the large tub with a detective novel and sometimes even a glass of wine.

Julia laughed uproariously at my suggestion. "A cat who's used to wandering the streets day or night would be content enclosed in one floor of a house? Oh, dearie, you really don't know much about cats, do you?" She patted my arm affectionately as we walked along. "And you know you have to have a sandbox for him to do his business too," she added, giving me a skeptical look.

Ugh. For someone who prided herself on being pragmatic and thoughtful, I realized I really hadn't been thinking this all through. But my optimistic self and energetic internal imp assured me that everything would work itself out. The first thing I had to do was get the cat to the vet. I could worry about the rest later.

By now, we'd reached the first of the shops and merchants. The place was mostly an open-air market, with the street closed off to vehicles except for the trucks that came in in the morning to deliver the products and in the late evening to pick up what was left along with any empty crates or other items. The vendors had street carts or stalls with awnings filling the *rue*. Some had storefronts—like the fishmonger and the butcher—but the sellers of fruits, vegetables, flowers, and the like were out in the street.

Everyone knew everyone. The vendors knew their customers and the shoppers knew each other because we all lived within walking distance, and we all visited regularly. It was an utterly strange and wonderful experience shopping for food in Paris.

Everyone said "Bonjour!" and "*Bonne journée!*" to everyone else, and many of the shopkeepers insisted on shaking my hand in greeting as well. It was energetic and frenetic and loud and, on this crisp, sunny February day, the smells of coal and wood-smoke and cigarettes filtered through the air and mingled with the smells of *freshness.*

The food for sale here seemed so much more fresh than at home. I don't know if I could really smell the potatoes and wrinkled apples Madame Marie was selling, or the few, precious oranges in Mademoiselle Inga's cart, but I *felt* like I could. And I suppose that's all that mattered.

We were just approaching Madame Marie, better known as Marie des Quatre Saisons, because she had the best vegetables in the market during all four seasons—not to mention all of the gossip—when I heard someone call my name.

"Oh, Mademoiselle Knight! You are here! Bonjour!"

I turned to see Clarice Pillon, who worked as a day maid for a well-to-do family not far from the market. She was, as she often was, walking the dog belonging to her employers. Madame Flouf was a medium-sized, champagne-colored poodle. Today she was wearing a pink wool coat trimmed with a mink collar—yes, I mean the dog, not Clarice.

I'd never seen dogs dressed in clothing until I came to Paris, but after being exposed to Oscar Wilde and his array of tiny bow ties and an occasional tuxedo jacket or vest, I had become used to it. Still, it amused me when I saw the poodle dressed more fashionably and expensively than Clarice herself, who wore a simple brown tweed skirt.

"Bonjour," I said, slipping away from Julia and Madame Marie, the latter of whom had been looking at me with great contem-

plation while extolling the virtues of her beets and turnips—
which meant the old woman was poised to quiz me over my dat-
ing life. I was happy for an excuse to avoid that.

"Ah, Mademoiselle Knight, I am so glad to see you today.
Now, sit, madame, if you please," she said bending slightly to
speak to the poodle, whose head was about the height of my
stomach. The dog promptly sat and looked around from beneath the sproing of curls on her forehead.

"So Madame Flouf has fully recovered from her adventure a
while ago?" I asked, petting the soft, springy curls.

In December, Madame Flouf had gotten away from Clarice
and been out all night on a very, very cold night—the night a
woman named Thérèse Lognon had been murdered in Julia's
apartment building. That had been the first murder investigation I'd gotten involved in, and since Clarice had been out all
night searching for the missing pooch, she'd caught a glimpse
of the killer—a fact which had come in handy in identifying who
it was.

"Oh, yes, she has. She was very, very naughty that day, but she
doesn't *ever* want to spend a night out like that again, do you,
madame?" She scratched the poodle under the chin, then turned
her attention back to me. "But, mademoiselle, I need your help.
I mean, my *sister* needs your help."

I had never met Clarice's sister, but I knew who she was because I'd been the recipient of a glorious pair of shoes through
her. Mathilde Pillon worked in a fashionable shoe boutique—
Godot & Block—and on occasion, a pair of custom-made shoes
might not meet the needs of the customer, or they might have
some tiny flaw . . . and so they couldn't be sold.

That was why Clarice was always wearing unusually fashionable shoes instead of the boring, black, thick-soled ones, and
why I'd become the recipient of a pair of dark red Mary Janes
since I wore a size six and Clarice did not (she wore a size eight,
and apparently Mathilde wore a size seven). Poor Julia wore a
shoe size so large most places didn't even make them in Paris,
for anything over a size ten was unheard of in the shoe shops
here. The shoes I had inherited had a little scratch on one side

and so been rejected by the customer. But I certainly didn't mind and I knew no one would notice.

"What's wrong?" I asked.

"Oh, Mathilde, she says that someone broke into the shop last night, and Monsieur Block, he does not want to call the police! Mathilde says that she is very afraid to go back to work until the thief is caught!" Clarice had a spray of freckles over her fair skin, and this morning they stood out even more sharply than usual as if to emphasize her anxiousness. "And I don't blame her!"

I was nodding as I listened. When she stopped speaking and looked at me inquiringly, I said, "But how can I help Mathilde?"

"Oh, but she wants you to find out who it was!" Clarice said, her brown eyes wide with hope beneath hair almost as springy as Madame Flouf's. "You were so very smart when Mademoiselle Lognon was killed! Why, you asked me all of the questions, and you are *much* more trustworthy than *les flics*!" She made a dainty sort of *peh* sound of disgust.

Clarice's opinion of the police wasn't an unusual one. During the German occupation, most of the police force had collaborated with—or somehow assisted and supported—the Nazis in their horrific actions, including the rounding up of Jews to send them off to concentration camps or worse. The Parisian memory was not the least bit short, nor was its judgment lenient, when it came to who was a collaborator versus who resisted—or at least remained neutral—during the war years. That mistrust of the authorities continued to permeate their daily lives and interactions with authority five years later.

Not for the first time, I wondered, uneasily, what Merveille had done during the war. Had he been a collaborator? I couldn't deny that if I learned he had been, it would completely change the way I felt about him.

Not that I felt anything in particular, really; just that I had a high opinion of him as a detective and a seeker of justice.

"I see," I said, taken aback and yet intrigued at the same time. "Mathilde wants me to investigate the break-in and catch the culprit."

Clarice nodded vigorously. "And I told her about what happened before, when you were investigating the poisoned wines, and the old restaurant on rue Las Cases and how you captured—"

I broke in with a laugh. "I didn't actually capture anyone. And I'm flattered that she wants my help." I hesitated. I couldn't deny my interest in poking my nose into a situation; especially being sanctioned to do so. "But what does Monsieur Block think about this? If he's called in the police already . . ."

"But that is what I said! He has not!" Clarice said earnestly. Madame Flouf was getting restless; the dog had risen from her seated position and was tugging gently on the leash. Clarice reached down to calm her with a pet on the head. "He doesn't want *les flics* around at all. His wife was a Jew, you see."

I nodded, sobering. "And so Monsieur Block will be receptive to me looking around?"

"*Bien entendu,*" Clarice said with very wide eyes, which made me suspicious that Monsieur Block might *not* be receptive to someone poking around.

Still. I liked the idea of utilizing some of the tactics I'd learned about crime scene investigation from the books and journals my father had innocently sent me.

And along with that, there was the undeniable bump of pleasure I'd felt from Clarice's praise—especially welcome on the heels of Merveille's flat dismissal.

"All right," I said with a smile. "I'll do what I can."

Clarice was very enthusiastic. She even offered to bring over something for dinner for my messieurs that evening in exchange for my going to meet with Mathilde and Monsieur Block. Apparently, along with my abhorrent singleness, my lack of cooking finesse was common knowledge in the market. I wasn't certain whether to be mortified or grateful.

I decided it was much better to be grateful.

"Yes, you see, Henri, who is Mathilde's boyfriend, works at a brasserie," Clarice went on. "And so I can get a very nice meal from him and bring it to your house for Messieurs Saint-Léger and Fautrier when I get done with work. *He* does not want Mathilde working where there is someone breaking in!"

Although I doubted a thief would return to break into a shop after he had already done so, I agreed that I would go right away to Godot & Block and speak with Mathilde and Monsieur Block about the situation.

"Your reputation is preceding you, Tabs," Julia gushed when I told her about the situation, safely out of earshot from Madame Marie. I was determined to avoid the vegetable seller and her matchmaking questions, so I merely gave her a little wave and a gay "Bonsoir!" as Julia and I started back home. "Mark my words, this won't be the last time you'll be asked to do something like this! Pretty soon, you'll be as famous as Tuppence Beresford or Nancy Drew!"

I laughed. At least she hadn't compared me to Miss Marple.

Julia was still chattering. "I'd attach myself like a clingy *barnacle* and come along with you, but I've *got* to get working on that stock. It's going to be the richest, most golden and lush broth I've ever made! Absolutely spectacular! And when I drench that delicate, delectable *ballotine de veau* with it . . ." Her eyes had gone misty and she clasped her hands in front of her chest as if embracing a loved one. "Paul's not going to know what *hit* him when he tastes it."

"He's a lucky man," I said.

"Speaking of lucky men," said Julia, giving me a meaningful look. "Don't think I didn't notice how you avoided telling me about what happened when you went to the police station today. Did you see him?"

"No, Inspecteur Allard wasn't at the station," I told her quite honestly. "I wasn't there very long anyway, but I did get my coat," I said quickly and succinctly in hopes of avoiding any more questions. I wasn't certain whether I would lie to her or not, so I decided I'd prefer to avoid the situation. I certainly wasn't going to tell her that the picture of Marguerite had disappeared.

Julia seemed disappointed, and I changed the subject before she could ask anything else. I kept her talking about the precious stock she was making, and the fact that Paul's birthday was coming up.

We parted in front of my house and I gave her a hug before

going up the walkway. Godot & Block was on the Right Bank, not very far from Maison Lannet, and so I was going to drive over there.

After assuring my messieurs that their dinner was going to be delivered by Clarice and that I wasn't certain when I'd be home, I hustled out of the house. It was getting close to four thirty, and Clarice had told me the shoe shop closed at five.

It was not a surprise to me that Godot & Block was located in the same area as many of the fashion ateliers. In fact, it was on rue Jean Goujon, which was a street that ran at a forty-five-degree angle to avenue Montaigne, where Maison Dior and Maison Lannet were stationed. It wasn't until I found the storefront of the shoe shop that I realized its backside was across from the backside of Maison Lannet.

My internal sprite, the one that spurs me into doing impetuous and sometimes foolhardy things, was ecstatic. Could it be a coincidence that there was a break-in at Godot & Block, a shop located just across a small alley and courtyard from Maison Lannet, on the same night that a killer exited that way? Surely not.

Surely not! said my imp more emphatically.

Was it possible that the break-in at the shoe shop was caused by the killer, trying to get away without being caught?

All of these thoughts bounded through my head as I approached the storefront. The window display featured six pairs of shoes, each gorgeous and crafted of well-tooled leather.

Some shops have a little bell that tinkles when a person walks in, but I'd noticed that in these fine, high-end places, it was not the case. That was because there was always a polite, efficient, and perfectly groomed vendeuse waiting to greet anyone stepping over the threshold. In this case, the saleswoman was instantly recognizable to me as Mathilde Pillon.

She had the same face shape, fair skin, and large brown eyes as her sister, but in her case, the freckles were mostly obscured by makeup. She looked as if she might be the elder sister, being in her late twenties.

"Bonjour, Mademoiselle Pillon," I said, offering my hand to shake hers. "I am Tabitha Knight. Your sister sent me."

You would have thought I'd just announced she'd won a million francs.

"Oh, mademoiselle, oh, *oh*! I cannot believe it! Thank you so much! Oh, this is terrible, you see, only *terrible*! Thank you, thank you!" She'd taken my hand with both of hers and was grasping it tightly. "But you know, I simply cannot feel safe here with all of this! *All* of this!" She cast a dark look toward the back of the shop where, presumably, Monsieur Block was lurking. "And *he* does not seem to care that I am now *terrified* to come to work! *Terrified!* First there is a murder and now there is a break-in! What if the killer comes back to do *me* in?"

I managed to extricate my fingers from hers. "I will do whatever I can to help. Now, could you show me where this break-in happened?"

I was fully expecting to be taken to the back of the shop where the rear door of Maison Lannet would likely be visible from across the pitiful courtyard I'd seen last night, but to my surprise, Mathilde simply spread her hands to encompass the area where we were standing.

"It was here. And when we came in this morning, the shoes—they were all over the floor. Out of their boxes. All of the orders jumbled up! Two pairs of the shoes for Madame Outhier and one set for Comtesse Brigitte will have to be remade, for they were scuffed and scratched. And, oh, for Madame Joilliet! She will be frantic about it!"

Of course I resisted the urge to ask whether Comtesse Brigitte wore a size six like I did. I was a professional. "Was anything taken?"

"Only a few francs. They were in the drawer. Every day, Monsieur Block takes all the money with him just before closing, and then to the bank or in the morning, you see, so there isn't much to tempt a thief. And then *I* am here by myself, you see, to do the closing up! And I do *not* want to be here by myself any longer! And Henri, he is very angry and he does not want me here alone either!"

"And what about Monsieur Godot?" I asked. "Does he come in to work every day too?"

"Oh, he is dead many years now. It is only Monsieur Block and his little assistant, Pietro."

I nodded, trying to look like the professional I was determined to be. "How do you think the culprit got in? Through the back door?"

"*Non, non, non!* They came in through here, this door. It was open a bit when I got here this morning."

"You were the first person here, then?" I asked. "Is that normally the case?"

"*Oui,* of course. I will be here to open the shop and turn on the lights. Every day. Every morning. *Alone.*" She stressed the fact of her solitude once more. "I have told my Henri about it, and he is very upset about it. He and Monsieur Block—they do not get along. And now he is even more angry at him."

"Did you notice anything on the floor or near the entrance? Footprints? A cigarette butt?"

"I didn't look at the ground, mademoiselle. I went to open the door and I found that it was already opened, and then, *oh no!* You see?" She made an energetic gesture near her head suggesting that her brain had gone fluttery or exploded or otherwise malfunctioned. I got the message.

"Yes, I see. Um . . . how do you think they got in? Was the door or lock broken?" Even as I asked, I went over to the door and opened it to look at the outside. It was getting dark on the street, but since I had remembered to bring the small flashlight I'd recently purchased, I was able to see that there were a few faint scratches and markings near the keyhole. It was very possible someone had picked the lock. Or it might only have been carelessness of someone trying to fit in the key. It was difficult to tell.

I had lockpicks, thanks to my father, but I hadn't thought to bring them. If I had, I'd have tried to pick the lock myself to see how easy it might have been.

"What do you see?" Mathilde crowded me as I examined the door.

"It is possible someone picked the lock." If true, that was yet another blow to my theory—well, my hope—that the killer from Maison Lannet had used the shoe shop as an escape. He or she wouldn't have forced open the front door from outside; they would have been coming in through the back door of the shop then possibly out the front.

"Ah! You see! It is terrible! Even the locks won't keep them out!" Again Mathilde glared into the back of the shop. "And he, Monsieur Block, does not even care the *least* for my safety!"

I was now very eager to meet this Monsieur Block, with whom she was quite disgusted.

"Why is he so intent on not reporting this to the police?" I asked.

Mathilde shrugged. "That, I do not know. He says to me that it was even possible my beau Henri who did such a thing as a joke so that I would quit this job and find another one—which is not even funny. Monsieur has always hoped I would like his son instead of Henri, and so they are always fighting with each other! And so if he can put my Henri in a bad light, and tease me about him, then he thinks I will want to see Charles Block? *Peh.* Of course not!"

I nodded, a little confused about the correlation between a break-in and the absent Henri, but I could certainly relate to the idea of wanting to pick my own boyfriend instead of being match-made.

"Do *you* have any idea who might have done this?" I asked.

"No, no, I do not!" Her voice was tight with gathering tears.

"All right. I'll look around. Perhaps I should speak with Monsieur Block?"

I wanted to ask more questions, but I couldn't think of any. I suddenly felt as if I were out of my depth. Mathilde had no information, could tell me nothing, and there weren't any handy clues just sitting on the floor for me to find.

Maybe this detective stuff wasn't as easy as I thought.

Still . . . I began to look around the shop, knowing it was probably futile. After all, people had been in and out all day long. Any clue to the thief's identity would have been obliterated.

"Did you have a lot of customers today?" I asked, peering under one of the four seats where someone might sit to try on shoes. There was no dust underneath—a testament to Mathilde's efficiency—and the foot measuring tools were neatly stacked nearby.

"Oh, *oui*, mademoiselle. You see, there was a *murder* last night on avenue Montaigne—did you not hear? And that is why I am so very frightened!—and of course everyone had to come out and see about it." Her eyes were round. "And so, yes, we had many people coming through the door today, asking many questions. And not about the shoes!"

I sighed. Drat.

I was just rising from my futile investigation when the shop door opened. To my surprise, I recognized the young woman who came in.

It was the mannequin from Maison Lannet whose short, cropped hair I'd admired.

CHAPTER 6

"AH, MATHILDE!" CRIED THE MANNEQUIN. THE TWO WOMEN embraced. "It has been so horrible! Just *horrible!*"

"Oh, Lisette!" cried Mathilde, patting the other woman on the back. "It is only the most terrible day! I am so sorry for you! But I am so glad you have come! And now we have even more tragedy! Look, do you see?" She took the mannequin—Lisette—by the arm and drew her to the front door, where she opened it and pointed to the markings I had noticed around the lock. "Someone has broken in here too!"

"*Non, non,* it cannot be true!" cried Lisette. "Was it the killer? No, it couldn't be!"

This went on for another few moments as I tried to decide how to interrupt. At last, the dramatics waned and the two women turned to face me. Lisette's eyes were puffy and her mascara had smudged beneath them. She removed her hat, which had been knocked askew during their embrace, and I automatically noted that her short, thick hair didn't look wild or staticky the way mine would.

"This is Mademoiselle Knight," said Mathilde, holding her friend's hand tightly. "She is going to help prove that Henri didn't do this. Maybe she can help you too?"

"Oh, oh, I know you!" cried Lisette, still in a tight, high voice. I wondered if that was her normal tone. "You were there yesterday, *non?* For the showing?"

"I was, yes. I was the one who found Madame Lannet's—Madame Lannet."

"Oh, oh, how terrible it must have been! And to think I had only just gone away! What if the killer had come for me instead?" A hand rose to cup her throat in an echo of the strangling lace. "It is frightening to think of it!"

"Terribly frightening," I said, then went on quickly in an effort to keep her from going off again, "Do you have any idea who might have done such a thing?"

"Me?" Her brown eyes, perfectly almond-shaped with thick lashes, went wide into circles. "But, no, of course not! It was a strangler, like they had in London, *non*? A person who just comes upon an innocent woman and—*kitz*!" She pulled an imaginary rope tight around her neck and stuck out her tongue while her eyes bulged.

I sighed internally. I didn't for one minute think that the person who killed Madame Lannet had wandered in randomly off the street, happened upon a piece of lace, and strangled her.

I decided to try again. "But it was a piece of lace that was used. Surely a person who is just coming in off the street with the intent to kill someone would have brought their own—er—method of strangulation with them. Was the lace from one of the workshops at Maison Lannet?"

I realized it was a bad question as soon as I asked it. The lace would have been taken along as evidence, and so there was no way Lisette would have seen it. "Do you know, did Madame Pineau recognize it? Perhaps what frock or gown it was from? The lace."

"Oh." Lisette looked at me, for the first time that wild, fearful look ebbing from her eyes. "Why . . . yes. She said it was for the Field." At my confused look, she explained, "The evening frock Madame Lannet has named the Field."

"So the lace was definitely taken from the workshops of Maison Lannet," I said. "Which means that whoever it was who killed Madame Lannet didn't plan to do so, but took advantage of the situation. Where is that lace kept, mademoiselle, do you know?" I went on, putting aside the fact that I was supposed to be investigating a break-in, not a murder.

"Oh, but it is a special lace, you see," Lisette said. All vestiges of her dramatics had faded and she was far more thoughtful and calm. "I think only Madame Lannet and perhaps Madame Diot—she is the *première main,* in charge of all the workers—would know where it is. It is for the special trim on a frock for Madame Joilliet. She likes the lace . . . ah, perhaps even too much of it . . . on her frocks. And I think it has only come in from a special order from Alençon."

"So you're saying this particular lace wouldn't have been easy for anyone to find and use. In other words, it wouldn't have been the first one at hand for a killer to grab."

"*Oui*. But all of the fabrics and trims are upstairs, you see. Where the workrooms are. Not in the *cabine*. But . . . Madame Lannet, she would perhaps have it in her office," replied Lisette, frowning as she thought. "If it has just come in, you see. She would want to look at it, check it, to make certain there are no flaws."

"And what about *Henri?*" Mathilde broke in with a little wail. "All of this about murders and lace, but what of *mon pauvre Henri?* Monsieur Block—*he* will accuse him! I know he will! Anything to break us up!"

I turned to her. "Yes, of course. I'm just attempting to determine whether these two incidents are connected. It appears . . . not," I admitted.

At that moment, a man appeared from the back of the shop—the infamous Monsieur Block, I deduced, by the fact that he wore a work apron and appeared to be in his forties or fifties with a surprisingly thick head of hair and a sparse mustache and beard. Surely too old to be the assistant.

"And what is all this?" he said. Smoke streamed in great puffs from his cigarette as if he were a locomotive engine.

Mathilde started, then quickly recovered. "Monsieur, this is

Mademoiselle Knight. She is here to help find out who it was that broke in last night. And it *wasn't* Henri!" she added with a burst of defiance.

"Peh," said Block, waving a hand. "Of course it was. He has that look about him. That shifty look. You can do much better than him!" His French, though fluent, had the tinge of a British accent. He turned his attention onto me, then his gaze dropped. "And you are not from *les flics*, mademoiselle?"

I realized he was assessing my choice of footwear, which was not, in this case, anything I was proud of. I resisted the urge to squirm by curling my toes inside my clunky but serviceable American boots—which had been sent to me by my parents for a Christmas gift.

"No, I am not a police agent. Monsieur Block, I'll do my best to determine who broke into your shop. Mathilde says there is nothing missing but a few francs?"

"*Oui.* A few francs, she says—as if it is nothing! *Peh.* But it is the ruination of the shoes—the shoes that I have slaved over so carefully, and now they cannot be sold and I will have to buy new leather for them! It is the *shoes*," he repeated, glaring at all of us as if we'd had the temerity to argue with him.

"Yes, I see," I replied. I knew that such a pair of custom shoes, handmade and finely tooled and designed, could cost upward of a thousand francs. "Do you have any idea who might have done this—besides Henri?" I added quickly when his eyes narrowed and his mouth opened, obviously to accuse the young man.

"No. No one. There is no one but that boy. He is a disreputable sort." He gave Mathilde a grumpy look punctuated by another puff of smoke and she shot him back a glare of her own. I got the impression that their relationship was as strong and comfortable as that of my messieurs, despite their solid disagreement on this point.

"But why would Henri do such a thing? It would only create a problem for his girl," I said reasonably. "Surely he wouldn't want to do that."

"*Non!* Of course he would not," Mathilde said.

"You said the shoes have been ruined, monsieur," I went on.

"The shoes—many shoes. They are ruined."

"Yes, of course. But if it was only a thief, maybe the shoes would have been taken to sell instead of only damaged and left behind. After all, your work is very valuable. Maybe the person who did this only wanted to cause you trouble—so that you would have to remake the shoes, perhaps not finishing an order on time. And that you might not have the proper tools to do it? Perhaps to disrupt your relationship with your customers, *non?*"

The cigarette Block had clamped between his lips sagged. "What are you saying? That someone has destroyed these things purposely? To ruin my business?"

"It's very possible. What sort of damage was done to the shoes? Is it something that might have happened by accident when they were thrown about, or is it something that perhaps only a shoemaker would know to do in order to ruin a shoe? Something deliberate?"

I could see that my questions were causing him to consider another option, and I admit I was proud of myself for thinking of that angle, when only a few minutes ago I was stymied.

"But . . . that is possible," he said, giving Mathilde a reluctant look. He turned away and went swiftly into the back room, leaving us alone.

"*Merci*, Mademoiselle Knight!" Mathilde said, her cheeks flushed with pleasure as she took my arm. "You have saved Henri!"

"Don't thank me yet," I replied. "I still have to find out who did it."

Monsieur Block returned as swiftly as he'd come. He was carrying several shoes, none of them a pair, and he dumped them onto the sales counter. "Ah! You see! It is as you said—the damage, it is not the simple scuffs or the scratches, *non?* I see it, mademoiselle! Now I see that whoever it was, they have poked the little holes with a hand awl, they have slit the stitches so that the leather is cut and the sole is broken. And so he ruined only one in a pair, but I must still buy the new leather for both to re-make them. For they won't match otherwise!" He looked up at me with an epiphany in his eyes. "This is someone who knew what to do to make these shoes so they cannot be used or sold."

"*Not* Henri!" cried Mathilde defiantly.

"*Non.*" Block gave her a wary look. "So it is not your Henri. *Ah!* It is that Philippe! It must be!"

"But of course it is!" Mathilde replied, clasping his arm as if they were friends again—which, it seemed, they were. "He is so angry that you have taken his clients! The *duc* and the Lady Joil-liet!"

"Ah, yes, of course I took his clients. He is a poor craftsman; anyone can see it!" said Block. His eyes glinted with fury. "A poor craftsman but with a big name and many friends. And so how will I catch him? How will I prove it?"

"I have an idea," I said. I was keeping an eye on Lisette be-cause I didn't want her to leave before I had a chance to talk with her. But she was wandering about the shop, idly picking up shoe models and even trying some of them on. I didn't know how well-paid mannequins were, so I didn't know whether she could afford those shoes, but she certainly knew good fashion when she saw it.

"What is it?" Mathilde asked.

"If it is this rival shoemaker—this Philippe—perhaps you could put it out that you've acquired a new, very valuable cus-tomer and that he will be picking up his custom-made shoes on a certain date. And you tell everyone about it. You talk about it very proudly and with great excitement. And so on the night be-fore this customer is to pick up the shoes, you lie in wait, se-cretly, here in the shop to catch him—because he will certainly come to destroy them before your great success."

"Yes! Yes! That is it! That is what we shall do! And we will cap-ture him with our bare hands!" Mathilde was delighted. "And Henri, he will wait with you, monsieur," she went on placidly. "He will help you to capture that Philippe."

Monsieur Block's face fell. "But a new customer who has a large, special shoe order . . . why, where can I find that? I cannot lie, for the lie will be found out. Everyone knows everyone here, you see?"

I smiled. "I can help you there as well. I can give you not one, but two famous, well-known customers who will go along with this scheme."

"And who is this?"

"Maurice Saint-Léger and Rafael Fautrier."

His eyes popped wide, then narrowed. His cigarette pumped out more smoke. "But you cannot do that. They—why, they already do the shopping with Monsieur Fath."

I continued to smile. "They will do it for you, for this purpose, at least. I am Monsieur Saint-Léger's granddaughter. I can promise you they will both do as I ask."

Monsieur Block's face blossomed into an expression of shock, hope, and then pleasure. "But, mademoiselle, this I did not know! How is it that the granddaughter of Monsieur Saint-Léger is—is—doing *this*?" He gestured to the space at large.

"But, you see, she was the one who found the killer with the poisoned wines," Mathilde said proudly. "My sister knows her well, Clarice, and mademoiselle even wears a pair of your shoes, Monsieur Block."

His attention dropped to my feet again. "She certainly does not."

While Mathilde explained how I came to be in possession of a pair of deep red Mary Janes I was obviously not wearing, I took the opportunity to wander over to talk to Lisette, who'd taken a seat to try on a pair of pale blue evening shoes.

I noticed, again, how attractive her hair was—tousled but not out of control and frizzy; feminine yet not long in length. I was determined to find out who cut and styled it for her, but murder was the more pressing topic.

Lisette seemed more than willing to talk to me, for she said, "I was listening to what you said there about the break-in, and it's smart. Do you think someone only wanted to hurt Maison Lannet and so that is why they did away with Madame?" She'd calmed from her earlier dramatics and although her voice was still high, it wasn't tense or tight as before.

"It's possible. Did Madame Lannet have anyone who might have wanted her fashion house not to succeed? To have her business ruined? And remember, whoever did it would have to have been able to come into the shop and find their way around easily."

"I don't know about anyone who would want to rival her as someone has done to Monsieur Block," Lisette said. "Maison Lannet is very new. The madame has only been approved by the Chambre Syndicale last year, and so this is her first collection. She has not had the time to make rivals, you see? But there was quite a lot of excitement about her collections. We have been busy every day for the shows since the collection opened."

"Where was Madame Lannet working before she opened her own house?" I knew Inspecteur Allard—and now Merveille— would be asking these same questions, but I wasn't there to hear the answers and of course my internal sprite was egging me on now that I'd had success—I hoped—with the shoe shop break-in.

"She was with Monsieur Dior, of course," said Lisette, giving me a strange look. "And before him, she was with Lelong."

"Madame Pineau seems to think that Monsieur Dior was envious of Madame Lannet and that he might have committed the crime."

As I had hoped, Lisette burst out laughing. "*C'est ridicule!* Of course Monsieur Dior has no concerns over Madame Lannet. After all, he left Lelong to make his own house. It happens, you see."

"Were you at Maison Dior before coming to Maison Lannet?" I asked.

Her eyelids flickered and her gaze bounced away. "*Non.*"

I waited. Merveille had unwittingly taught me that silence was an excellent tactic to get someone to speak even when they were reluctant to do so.

It took only a moment. "I was nowhere before Maison Lannet," she said, her voice tightening up again. "I was only a shop-girl in a *prêt-à-porter* clothing boutique. But Madame Pineau, she came into my shop one time and she looked me over and she said that I should come to avenue Montaigne and see about a job." She cast me a sudden, vehement glance. "I was not a prostitute!"

As it had never occurred to me that she might have been, I only blinked and said, "Of course not."

"But you see, that is what they said, only to be mean! The others," she spat.

I was having a difficult time following her logic, so, again, I let her speak.

"The ones at Dior and at Fath! And Lanvin! The mannequins. You see, not so long ago—in '46—the law changed and all of the brothels were closed. And when Monsieur Dior put it about that he was hiring pretty girls for his atelier right when this happened, why, they all came.

"*Les prostituées* lined up, crowded the place, you see, because they needed a job! So many of them came, there was no room to walk inside." Now her eyes danced with a bit of humor. "Madame Pineau said as how there were so many who came that day, all of them were *prostituées*, but none of them suitable. Ah, but there was only *one* who came that day who was suitable and was hired, but she was not a prostitute. She is becoming famous now for Dior, you see. Marie-Thérèse is her name."

From this anecdote, I was able to extract one relevant piece of information. "Madame Pineau was there at Maison Dior too?"

"Oh, *oui.* And that is why the other girls like to tease and ask whether I was a prostitute. Because they know about that day, and Madame Pineau was at Dior during that time and she found me, you see, and so they think it is so about *me!*" Her eyes glistened with angry tears. "Only because I was first a shopgirl and not—*beh!*" She spat in disgust.

"I see," I said, although I wasn't certain I did. "When did Madame Pineau leave Dior?"

"Why, she left when Madame Lannet did, of course."

"When they left Dior to start Maison Lannet, was there a problem with Monsieur Dior?"

"But no, as I have said. Not at all. He was not happy, of course, but to hear it told, he was only concentrated on his work. He knew Madame Raymonde and Madame Bricard would take care of it all. And so they have. Dior is the top of the haute couture world." She sounded a little wistful.

I nodded. I knew there were more questions I should ask, but I couldn't think of any at the moment. In an effort to keep her interest, I said, "If you don't mind my saying, your hairstyle is very pretty. Would you tell me where you get it cut? I have been thinking about doing the same with mine." I gestured upward, but with my hat still on, she surely couldn't fully appreciate the disaster of my hair.

To my surprise, she looked at me closely for a moment, tilting her head from side to side. "Take off your hat," she ordered, and I complied. I actually felt my hair explode with static electricity. It was a good thing I couldn't see it.

After another few moments of examination—which, to my surprise, included her reaching out and fingering some of my hair—and more head tilting, Lisette nodded. "*Oui.* I think it would be very, very beautiful on you, mademoiselle. This short cut. Not everyone can wear it, you see. But you, you have the face and the hair. And your eyes, they are big and the brows are dark and so do not get lost, and that is important too." She nodded once, as if the deed had already been done. "I will do it."

She'd surprised me again. "You? But I was hoping that your own beautician would do it—"

She was laughing. "Oh, but it is me, you see! I have cut my own hair." She flipped a hand through her locks and when she pulled it away, they fell back into place, tousled but pretty.

"You did that yourself?"

"Oh, *oui,* mademoiselle," said Mathilde, who'd joined us by now. "Lisette, she is an artist with the hair. *Une déesse.* I have told her many times she is being wasted as a mannequin. She has cut my hair too." She fluffed her own style, which was longer than the one I hoped for but no less attractive.

"I will do this for you because you have helped my friend, *non?*" Lisette said, wrapping her arm around Mathilde's waist. "Come, let us go."

"Let me get my handbag," said Mathilde, darting away as I balked.

"You want to do it now?" I said.

"But why not?"

Yes. Why not?

I reached up to touch my hair, which nearly brushed my shoulders. That was going to be a lot of hair cut off. I felt a rush of nerves. Did I *really* want to do it?

"Come, come, mademoiselle," Lisette said impatiently. "Let us go. Mathilde! Hurry up! We are cutting Mademoiselle Knight's hair," announced Lisette.

"And what a transformation it will be!" Mathilde said as she reappeared with her handbag. She spoke with far more excitement than I was feeling.

"But first, a little dinner, *non?*" Lisette said, patting her tummy. "I have not been able to eat all day, and now at last, my stomach is settling."

"Oh, *oui*, and I will go with you too," said Mathilde. "Monsieur Block, I am leaving now!" she called back.

I might have heard a grunt from the back of the shop, but I wasn't certain. By then, I was being swept out of the front door of the shop and down the street.

There was a little cafe where we sat at a tiny table inside and quickly ate cheese and tomato baguettes. By the time we had finished, we were all on a first-name basis and the sun had dipped behind the buildings in the west. I was enjoying the company of my two energetic companions and we were all laughing about Monsieur Block and his backhanded matchmaking when we came out of the boulangerie. The streetlights had come on and the shops were all closed. People were going to dinner or heading home after work.

"Oh, *zut.*" Lisette stopped suddenly on the street. "My scissors are at Maison Lannet. I keep them there, you see, for the touch-ups." She flicked a finger at her head. "We will have to go there first to get them."

"But it's closed up as a crime scene," I said, although my internal sprite was doing cartwheels at the possibility of getting back inside the building.

Lisette shrugged. "I have a key, of course."

"Who else has a key?" I asked immediately. I wasn't certain it mattered; for the shop hadn't been locked when I came in and found Madame Lannet. Anyone could have come inside.

"Madame Pineau, of course, and myself because I come early and stay late sometimes, and Madame Guillaume, the *première* of the workers. Maybe one of the other mannequins too."

I warred with myself. Was it wrong to go back inside the crime scene? It had been more than twenty-four hours. Surely the police had done what they needed to do. Merveille was very efficient. And we were only going inside to get a pair of scissors.

Obviously, my zest for adventure and curiosity won out.

I was only mildly surprised when Mathilde directed us back to Godot & Block. "We will cut across the courtyard so we don't have to walk all the way around the block, *non?*"

The shoe shop was dark and silent, and I felt the tension from Mathilde as she unlocked the front door. I could understand why she would not be thrilled about the idea of coming here alone early in the morning or later in the afternoon when it was still dark.

She turned on only one small light for us as we walked briskly through the front part of the shop back through the empty workrooms.

As I had already realized, the back door of Godot & Block led into a tiny courtyard with a narrow alley exit—the same courtyard and alley shared by the back of Maison Lannet. There was no light outside the back door, and the deserted, wintry court-yard added to the creepiness of the situation. As we picked our way across, trying to avoid anything disgusting, we startled a cat who'd been rooting in a trash can. He hissed at us, then went back to his digging. He reminded me of my own Monsieur Alley Cat, and my intent to get him medical attention.

Lisette unlocked the back door to Maison Lannet, and Mathilde and I stepped into the same corridor where I'd found the metal cylinder last night. This was the hallway through which I was cer-tain the killer had passed.

The building was silent and shadowy, and I felt the sudden hesitation in Lisette's movements. It must have finally sunk in that this was the place a woman had died only last night.

Lisette paused. Mathilde grabbed my hand in a death grip, as if she were afraid a killer—or a ghost—was going to erupt from the shadows.

After a moment, I heard Lisette exhale a shaky breath, and then she reached out and pushed the light switch. The flood of light that filled the short hallway was welcome, as were the other lights Lisette turned on as we made our way to the front of the building.

Everything was quiet and still. Mathilde gripped my hand as well as Lisette's as we started toward the grand staircase that would take us to the first floor where the salon was located. De-spite the lights Lisette turned on along the way, I could hear short, unsteady breaths coming from both young women.

When we got to the stairs, I gratefully extracted my hand from Mathilde's death grip, for the treads were too narrow for the three of us to walk abreast. Lisette led the way up with Mathilde fairly sewn to her side.

"I wish Henri were here," I heard Mathilde wail softly.

We climbed to the first floor, past the salon, then kept going to the second floor, where the *cabine* and Madame Lannet's of-fice were located.

As we got to the top of the second flight of stairs, I stopped suddenly.

"Cigarette smoke," I said softly, sniffing. Yes, there was the definite scent of smoke in the air.

Someone had been here recently.

CHAPTER 7

MATHILDE AND LISETTE TURNED.

"What is it?" the latter asked nervously.

"I smell cigarette smoke," I said, keeping my voice quiet. "Someone has been here recently." I knew it couldn't have been Merveille poking around the scene, for I'd never seen him smoke.

"*The killer!*" Lisette whispered, her eyes wide.

Mathilde made a quiet sound of fear and huddled so close to me, dragging Lisette with her, that I was afraid we'd tumble down the stairs. I gave her a gentle push. "Keep going."

"But—"

"It's okay," I said, and maneuvered us safely to the top of the steps. "There are three of us and only one of him," I said, allowing my voice to carry. "And Henri will be here any minute now, won't he?"

Mathilde gaped at me, opened her mouth to argue, then Lisette elbowed her and she squeaked out a "Yes! Yes, he is coming!"

I pulled away from clinging hands and tried to follow the scent of smoke, but although it lingered on the landing, it didn't seem to be particularly thick anywhere. It was also fading.

How long did cigarette smoke linger in a space? If I knew that, I could guess how long ago the person had been here.

I wondered if I should call Merveille to tell him someone had been here, but immediately and vehemently rejected that idea. He would be furious for many reasons.

Instead, I decided to look around. Hoping that if the intruder was here, I'd scared him—or her—off from attacking us, I boldly walked across the landing, trying to sniff out whether the tobacco scent was stronger from any particular direction.

I couldn't tell whether it was, but I went into Madame Lannet's office. It was dark and silent, and it appeared much the same as it had been last night.

When I turned to go back out, I nearly ran into Lisette and Mathilde. They were nearly glued to each other, and, it seemed, wanted me to join the crowd. I kept my distance, preferring to be able to breathe and move readily. Lisette had taken up an umbrella from somewhere, presumably as a weapon—a ploy with which I agreed. I patted my skirt pocket and felt the comforting weight of my tool knife, but I didn't take it out.

"Where are your scissors?" I asked Lisette in a normal voice.

"They are upstairs by the workshops in the locker where I can keep all of my belongings. Madame Pineau does not like the clutter *dans la cabine,* as she says, for someone might see it when they visit Madame Lannet's office." She gestured to the stairs that led to the third floor—a far more utilitarian flight than the sweeping staircases we'd just climbed. "We are only to freshen our makeup and add perfume in the *cabine.*"

Once again, I boldly led the way up the steps, with the two others close on my heels.

The hair at the back of my neck prickled as we climbed, for I was certain the smell of cigarette smoke lingered up here as well. Stronger, perhaps.

"Would Madame Pineau be here tonight, do you think?" I asked Lisette as we got to the top. There was a small landing with three doors, and another set of stairs to the fourth and highest floor.

"I don't know. Why would she come to this place after what happened?" she asked, probably unaware of the irony of her question.

"Does she smoke?" I asked. What would the killer—if indeed it was the killer whose cigarette I was smelling—want with these upstairs rooms? The workshops, I assumed. I knew that in order to be granted haute couture status, the couturier had to employ a certain number of seamstresses, known as *les petites mains*, and crafters on-site.

"Madame Pineau? No, she does not smoke. She does not let anyone smoke here in the workshops or in the *cabine*. She claims it makes the fabrics smell." Lisette's tone suggested she was in stark disagreement with that position. "But she cannot keep the clients from smoking in the salon, can she?"

"Well, someone has been smoking here," I said. "On this floor, I think."

Lisette and Mathilde sniffed audibly, then nodded. "*Oui*, I can smell it here too," said the mannequin.

"Let's get your scissors," I said, suddenly feeling the strong urge to leave.

"Yes, of course." Lisette slipped past me and darted into one of the rooms.

Despite—or maybe because of—my sudden desire to leave, I pushed open one of the other doors.

It was obviously one of the workrooms. The space was large with many tables and only two stingy windows. When my attention landed on the figure of a person standing in the shadows, I nearly had a heart attack. From Mathilde's quickly stifled gasp and the sudden, talon-like grip on my arm, I knew she'd thought the same. I realized quickly that it was only a dressmaker's dummy, but my heart was still pounding, my knees trembling. There were several of those dressmaker forms littered about the room, most attired with the model of a frock or gown in some stage of creation.

I felt on the wall for the light switch. I don't know why; we were supposed to be getting Lisette's scissors and leaving. But I suppose I wanted to see what a haute couture workroom looked like—and maybe even catch a glimpse of some of the gorgeous gowns in process.

I pushed the button and the lights came on, illuminating the room as bright as the sunniest day.

Mathilde screamed in my ear, but I hardly noticed because I, too, had seen the crumpled figure lying in a dark, shiny pool of blood. The same ugly red saturated the front of the woman's dress where a large pair of sewing scissors protruded. Its benign oval handles gleamed innocently.

Lisette rushed up as I yanked away from Mathilde's death grip and moved to the body.

It was Gabrielle Pineau.

Careful not to step in the blood or to disrupt anything, I lifted a wrist to feel for a pulse. There was far too much blood for her to be alive, but I had to check anyway. There was blood all over her hand, as if she'd clutched herself at the wound or tried to pull the scissors free. The blood was smeared and still a little wet, which made me nervous. She hadn't been attacked very long ago.

"Call the police," I said over my shoulder, trying to ignore the squeaky sobs from Mathilde and the panting, half-crying breaths from Lisette as they huddled in the doorway. I drew a deep breath, and, resigned, added, "Ask for Inspecteur Merveille to come."

As I'd expected, there was no pulse. Heaving a sigh, I eased back from Madame Pineau. The poor woman. It couldn't have been a pleasant way to die, and possibly not a quick one if she'd had time to try to pull the scissor blades free.

"Rest in peace, madame," I said. I hoped she *would* be at peace with her beloved Rose-Marie, whatever their relationship might have been.

I rose. Mathilde had gone with Lisette to make the telephone call, and I wanted to look around the room . . . but another part of me wanted to fly the coop before Merveille arrived and pinned me with that cold, frustrated look when finding me at the scene of yet another dead body. The novelty of being an amateur detective was starting to wear off, and even I was beginning to wonder why I seemed to attract these tragedies.

Only a few weeks ago, I'd been in the position to stop a death from happening and I hadn't acted. I knew it wasn't my fault, but I still carried some of that guilt. And now, two people were dead in less than twenty-four hours—both in a place I had just visited. I knew it was ridiculous, but I couldn't help but feel as if my visit to Maison Lannet had precipitated these deaths.

I blinked at the sudden sting of tears in my eyes. It truly wasn't my fault, none of this was, but I couldn't help but feel somehow responsible. Not that Madame Pineau's body wouldn't have been discovered if I hadn't wanted my hair cut. . . .

I wandered around the room, a little listless, but still looking for something. I assumed Lisette and Mathilde had gone down to the second floor to use the telephone in Madame Lannet's office. I was looking sightlessly at a gorgeous, rumpled pool of blue taffeta when I heard a noise from above. It sounded like a quiet thump.

I bolted from the room, bringing a chair with me and yanking the tool knife from my pocket. I headed for the bottom of the stairs to the fourth floor, shouting for Mathilde and Lisette. "He's still here! Help me catch him!"

I did not expect the two young women to help me capture a murderer. *I* didn't really want to capture a killer. But I wanted the culprit to know that I'd heard him and that there was no escape. I stood at the bottom of the stairs that led up to what must be more workrooms—I certainly wasn't going to go up there! He'd have to get by me, the chair I would brandish like a lion tamer, and my tool knife.

"The police are on their way!" I shouted up the stairs.

The sounds of bounding footsteps from behind me heralded the return of Mathilde and Lisette.

"What is it? What is happening?" cried Mathilde.

I explained and she shrank back a little. But I saw that she now held her own umbrella with its pointy ferule at the ready. The three of us stood there at the bottom of the stairs, ready to fight off anyone who might appear.

There was silence except for our breathing—not particularly

easy or slow, might I add—and we waited what seemed like a long time but was probably only a minute or so. Nothing happened.

Then the obvious thing occurred to me. "Is there a fire escape?" I asked, cursing myself for my stupidity. Of course there was a fire escape at the top of a four-story building. And surely that was the way the intruder had used to escape. I was rattled; that was the only explanation for my lack of cognition.

"But of course," said Lisette. She lowered her umbrella.

"One of you go down and wait for the police," I said as I charged upstairs, leaving the chair behind but holding my tool knife—now closed for safety—at the ready.

The stairs ended in a large, open space with a lower, vaulted ceiling—not unlike my living space at home with Grand-père. The last bit of dusky light filtered in through several dormer windows, but when I found and pressed the light switch, everything lit up brightly. Work tables were arranged in long rows, and there were more dressmaker dummies scattered about, along with a large surface for cutting swaths of fabric. Another door at the end of the workroom was open, and it looked like it might be storage. There were no sewing machines in sight, for all haute couture works were required to be completely sewn by hand.

I didn't smell any cigarette smoke, but I did feel a waft of chilly air. I was furious with myself for forgetting about the fire escape although I don't know what else I would have done differently; contrary to some people's opinions, I certainly wasn't going to rush upstairs and confront a killer—I hurried through the workroom into the back storage room.

Yes. He or she had come through here—a window at the far end was ajar, and when I opened it and poked out my head to look down, I saw the rickety fire escape stairs zigzagging away below. No one was in view, but I waited and watched for a moment, my breath puffing white in the chill air, hoping I might see the intruder running away on the ground. He couldn't be that far ahead of me and it would have taken him some time to get down the stairs.

Unless he went across . . .

My head snapped up so fast I bumped the back of it on the window sash above me. It was possible, for the rooftop of the next building couldn't be more than three feet away, and it was slightly lower than the window I was looking out of.

I could easily jump the distance of a yard; not that I would want to, at this height, but I could if I was being chased and needed to get away. The intruder could have gone out the window and across, then scrambled over the peak and out of sight.

The shapes of dormers, chimneys, antennas, and soldierlike chimney pots broke the surface of the dark, slanted stone surfaces. I peered into the growing dusk, scouring for activity among the rooftops that sprawled before me in uneven rows of erratic heights and shapes. There was an infinite number of ways the killer could escape once vaulted across the span— through any window or across any balustrade or down any flight of fire escape stairs.

Whoever it was, was long gone.

I eased myself back inside, frustrated and annoyed. I'd been in the same building with the killer *twice* now, and I had nothing to help identify him or her, except the faint smell of cigarette smoke.

What would have happened if Mathilde and Lisette and I had arrived here ten or fifteen minutes earlier? Would we have interrupted the killer? Maybe even saved Madame Pineau's life?

Frustrated, I trudged down the stairs to the third floor. Neither of my companions were there, and I assumed they'd gone together to the ground floor to wait for the police instead of splitting up. Since I had time, I might as well look around.

I started in the room where Madame Pineau lay. For the second time in less than twenty-four hours, I covered a dead body with my coat. There were plenty of pieces of fabric around, but I hesitated to take an expensive piece of material like silk or taffeta to cover a bloody body. I did lay a handkerchief over the wound before I put my coat down; I didn't fancy the idea of wearing a coat with murderous bloodstains on it.

I prowled around the room, weaving between dressmaker fig-
ures attired in the basic *toile* of models, tables, and chairs crowded
together. There were no signs of great disturbance except the
worktable closest to the victim and the doorway, where everything had been pulled or knocked off: a pool of ice-blue taffeta,
a pincushion that had tumbled to the floor, a pair of scissors. A
thimble. A threaded needle. Some sequins.

It seemed clear to me that Madame Pineau had been in the
room, possibly examining some of the work. She probably
turned as her attacker came in, and he rushed toward her to
stab her in the heart. She'd been taken by surprise and quickly
overpowered, which explained why there wasn't much sign of
struggle.

Sadness swept over me again, thinking about how the poor
woman must have been feeling, here alone in the atelier after
the tragedy of last night. Perhaps she'd been looking over the
pieces of clothing, wondering if any could be finished or somehow salvaged now that the couturier was gone.

Or maybe she was just grieving over gowns and frocks that
would never be finished, never be worn, never shift and slide,
whisper and rustle, fabric against flesh as they'd been lovingly
designed to do.

My heart felt pinched when I left the room. I could hear
voices from below, including that of at least one male. Probably
the street police agents sent from a local station. Merveille likely
wouldn't have gotten here so quickly.

Even so, I knew I was running out of time to poke around, so
I bounded down to the second floor where the *cabine* and office
were located—and where I'd first smelled the cigarette smoke.

I wondered if the intruder had been snooping around in the
office. After all, I had interrupted them yesterday. If they'd been
looking for something, that was a good reason for them to come
back once the coast was clear.

My diligence was rewarded, for almost immediately, I spotted
a white cigarette butt on the floor just inside the office door. It
had to be from the intruder if what Lisette said was to be

believed—that no one was allowed to smoke except in the salon. I hadn't noticed yesterday, but now as I looked over at Madame Lannet's desk, I confirmed the lack of an ashtray among the scattered papers and fabric. Nor was there one on a stand near the chairs.

No, smoking was not permitted in this room.

I was still wearing gloves, so I picked up the cigarette butt. It had been smoked almost down to the end but I could still make out the spare, slender letters spelling the brand: LE PHÉNIX VIE. There was no lipstick on it, which was another point toward the intruder being a man.

I wrapped the butt in a handkerchief and stuck it inside my pocket so I could continue to look around. I heard footsteps and voices coming up the stairs from the ground floor and knew I had to hurry.

At first glance, nothing looked any different from yesterday—the desk was still messy, there was a dressmaker's dummy still cloaked in the muslin of a half-finished model, pieces of fabric strewn over the back of a side chair, sketches of designs in various stages on the desk, floor, pinned to a large board on the wall. The voices had reached the landing, but they kept going. Lisette and Mathilde were taking the police to the scene of the crime one floor above.

I breathed a little easier and came around to the side of the desk where Madame Lannet would sit—a perspective I hadn't made it to last night. The chair was a heavy one and it was pushed away from the desk at a strange angle—half facing the empty wall behind it—as if someone had risen quickly and suddenly, shoving it back so hard that it spun away and bumped into the wall. At least, that was how it struck me.

For that reason, I didn't touch the chair. I looked down at the desk and, still with my gloves on, carefully pulled out each drawer to look inside. I was probably wasting time, for surely the police had been over everything in this room already, but it seemed the thing to do.

Plus, I was nosy.

Nothing strange or unusual in the drawers jumped out at me—there were invoices due to be paid, many of them to Outhier Textile Entreprise, and a stack of bills to be sent to clients. I recognized some of the names—Joilliet, Brigitte, Grenech—simply because they were the ones that tended to be mentioned in the newspaper or on the radio. Such ostentatious clientele for a new atelier was impressive.

There were pens, lead pencils, colored pencils, paintbrushes, and watercolors in another drawer—obviously for Madame Lannet's sketches. Another drawer with onionskin paper for tracing and transferring designs, and another with heavier stock for the original drawings. Files of clients, all looking very new, as one would expect from a brand-new *maison de couture.*

The hair on the back of my neck prickled as I heard a firm, efficient tread on the stairs coming from below. I knew it was Merveille. Heaven knew I'd heard him walk up the stairs enough times.

I admit it—my stomach did a funny little flip, but I knew it was because it was probably going to be awkward and unpleasant when we spoke. It would be even more so if he discovered me in here, snooping around. Since the office door was wide open, all he had to do was glance inside as he passed by and he'd see me. . . .

Ugh. Yes. I did it.

I dropped to the floor behind the desk in a crouch and prayed with all my might that Merveille would keep going and not come in here to look. If he found me in such an embarrassing, undignified position I wasn't sure how I'd recover.

The steps paused at the top of the stairs. The hair on the back of my neck was standing straight up and I was feeling a little clammy, with an unpleasant churning in my stomach. *Please keep going.*

When the steps started up again, moving away, I exhaled in a rush. I was just about to pull to my feet when I saw something glint under the desk right above my head. It was a key, taped to the bottom of the kneehole in the very farthest corner from where Madame Lannet would sit.

I reached for it even as I wondered how the police had missed it. The key and its tape came loose easily, and I scooted back out from beneath the desk. As I did so, I saw something else: a tiny piece of fabric—hardly more than a few frayed threads—caught on a strip of decorative metal casing around the kneehole opening.

The small fragment had caught on a tiny, sharp point that was out of line near the bottom and fluttered there as if to say, "At last, a clue!"

If it had been my desk, I'd have fixed that rough edge because I would have kept catching my stockings on it and ruining them. Either Madame Lannet was more careful than I tended to be, she didn't care if her stockings had ladders, or the bent piece of metal was a new development—possibly even by whoever had left the scrap of cloth.

I had a magnifying glass in my pocketbook, but I'd dropped my purse when I saw Madame Pineau on the floor. All I could do now was get as close to the small piece of cloth as possible and peer at it. It was dark, and based on its location and the type of fabric, I would suspect it was from a long skirt, or, more likely, a pair of trousers—which, again, would suggest a man.

Much as I wanted a better look, I wasn't going to remove the frayed piece. Not only would Merveille want to see where and how it had been caught, but I didn't want to be accused of interfering in an investigation.

Of course, I also had a cigarette butt wrapped in a handkerchief in my pocket that had been removed from the scene. And a key that had been taped beneath the desk.

I sighed. I would put them both back. Now that there was another death in the atelier, the *inspecteur* would go over the whole place again with a fine-toothed comb.

I had just re-taped the key in its spot when I heard footsteps again.

"And where is she?"

The familiar voice had me bolting from behind the desk and toward the door of the office.

I *think* I managed to get into the hallway before Merveille saw me dart out of the office, but since I was a little out of breath—and probably flushed—from the breakneck movement, he probably wasn't fooled.

"Mademoiselle Knight, I understand you were the one to discover the body of Gabrielle Pineau."

I had to hand it to him—his voice was devoid of any accusation, frustration, or even exasperation. Definitely not a lick of humor. His words were unemotional and calm. His expression was the same. Even his eyes, those cool, stone-gray ones, appeared merely expectant as they looked at me from beneath the brim of his fedora.

"Yes," I said. "And I found this on the floor, just there," I added as I pulled the handkerchief with the cigarette stub out of my pocket. "I smelled smoke when we first got to this floor, and so I was—well, I was looking for signs of a cigarette, obviously. Lisette said that Madame Pineau did not allow anyone to smoke above the first floor."

I suppose it was testament to our history—such as it was—that Merveille and I wasted no time on chitchat or obvious questions. He'd opened the subject, and the conversation picked up from there without any filler. I didn't feel the need to fill in whys or hows.

He took the handkerchief, opening it for a brief look at the cigarette butt, then handed it to an agent hovering in the background. "Mademoiselle Feydeau has already explained what the three of you were doing here, and that she had a key because she worked here," he said, still in an agreeable, almost friendly voice. Which made me nervous.

"Would you like to take my full statement now, Inspecteur?"

"Of course, mademoiselle."

We glanced up as two men came into view, climbing the steps from below. They were carrying a stretcher and obviously headed to the third floor.

Merveille halted them with a gesture. "A little moment, if you please." He looked at me, then made a motion for me to precede him up the stairs.

Gabrielle Pineau's body remained undisturbed, although I could tell that my coat had been moved so Merveille could look at her. Mathilde and Lisette were sitting together on one of the lower steps of the narrow, utilitarian set of stairs to the other work areas.

"Please, mademoiselle," said Merveille with another of his spare but effective gestures.

I spoke. "As you know, we came here to retrieve something from Lisette's—Mademoiselle Feydeau's locker. As we got to the top of the stairs of the second floor, I smelled cigarette smoke, and so I looked around to see if anyone was here. I didn't see anyone, and so we continued climbing up the steps. I got to the top of the third floor first, and smelled cigarette smoke again."

"Ah, he is the dedicated smoker, our intruder," murmured Merveille.

"It appears that way." I wasn't sure what to make of that comment; normally, the *inspecteur* wouldn't interrupt during a statement, and certainly not to say anything that even hinted at the slightest bit of levity. "So I suppose I knew someone was here or had been here recently. I turned on the light in the room, and there she was. I could see that she was likely dead, but I did check her pulse to make certain. I didn't touch anything else."

I didn't need to point out that Madame had blood on her hands and what it meant, nor that I had covered her. Nor did I need to remind him I was wearing gloves.

"Mathilde—Mademoiselle Pillon—was behind me and when she saw Gabrielle Pineau, she screamed. I think that might have alerted the intruder, because then I heard a thud above me. I . . . uh . . . grabbed a chair and called for help and went to stand at the bottom of the steps." My cheeks grew hot under his regard, which clearly read: *And you meant to do what with this chair?*

I soldiered on. "After a moment, I realized whoever it was probably went out through the window and down the fire escape— or across to another roof. I ran upstairs and found the window ajar. No one was there, and no one was in sight either above or below."

As was his habit, Merveille did not take notes; however, the police agent to whom he'd given the cigarette butt was busily scratching on a notepad with a pencil.

"And then, mademoiselle?"

"I came back down here to, uh, look around while we were waiting for the police to arrive."

He nodded gravely. "And then you went down to look around some more, perhaps?" He nodded toward the steps we'd just climbed.

"Yes. I found the cigarette butt on the floor, as I said."

"And nothing else, mademoiselle?"

I had definitely not fooled him, dag-nabbit. I gritted my teeth and said, "You might want to take another look at the desk. Under it."

Those gray eyes held mine for a moment and I felt like the floor was falling away in front of me. I hoped my face wasn't as red as it felt. All he said was, "Very well, mademoiselle."

"Is there anything else?" I asked, suddenly ready to be gone from there.

"No, mademoiselle."

I looked at Lisette and Mathilde, who bolted to their feet at his dismissal. They were even more grateful to be leaving than I was.

I assumed that, due to the unexpected events of the evening, I'd head back home and perhaps have my hair cut another day, but Lisette wouldn't hear of it.

"*Non, non, non!* But we *must* do your hair tonight. It will help me to think of something other than *la pauvre madame,*" she said, taking my arm in a friendly grip. "And the so very stern *inspecteur!*" She gave a little shiver.

Since I didn't have to go home to see about dinner, and since I, too, wanted something other to think about than Madame Pineau with her horribly bloodied bodice—as well as the very stern *inspecteur*—I agreed.

Lisette's flat was a room in a residential hotel, but it was only three blocks from avenue Montaigne.

A dour-looking woman of seventy eyed us from the front desk as we strode in. Lisette waved gaily and smiled, asking if she had any messages.

The woman unfroze enough to smile back—which made her face crinkle everywhere like pleated taffeta—and replied, "Not since you were just here, Lisette."

"*Merci,* madame," Lisette said. "Bonsoir!"

The three of us started up the stairs to the third floor, chattering all the way.

We were nearly to the top of the second flight when the lights suddenly went out, plunging the stairs and hallway into darkness.

CHAPTER 8

MATHILDE GAVE A QUIET SHRIEK OF SURPRISE AND CLUTCHED AT me as I smothered a gasp, nearly bumping into Lisette. It was pitch black, for there were no windows on the stairway.

"*Merde!*" exclaimed Lisette, who didn't sound as shocked by the sudden darkness as I felt. "The stupid lights. They are supposed to stay on for thirty seconds, and then go out, but now it is only twenty seconds, I think."

Grumbling, she stomped the rest of the way up the steps. Mathilde's grip on my arm eased and I followed, my heart rate settling back to normal. Mathilde took up the rear, still very close on my heels.

I was aware of the Parisian light-switch timer conundrum. In an effort to save money on electricity, many lights in hallways and on stairways in hotels and *pensiones* or other public buildings would stay on only for thirty seconds once activated, and then go out. This practice had started during the war but continued even as other rationing had ended. In areas of the city, full neighborhoods still had regular, scheduled blackouts in order to conserve the flow through the system. Julia had come home early from Le Cordon Bleu more than once because of this.

Until I began investigating murders—that is, until this very moment—I never thought about how beneficial such a thing could be to a killer.

Lisette had turned on the lights again at the top of the stairs, so we had another twenty or thirty seconds of illumination as she fit her key into the lock of her door. It opened into a surprisingly spacious room. I didn't have much of a chance to look around or take in the details, because she immediately set to work on getting me ready for my haircut: propping me on a chair from the small dining table, then draping a towel over my shoulders.

"Are you sure this is a good idea?" I said, wishing Lisette had positioned me in front of a mirror so I could watch the process.

Maybe it was better she hadn't.

"Ah, but it will be *magnifique* on you, Tabitha!" cried Mathilde.

"That it will," said Lisette, already fussing with my hair—running her fingers through it, up from the base of my neck and through the scalp, tugging lightly at it—as if to determine the best approach. "You have far too much of this"—she held up a thick lock—"and it is messy and unruly and it does not like to behave, *non?* It stands out like you have been struck by lightning, *non? Je suis très brilliant.* You will be the sexy, sensual, powerful goddess when I am finished," she boasted in a very French manner.

I stifled a laugh. That was going a bit far, but I appreciated her sentiment. I also believed Mathilde because she entrusted her own hair to Lisette. And so I accepted a large glass—which looked more like an old olive jar—of red wine for courage, and closed my mouth.

The first snip of hair had me a little nervous, but by then it was too late to turn back. A few more snips had me wanting to squirm, especially when a large, long lock of hair fell onto my lap. That was an *awful* lot of hair.

Was I going to look like a *boy?* I glanced at Mathilde to see whether she was aghast by the way I was looking, but she was flipping through a magazine and didn't seem to be paying any attention to us.

I took a very large gulp of wine. Then, in an effort to distract myself—and hopefully *not* to distract Lisette—I said, "Do you know why Madame Lannet would have a key taped underneath her desk?"

"Oh, no, but what kind of key?" asked Lisette, still snipping.

"It was a small key. Not like for a door but maybe for a small box or a drawer."

"Mmm. *Non.*"

Snip. Snip, snip.

"What about Madame Pineau? Would she have such a key?" I had come to the conclusion that the key had probably been hidden after the police searched the office following Madame Lannet's death, which implied that Madame Pineau had been the one to tape it there.

Lisette shrugged and made a noncommittal sound. "I do not know."

"Do you know anyone who smokes cigarettes who might have been at Maison Lannet?" I went on.

"No." *Snip, snip*—Lisette stepped back suddenly and gaped at me. "Is that the killer?"

"Probably. I found a cigarette butt, and since you said that no one is allowed to smoke above the salon, it appears that the killer prefers Le Phénix Vie."

"It is terrible. All of this is terrible!" Lisette cried, then returned matter-of-factly to her work.

The piles of hair falling on and around me were *really* concerning. I tried not to look at them. Mathilde was still engrossed in her magazine so she was no help to me for an impression of whether what was happening was good or horrific.

I concentrated on other things I could ask Lisette in hopes of learning something relevant. Of course, if I learned anything relevant, I'd have to pass it on to Merveille, and that would be . . . uncomfortable. Still, I plowed on. "Do you have any idea how successful Madame Lannet's atelier is? Is it making money? Is it making a profit, I should say?"

"Ah, business is good, I think," said Lisette, frowning slightly as she crouched a little to give my bangs some attention. "I do not have any impressions that there are bill collectors. I have always been paid on time, and so have the other mannequins. And it is so early, you see, for only the first collection was just released but we had many, many showings and there were many orders, I think."

That seemed to gibe with what Madame Pineau said when Charmaine tried to order a gown.

"But only, the business of fashion is not so *very* good for anyone," Lisette went on. "There are clients, *oui*, but there are perhaps not enough of them. The clients, they spend the money, but since the war, there are just not so many of them." She shrugged. "Is that not so, Mathilde?"

"What is it?" Mathilde looked up.

"There are not so many clients for the fashion, even with the war over, *non*?"

"Ah, *oui*. Monsieur Block, he says the same." Mathilde tsked and returned to her magazine.

I had taken to not looking down any longer, for the pile of hair continued to grow alarmingly. My stomach was doing nervous flips. How long would it take my hair to grow back? Was I going to have to hide away for months? Wrap my head in a scarf whenever I went out?

To distract myself, I tried another tactic. "If the fashion business is not so good, then how was Madame Lannet able to start her atelier? Surely it cost money to lease the building and decorate and furnish it, and then to buy all of the supplies, pay the workers, and to get the approval by the Chambre Syndicale, and so on. It must have taken a lot of money, and she was only working for Dior, so where did it all come from?"

"Ah, *oui*, that is a question, *non*?" Lisette stepped back to look at me head-on, then grabbed a hank of hair on each side of my face and gently tugged them down along my cheeks to measure whether they were the same length. With a little sound of approval, she released them and snipped at the left side as she continued her explanation.

"As I understand, it was some Monsieur Outhier who came to Madame Lannet and he offered her the money to start it up."

The name Outhier had been on some of the invoices I'd seen in Madame Lannet's office. "Do you know anything about Monsieur Outhier? Why he would want to invest in Madame Lannet?"

"Ah, *non*, not so very much." Lisette was now snip-snipping straight across the nape of my neck. I could feel the cool steel from the outside of the blade against my skin and it felt *really* close to the bottom of my head, near the top of my neck. My hair was going to be *really* short back there. I suppressed a nervous shiver.

Lisette went on. "I think he is very rich and he has a wife who likes very nice clothing. That is all."

"Did Monsieur Outhier know Madame Lannet very well? What I mean is, I wonder how he came to know her and decided to pay for her in particular to start a *maison de couture*," I said.

"That I do not know," said Lisette with a shrug of indifference. "Perhaps he or his wife knew her from when she was at Dior or Lelong?"

Lisette might not know, but I was interested in finding out more. Now that Maison Lannet was to be in business no longer, where did that leave Monsieur Outhier and his investment?

I couldn't help but think of Monsieur Block and his rival, the so-called Philippe. If what I suggested was true about the destruction in the shoe shop being an attempt to ruin Monsieur Block and make a bad name for him or to steal his customers, could the death of Madame Lannet and her *première* be not only a way to destroy the couturier herself, but also affect the man who'd invested in her shop?

If the shop was ruined and closed down, then surely Monsieur Outhier would have a large loss. And his wife would not have her fashions.

Then another thought struck me. "Were there any other designers who wanted to start an atelier, who might have thought *they* should have been chosen by Monsieur Outhier?"

"Mm. *Oui*, I think there was Robert Illouz. He was not so very happy when the news came that Madame Lannet was getting the money to open her atelier and was leaving Dior."

"This Robert Illouz—so he is a designer too?"

"*Oui*. He was at Maison Lelong with Dior and Madame Lannet during the war. They *all* designed for the Germans," she said with a grimace. "They had no choice, I think . . . But . . . there were many who had a choice, and there were those who *did* choose." She scoffed, her face twisting with disgust. "And others . . ." Her expression sobered as she gestured to me and then to the piles of hair on the floor. "Others paid for their choices later with *les tondeurs*. Even those who tried only to survive."

I knew what she referred to—the head-shaving of women who slept with German soldiers, either willingly or perhaps not so willingly. They had been known as "horizontal collaborators" or "German mattresses," and during the celebratory riots after the liberation, *les tondeurs*—the shearers—rounded up women who had been suspected of collaborating with the Germans . . . whether they had done so or not . . . and they shaved their heads.

I couldn't imagine the humiliation those women suffered, whether or not they'd willingly liaised with the occupiers. Here I sat, getting only inches cut off my very thick and long hair, terrified about how I would look and whether it would affect my femininity . . . and these women were publicly, forcibly, violently shorn to the scalp.

I shuddered. Lisette seemed to follow my thoughts, for she spoke. "And that is how I became the goddess of the hair." She spoke with understated bravado, suddenly sober and quiet. "It was my friend Paulette . . . she did not have the choice to say no, you see? She had to feed her baby. There was no other way."

She had stopped snipping at my hair and now she stood in front of me, hands on her hips, face set in grave lines. "And *les tondeurs*, they shaved her and the others—right there in the square. And they drove them through the streets in the back of a wagon for all to see." Lisette's eyes glittered with tears of fury. "People spat at them, and threw things, and even some claimed her baby was from a German! And he was not! Oh, he was not. His father was in a war camp!"

"I'm so sorry. That must have been terrible." My throat burned.

I could only imagine how horrifying and frightening—and how unfair—it must have been.

"It was terrible. She cried, Paulette, for days. She would not go out, for even with her head covered, everyone who saw her, knew what it meant." Lisette sighed, blinking rapidly.

After a moment, she went back to her work snipping at my hair as she continued speaking. "When her hair began to grow back, I helped her to make it look . . . eh . . . deliberate, you see? The short style. To make it chic and pretty. And there were others too, who heard and came to me . . . And so now, *je suis la déesse des cheveux.*" Her smile was rueful as she spread her hands. "It was all I could do to help."

"I'm certain Paulette and the others were grateful," I replied. "That was so kind of you."

"And what else could I do? Nothing but that little thing."

Her expression changed from one of intense regret to focus as she lifted the scissors once more. "And now, to finish this . . ."

Snip, snip . . . snip.

I was suddenly feeling much better about my prospects in having less hair, and I still had questions. "What is this Robert Illouz doing now? Is he still designing?"

"He is still with Lelong, I think. Or perhaps he has gone to Dior . . . I do not know. *Ah. Oui.* There we are." Lisette suddenly stepped back from my hair and began to circle me slowly, examining her work with sharp, critical eyes.

"*Oh!*" Mathilde at last looked up from her magazine, then hurried over to stand in front of me. Her eyes were wide and she covered her mouth with two hands.

I couldn't tell whether that was a good "*Oh!*" or an "Oh, *no!*" exclamation, and I bit my lip nervously.

But then Mathilde took her hands away and I could see that she was smiling. Big, wide, and happy. "But it is *beautiful.* You are beautiful! So *chic* and *glamorous!* You look like a real Parisian woman!"

"Let me see!" I demanded, sliding off the chair.

Lisette thrust a mirror into my hands. When I brought my face into the reflection, I gasped.

"Honestly, Tabitha dear, if I didn't know and love you as well as I do, I would really think there might be something *wrong* with you! Finding dead bodies all the time! Ye gods!" Julia crowed and cackled and nudged me with a loving elbow (her hands were full) as I came into her kitchen late the next morning. She'd just returned from her morning class at Le Cordon Bleu and had insisted I come over to catch her up on things.

As was my habit, I tossed my coat over a chair and considered my next move—that is, how to navigate to a seat at the table without getting mowed over.

Julia was, as usual when in the domain of *la cuisine*, a cyclone. But she was a contained, orderly cyclone. Instead of leaving destruction in her whirling, spinning, churning, stirring wake, she left behind smoothly formed breads, neatly trussed chickens, perfectly sliced potatoes and julienned carrots . . . all of it delicious and decadent and aromatic.

At the moment, she was arranging items on the table across from me: butter and several rolled-up cloths which I thought might contain some sort of pastry dough. She'd retrieved the rolls from the cold box that hung outside the tiny kitchen window. One piece of paper-thin pastry already lay flat on a wooden board.

"I know. I'm beginning to wonder about me myself," I said, slipping past and around her to take a seat at the table. "But Merveille—"

Drat. I stopped talking, but it was too late.

"Merveille?" Julia asked, stopping suddenly—which is a rare thing to happen when she is in the midst of cooking and provides pointed emphasis to her reaction.

I capitulated and explained, "Inspecteur Allard had to leave town because his family was in an accident, and Merveille was assigned to take over the case."

Julia, who had finally picked up the butter and began swiping small chunks off it with a knife, said, "And when did you learn this, Tabitha?"

I did the only thing I could think of. I yanked off my hat.

Julia shrieked, the brick of butter slipping from her hands to thunk onto the table. "*Tabitha! Your hair!*"

Grand-père's and Oncle Rafe's reactions this morning had been similarly vociferous. Fortunately, after their immediate shock, both had assured me that my new hairdo looked *magnifique* and that I was *une déesse*. I had accepted the compliments with a bit of reserve; after all, despite their elegant ways and fashionable sense, they were still men and I well knew I wasn't anywhere close to being a goddess. I was, however, a woman with, suddenly, *very* short hair.

"It's . . . *my God*, you look *spectacular!*" Abandoning the butter and her pastry, Julia was looking at me from all angles, and her dancing eyes and the broad smile on her face didn't lie. I could tell she liked it.

"I'm still getting used to it," I told her, shaking my head a little. "It feels a lot lighter. But best of all, it doesn't turn into a wild, staticky mess when I take off my hat."

"Merveille is going to swallow his tongue when he sees you," Julia said. "The cut looks absolutely stunning on you. It's just so *luscious* and *delicious* the way it curls just like that, around your ear and almost touching your chin—and leaves your long neck bare. There's a lot of pretty neck exposed there, Tabs. You'd better wear a scarf when you go out in the winter, but be as generous with the perfume around your earlobes as I am with butter in the kitchen! But when did you do it?"

Having not completely avoided the topic of Merveille with my distraction, I sought to keep my friend from circling back around to it and explained about Mathilde and Lisette. "And that's how it turned out that I found Madame Pineau," I concluded.

Julia shook her head, the last vestiges of glee fading from her eyes. "The poor woman. Stabbed with a pair of scissors. How awful."

"It was terrible."

"Two deaths at the same place in two days," mused Julia, returning to her work. She was still slicing off little swatches of butter, then sprinkling them generously on the layer of thin pastry dough. Then she unrolled one of the towels to reveal, as I had suspected, another paper-thin layer of dough. She laid it on top of the butter-speckled layer and plopped more chunks over this new layer.

I nodded. "Yes, and I've been thinking about it. It's got to be the same person, but the methods are so different. Madame Lannet was strangled from behind with a length of lace. And the interesting thing is, Lisette said it was from a special order of lace that might have come from Madame Lannet's office instead of the workrooms. But Madame wasn't killed in the office—she was killed in the *cabine*."

"Whoever it was came up behind her while she was sitting at the vanity," Julia said.

"Right. And it seems that she'd probably have *seen* them come in behind her—through the mirror, I mean—and would have sprung up out of the chair if she wasn't expecting them, or if they were someone she didn't trust or know. Right?

"I think it's a man," I went on, then explained about the frayed scrap of material I'd noticed on the bottom edge of the desk kneehole. "If she had gotten up from the desk and turned toward him when he came in—if she wasn't expecting him or was afraid of him—he wouldn't have been able to strangle her from behind . . . probably, anyway."

"The things had been knocked off the vanity," Julia commented. "And the chair overturned, which agrees with your scenario. She was struggling to get away while the lace was tightened around her throat from behind." Her expression was sober as she carefully began to unroll a cylinder of another paper-thin layer of dough.

"Yes," I said. "And I've been thinking about the lace. It seems a little strange that he—I'm just going to use that pronoun for now, but it could still be a woman. I don't think it would take that much strength to strangle someone if you caught them by surprise from behind. Anyway, he would have had to have gotten the lace from her office, then come into the *cabine* to kill her, then went *back* into the office to rifle around and knock me into the desk."

"Yes, it seems strange, because he could have used something else to kill her with," Julia said, frowning. "Instead of the special lace, I mean. So why make the extra trip? Unless there wasn't anything in the *cabine* that could be used."

I shrugged. "I don't know. It just seems as if he was rooting around in her office for something and she found him there, then he would have killed her there in the office."

"Or maybe they were in her office and they went into the *cabine*, but he grabbed the lace from the office on the way and brought it with him, waiting for an opportunity to take her by surprise. Maybe he knew she was going to sit down at the vanity. Maybe she didn't sit down at all, but the chair just got knocked over during the struggle.

"Either way, it seems as if he at least *planned* for it a little bit— to bring the lace with him from one room to the other. It wasn't a crime of passion," Julia mused.

"I get that impression too. He may not have come to Maison Lannet intending to kill her, but he definitely didn't just grab the first thing he saw and murder her on the spot. So that means something must have changed during the time they were together that made him decide to kill her. She said or did something that angered him."

"Either way, it had to be someone she knew," Julia concluded. "Someone who was in the atelier with her when she was alone."

"Right. But she couldn't have been alone with him for that long, Julia. *We* were only gone for maybe twenty or thirty minutes at the cafe before I came back for my glove, and she was dead but still warm."

"True. Unless Madame Lannet wasn't there at the shop when we were there—after all, we didn't see her, did we?—and then she returned after it was supposed to close. Maybe he was with her when she came back and sent Madame Pineau off for dinner."

"But then Madame Pineau would have seen him," I reminded her.

"Yes, that's true." Julia frowned in thought. "It's very confusing. And we can't ask Madame Pineau now, can we?"

"No. And maybe that's why she is now dead. I think that Gabrielle Pineau's death was less planned and more of a spur-of-the-moment, reactionary murder. I think the killer was there last night because he was looking for something. He'd come back because he didn't find what he wanted the first night. Or he wanted to get rid of Madame Pineau for some other reason."

"But you said you found Madame Pineau upstairs from the office."

I nodded. Julia *had* been listening to me, even while she was making whatever it was she was making. And whatever it was, it was going to be delicate and *very* caloric. The amount of butter she was using was breathtaking.

Which meant, of course, that I desperately wanted to eat the final product.

"Yes. He killed her upstairs, but there were more signs of a struggle. She tried to defend herself, and he stabbed her from the front. I wonder . . ." My voice trailed off as I remembered the desk chair. "I wonder if maybe he was looking at something in the office at Madame Lannet's desk—and maybe he heard Madame Pineau upstairs. The way the chair was positioned, it looked like someone had shoved it away fast and hard as if to quickly get away from the desk."

"That's how he left the fragment of material. He was in a hurry."

"Right," I agreed. That had been my own conclusion. "So he was looking around, heard her coming, shoved away and then . . . went upstairs to kill her?" I frowned. That didn't make much sense.

"Or . . . what if *she* was at the desk and heard something upstairs and went up to find out what it was, and that's when he attacked her. He could have grabbed a pair of scissors right there—you said they were in the workroom, right? And that's why he caught her in the front—she came in to confront him."

I was nodding. "Yes, that makes much more sense. And then he went back to the office to look around some more, and when he heard us arriving downstairs, he hightailed it out of there."

"Or he'd finished looking in the office already and gone upstairs to search some more because he didn't find what he wanted, and that's when Madame Pineau heard him and confronted him. He could have left the scrap of cloth at any time."

I nodded. "That all makes sense. But what was he looking for? And has he found it yet? He *could* have found it before he killed Madame Pineau, and then stabbed her because she accosted him or tried to take it away from him or because she'd seen him there yesterday with Madame Lannet."

We looked at each other. My brain felt muddled. Nothing seemed really clear.

"So what's your next step?" asked Julia, as if reading my mind.

I hesitated then replied, "I don't know. I couldn't come up with any other things to ask Lisette. It's out of the question to think that I could get back in to Maison Lannet to look around again—and anyway, with Merveille in charge, there won't be anything left to find. He's very thorough."

To my relief, Julia didn't jump on the subject of Merveille. Maybe she was getting the message. Instead, she gave me an affectionate smile. "At least you're not denying your interest in investigating like you usually do, even as you go about doing just that."

I shot her an annoyed look, then smiled wryly. "I guess there's no use in pretending. If I'm going to keep randomly running into dead bodies, it must mean that I should do something about it, right? Why else would they keep showing up in my path?"

"And those books your father sent you don't hurt," Julia said. She'd finished layering the dough—which was so thin I could actually make out the pale yellow color of the butter beneath it—and was now cutting it into long triangles.

"*Croissants!*" I exclaimed, suddenly realizing what she was making.

Julia laughed. "Of course, dearie. I'll be sending some home with you. Your messieurs will love them slathered with butter and maybe some jam."

"There's already enough butter in them," I said, and swallowed because I was salivating at the thought. Breakfast had been unusually early because I'd had two tutoring appointments this morning.

"Bite your tongue, Tabs! There's *never* enough butter in *anything*," Julia told me seriously. Then her eyes danced. "Maybe you could bring one or two to Merveille when you drop in to see him at the 36."

"Who said I was—right. Never mind. I'm not going to prevaricate anymore. And bringing him some fresh croissants is as good a reason as any—although it's not like he can't get a fresh croissant on any street corner," I said wryly. "After all, this is Paris."

"I'm sure you can come up with a reasonable excuse, Tabitha. You've always been able to in the past," she said, giving me a knowing look.

"Well, I did ask him to share any news with me about Inspecteur Allard's family and I didn't bring up the subject last night, so I suppose that's a reason to stop by. If I can just get a look at the pinup board where he hangs all the information about the case, then maybe I'll have some ideas of what to do next. The thing is, Merveille might not like it, but I can help him. People are more willing to talk to me—especially women—than the police."

"Yes, but I doubt you'll ever get him to admit he needs your help," Julia said.

"No, but he certainly isn't going to ignore any information I might give him," I said. "Grand-père and Oncle Rafe are insisting I go to Maison Dior for an appointment with them. They want me to pick out a gown for the grand reopening of Maison de Verre," I told her with a little roll of my eyes. "We have an appointment for late tomorrow afternoon. A private one—with Monsieur Dior himself." That had surprised me . . . then, upon second thought, it hadn't.

As a partner in a large, successful bank, my grandfather knew most everyone and had a large measure of influence in the city. And he and Oncle Rafe—whose reputation wasn't nearly as smooth, shiny, and innocent as my grandfather's—had worked for the Resistance during the Occupation. They were celebrated and respected by many.

Julia's eyes widened in astonishment and delight. "Tabitha! You're going to be wearing haute couture!"

"More importantly, I'm going to try and use the visit at Dior to see if I can learn anything more about Mesdames Lannet and Pineau when they worked at Dior," I replied with a sly smile. "I'm sure Grand-père and Oncle Rafe will help me do some investigative work while we're there."

"They will love that," Julia said as she began to roll one of the long triangles into the shape of a croissant. "But what about Monsieur Alley Cat? You haven't forgotten about him, have you? Paul suggested we loan you Minette's carrying case. I told him I'd be happy to have you borrow it, but I didn't think it would actually get any use." She chuckled heartily. "If you can get your stray cat in it without being clawed to death, I'll cook you and your messieurs dinner every night for a *week*."

"I'll get him in there," I said firmly. Dinner for a week? I'd cage a lion to have Julia Child cook dinner for us for a week. "Do you have any fish carcasses or skin I can use?"

CHAPTER 9

SOMETIME LATER, ARMED WITH FRESH CROISSANTS, THE CHILDS' cat carrier, and a brown paper sack of smelly, greasy cod leftovers, I took my leave from Julia.

I had also borrowed a large blanket and a pair of Paul's heavy gloves, and was feeling very optimistic about my chances of getting Monsieur le Chat de Gouttière safely into the carrier.

Julia, who'd been chuckling heartily to herself, waved me off with a bemused smile and a *"Bonne chance!"* The fact that I heard her raucous laughter follow me into the elevator just as the doors closed didn't give me any great confidence.

Even so, I had a plan.

Inside my little Renault, the glorious scent of fresh croissant warred with the rank odor of fish; the latter of which, Julia explained, was three days old from when she'd made the bouillabaisse broth. She'd saved it so that small portions could be included in Minette's dinner each night. Paul wasn't the only one who was well-fed in the Child household. Thankfully, the disgusting stuff had been kept outside the kitchen window in a closed metal box so as not to pervade the kitchen.

I managed to keep myself from eating more than one of the croissants—they were *divine*, hot, flaky, buttery—but that was only because I arrived at the quai before I could reach into the bag for a second one. It was just as well, because there were enough flakes all over my dark blue coat to make up half of another pastry.

The remnants of my meager lunch wafted to the ground as I climbed out of my car, and I knew the birds and perhaps even a cat or two would feast upon them. I had parked as close to the bench where I had seen Monsieur Alley Cat yesterday as I could, but it was still a half block away.

Today, the weather was spitting sleet and an occasional snowflake. The sky was a dull, featureless gray, with no sign of the sun's orb through the clouds. Everything appeared dull in color; washed out and drab—even the blue and yellow Pernod umbrellas, raised above some of the outdoor cafe tables in an effort to ward off the spritzing of sleet.

I felt a little foolish lugging a large blanket and a metal cat carrier down the street, but no one seemed to notice or care. Everyone I passed by was walking quickly, many with a trail of cigarette smoke wafting behind them, some with a leashed dog who sniffed inquisitively toward me and my bag of cod.

Fortunately, it wasn't windy, even this close to the river, so it wasn't unbearably cold. Still, Julia's point that I should wear a heavy muffler around my now bare neck was well-taken. I had to turn up my coat collar and wrap the scarf around my throat to keep warm.

I placed all of my cat-capturing gear on the bench where I'd recently encountered Monsieur le Chat and looked around. The feline in question was nowhere to be seen, but I wasn't dissuaded. The fish would lure him quickly.

I dumped a little of it on the park bench. Then I opened up the door of the cat carrier—which looked very much like a large metal makeup case—and used a stick to knock some of the fish inside. I turned the carrier so the opening faced away from me and toward the fish on the bench, reasoning that my quarry would simply follow the trail into the metal box. I was confident my heroic cat would make his way into the cage, and then I could close the door by flipping it down—*et voilà!*

I'd brought the heavy blanket as well, in case he didn't go inside the cage. I thought I could throw it over him while he was eating and bundle him up with it before he got away, then carry him wrapped thus to my car, being safely protected from his claws.

But, as often happens, the best-laid plans don't pan out. Although I sat there in the spitting weather for fifteen minutes, huddling inside my muffler and wishing desperately for a hot *café*, Monsieur Alley Cat did not deign to make his appearance. I had to chase away two other cats from the aromatic offering, however, as well as an inquisitive pigeon.

I was cold and damp and decided it was time to give up—for now. I packed up my gear, including the uneaten fish—yuck— and trudged back to my car. Maybe if I couldn't catch a cat, I could at least badger some information from Merveille.

As I've noted previously, the Direction régionale de la police judiciaire de la préfecture de police de Paris, also known as the DRPJ or *police judiciaire,* is located on the Île-de-la-Cité, not far from Monsieur le Chat de Gouttière's favorite bench. I managed to find a place to park and alighted from my Renault with the bag of croissants—now one more pastry lighter—and brushed off my coat once more.

As I climbed the steps into the regal building, I wondered if I was making a mistake by bringing croissants—quite obviously a bribe—to Merveille. What would he think of that? I decided I would make certain he knew they were from Julia, whom he'd met a number of times and in whose kitchen he had twice enjoyed a meal.

The same police agent was sitting at the front desk when I came in, but he was speaking to another visitor. That was fine with me. I slipped past the desk while the agent was looking down to write something and headed down the corridor to Merveille's office.

I was aware that my hands were a little clammy as I hurried down the hall. I wasn't certain whether I wanted Merveille to be in his office or not.

I passed two other police agents, but surprisingly, neither of them asked who I was or what I was doing. I wasn't sure how I felt about such absence of security in general, but in this case, I was grateful for their lack of interest. Especially when I arrived at Merveille's office to find the door—which conveniently sported a window—closed. The lights were off inside and no one was in view. The rack where he would normally hang his hat and coat was empty. By all indications, the *inspecteur* was out.

I hovered at the door.

I want to be clear that I had no intention of going inside. It would be an invasion of privacy, not to mention possibly illegal.

I'm pleased to say that I didn't even try the knob to see if it was locked.

But that didn't mean I couldn't stand at the window and look at his crime board—and the desk, which was neatly organized and still missing the photograph of Marguerite—which is exactly what I did.

Since the office wasn't very large, the place where Merveille posted all of the photographs, maps, and information wasn't a great distance from the door. Maybe twelve or fifteen feet. I could see everything fairly well from the window, and I divided my time between squinting at the crime wall through the glass and surveying the corridor in both directions to make certain no one was coming.

I could make out shots of both crime scenes and the weapons used at each one, as well as pictures of Lisette and several other women who I guessed were also employees of Maison Lannet. There were also photographs of two men. All of the pictures were too far away and the light was too dim for me to read the captions with their names—and I have good vision.

My hand crept to the doorknob. If I could just get a little closer . . .

No.

I stepped back, my hand falling to my side without even touching the metal knob.

I tried one more time to peer through the window and read the names of the two men, but it was simply not possible. With a sigh, I turned and started back down the hall to the front desk.

When I got there, I found the police agent whom I'd spoken

to yesterday now available to speak to me. I told Agent Fenèche at the front desk that I wanted to leave the sack of croissants for Inspecteur Merveille, instructing him to write in the message that they were from Madame Child. Before I handed over the bag, I offered Fenèche one of the pastries as a thank-you.

As I drove away from the *police judiciaire*, it was with a sense of frustration and aimlessness. Both of the tasks I'd set for myself—catching the cat and talking to Merveille—had been stymied.

And now the interior of my car smelled like rotting fish.

Since I didn't have anywhere else I had to be, and I didn't want the disgusting smell to get any worse, I decided to try one more time to find the cat. It was early afternoon and I saw no reason to rush back home.

Once again I parked, this time even farther away, and trudged to the bench with my cat-capturing tools. I set it up the same way I had before, with two small, but hopefully enticing, servings of fish, and I waited.

I had only been sitting there for a few minutes when I caught sight of the broken-tailed cat from the corner of my eye. Despite my relief that he was still around, I was careful not to move or to acknowledge his presence. Instead, I pretended to read a newspaper—*Le Monde*—someone had left on the bench.

After a few moments eyeing me from behind a broad chestnut tree, Monsieur Chat de Gouttiére sauntered toward the bench. I continued to peruse the paper and when I turned the page I saw a headline that caught my eye: MAISON LANNET DONE; OUTHIER DOOMED?

I forgot about my feline friend as I began to read the article. It was, as the headline suggested, about the sudden and violent demise of Madame Lannet and how it would affect the *maison de couture*'s investor Frédéric Outhier. But it was the photograph of Outhier that caught my attention, for I immediately recognized him as being the man in one of the photographs hanging on Merveille's crime wall. It was the same picture.

So Merveille was thinking along the same lines as I had been:

Was it possible someone was trying to ruin Outhier or otherwise damage him by destroying Maison Lannet? The thought made me smile and gave me a boost of confidence that my budding investigative abilities were aligned with that of a far-more experienced detective.

I suddenly remembered why I was sitting on a park bench and looked over. The fish was gone and so was the cat!

With a cry, I lunged to my feet, looking around to see if I could determine where the sly feline had gone. The cat shot out of the carrier at my sudden movement—stupid me, I hadn't even looked inside!—and bounded off into a nearby bush.

"Well, that served me right," I grumbled, staring after him for a few moments. I plunked back down on the bench, wondering whether I should put out more fish and hope Monsieur would take the bait a third time.

I saw nothing to lose by trying. I supposed I could always get more fish skins, and I didn't like the idea of taking it and its rank odor back to my car again.

Once more, I set the bait. This time I put some on the ground next to the bench, then on the bench as before, and then the rest of it inside the carrier.

I sat back down and picked up the paper once more. This time, however, I kept my peripheral vision attuned to the bench next to me. Monsieur le Chat de Gouttière must have been hungry for cod, for he hardly waited to slink out from beneath the spiny, leafless bush where he'd taken refuge.

He mowed through the fish offerings like an expert: first on the ground, then jumping lightly to the bench and scarfing down, and finally, with a glance at me, moving hesitantly into the carrier.

This time I was ready for him. I flipped the door down over the entrance and latched it in two swift movements. No sooner had I done so than the most horrific howling, screeching, yowling sounds began to come from inside. The case rattled and creaked and rocked with far more violence than I expected from a single cat. I had to wonder whether he'd somehow manage to break out despite the carrier being made of metal.

I collected far more looks on my way back to the Renault than I had on my way to the bench. The case I carried by its handle leaped and rocked wildly against me. The metallic thuds and sharp clangings of Monsieur le Chat charging and leaping at the sides of his prison alarmed me as well as the people I passed by. The yowling and howling added to the ambience. And the dratted cat was *heavy*. So not only was he loud and violent, he weighed far more than I'd expected.

By the time I got to my car, I was swearing under my breath and seriously reconsidering my heroic measures. The stupid case had been bumping, hard, against my thigh all the way to the car and my head was beginning to throb from where I'd hit it on Madame Lannet's desk.

And so I was not in the best frame of mind when I reached my distinctive cherry-red Renault and discovered Merveille standing there.

I can't imagine the sight I presented.

Actually, I can.

The image I imagine I presented has been burned into my memory forever: me, awkwardly cuddling a large bundle of blanket against one side with my left hand, slugging along a metal carrier in my other hand, whose rocking and lurching surely caused me to stagger while listing to my right. My hat was certainly askew, my coat was half-unbuttoned due to the aforementioned rocking and lurching, and I'm quite certain I smelled of rotting fish.

CHAPTER 10

"MADEMOISELLE, IF YOU WILL PERMIT . . ." AS HE SPOKE, MERveille stepped forward and briskly relieved me of the screeching, yowling, bouncing metal case.

He glanced down at it as it lurched and bounded in his grip, then at me, and I'm one hundred percent certain he just barely caught himself from laughing. He set the case on the ground next to my car where it continued to rock and rattle.

"It's the cat with the broken tail. The one who saved my life." I tried to sound dignified even though I was certain the *inspecteur* had lifted his nose and sniffed the air. In my direction.

I'm pretty certain he wasn't smelling my perfume.

"And you have decided to take him into captivity?" Was there the faintest tremor in his voice? A quiver of suppressed laughter?

I shot Merveille a dark look. "He's sick. I wanted to get him some medical help."

"I don't think Monsieur le Chat is as grateful for your assistance as you were for his," replied the *inspecteur*, probably wondering how a sick cat could be making so much ruckus. He wouldn't be the only one.

"Is there something you wanted, Inspecteur?" I asked, digging for the car key in my pocketbook. I'd given up and let the blanket drop to the ground. It was Julia's and the ground was damp and dirty, so I'd have to have Bet or Blythe launder it before I returned it, but that was far better than standing there clutching it to me while I talked to Merveille and dug blindly in my purse.

"I thought I recognized your car," he said.

That was probably true; my car was red, after all, and Merveille knew I often stopped in this area to feed the alley cat.

Before I could respond, he went on, "And I thought I would take the opportunity to thank you—er, Madame Child—for the croissants. I found them when I returned to the office." He was looking at me intently—not trying to catch my eye, but as if I were some sort of specimen. I think he was noticing my new hairstyle, although it was covered by my hat. Still, it was obvious that I no longer had thick, unruly locks of hair erupting from beneath the sides of my chapeau.

I nodded as my fingers closed over the Renault key deep inside my pocketbook. "I'll pass on your thanks to Julia."

He picked up the violently shaking, still howling cat carrier as I unlocked the door, then set it on the passenger seat. "You are taking him to the veterinarian, then?"

"Yes."

The cat let out a long, low, yowl that ended in a vibrating shriek loud enough to wake the dead.

Merveille lifted one brow, looking from the carrier to me and back again. "I would suggest, then, mademoiselle, that you are far away when the door of that case is opened."

I gave a pained chuckle and closed the car door. "Believe me, I will be. Um, I was wondering if there was any news about Inspecteur Allard's family."

"Ah, yes. And that is kind of you to ask." His expression sobered. "Madame Allard is still in hospital. She will require surgery for a fractured arm, but she is expected to heal well after. The two children are banged up with bruises and one has a sprained wrist—the daughter, it is—but they will recover as well."

"I'm relieved to hear it," I said. "It was a car accident, you said?"

"Yes." He looked very grim. "The French, we all drive so fast. It is very inconsiderate and dangerous. Car accidents cause too many injuries and deaths."

Something about the way he said that caught my attention. I

got the impression he wasn't speaking in generalities, but before I could ask, he said, "I do hope you are not planning to return to Maison Lannet, mademoiselle."

I shook my head. "There would be no reason to. I'm certain you were very thorough with your search," I added, flashing him a pert smile.

"Ah, and so honored I am by your confidence, mademoiselle," he replied dryly.

"It must be a man," I went on. "The killer."

"I am of the same opinion, mademoiselle, but do not take that to mean you should be poking your nose into this investigation. Despite how many bodies you might find."

"I certainly hope there won't be any more," I said with feeling. "But, Inspecteur, the fact that I *do* continue to keep stumbling over dead people leads me to wonder why it keeps happening to me . . . and whether it means I should—"

"*Investigate?*" Merveille rarely interrupted, but in this case apparently he was unable to hold his tongue. His eyes flashed. "Mademoiselle, please do not fool yourself into thinking that the finding of the murdered gives you permission to do such a thing. Detective work is a job for the police, not for . . . you."

I lifted a brow at him. "Not for me, a woman? Or not for me, Tabitha Knight?"

"Not for anyone who is neither a police agent nor a detective," he replied firmly.

At that moment, I had an idea. A wild, crazy, brilliant, *exciting* idea. "Well, perhaps I will join the police force here in Paris," I said blithely. "They do take women, don't they?"

This time, he wasn't able to control his reaction; his eyes went wide and his mouth opened in shock. "Mademoiselle—"

"Or, better yet," I went on just as disingenuously but I knew my eyes sparkled with glee, "perhaps I'll look into getting my private investigator's license."

He closed his mouth and stared down at me for a heartbeat or two. "I do believe you're serious."

"Of course I'm serious," I replied. "Why not? I find investigating crimes very interesting, and I'm not so bad at it. With training, and a license, I could get even better. And then you couldn't brush me off all the time." That last part probably wasn't true, but that didn't matter to me. I was suddenly having a wonderful time, teasing him. My little imp was in raptures, doing cartwheels through my head.

Merveille shook his head. "Just because you've stumbled over a dead body or two—"

"Seven," I said. "Seven bodies—so far. Eight if you count Thérèse Lognon, but I didn't actually find her. Even you have to admit that can't be a coincidence."

"No," he said. "I would not call that a coincidence. I would call it—" He shook his head, clamping his lips together again. His expression was one of barely contained frustration . . . with maybe, just maybe, a hint of levity in his eyes. "Mademoiselle Knight—"

"You can call me Tabitha," I said. "I'm American, remember, and we're just not so formal back home. Besides, you've already done it."

"That was in an extenuating circumstance," he replied. "You were ignoring me. The informality—it is not such a good idea in general."

I beamed up at him. "I promise I won't try and call you Étienne, Inspecteur. But this 'mademoiselle' thing is for the birds."

He just shook his head. But I thought I saw the corner of his mouth quiver.

"Did you find out what the key belongs to?" I asked, still enjoying trying to throw him off balance. Not at all an easy thing to do.

"The small key that was taped beneath Madame Lannet's desk?" he replied. "The key that was not there the first night, but appeared on the second one?"

"That's the one," I replied, pleased that he'd confirmed my suspicion that the key had been put there in between the murders of Madame Lannet and Madame Pineau.

"Not yet," he said.

"I asked Lisette—pardon me, Mademoiselle Feydeau—whether she had any ideas what it might belong to and she didn't."

"I see," he replied grimly. "And what else did you ask Mademoiselle Feydeau?"

"I asked her about the lace that was used to strangle Madame Lannet. She said that Madame Pineau had told her it was a special lace, a new order that had come in for a specific gown that was being made for a Madame . . . Joilliet I think was her name. And that the lace would have likely been in Madame Lannet's office because it was so special, which meant the killer didn't bring it with him and probably didn't plan to do away with Madame Lannet." I glanced at him to see whether he agreed, but his expression was stony. "She also mentioned Monsieur Outhier and his investment in Maison Lannet as well."

"You've been very thorough, mademoiselle," he said.

"I didn't seek her out to question her," I said. "But the opportunity arose and I took it."

"And you were with her at Maison Lannet last night for what purpose?"

"I'm certain you already know we were there to retrieve something that belonged to Lisette." For some reason, I didn't want to mention what it was or why she needed the scissors. I pushed on before he could ask. "Inspecteur, you have to admit that *I* have an advantage in investigating any case that you simply don't have."

"And what is that?"

"People will talk more openly to me than they will to you. *Especially* women," I said. "You're a police agent. And you have a . . . demeanor that can be off-putting to some people. Besides, you and I both know how . . . how . . . people feel about the police since . . . uh . . . the Occupation." My mouth dried a little as I realized we were getting close to a topic I wasn't certain I wanted to delve into.

His expression remained implacable. "*Oui*. And it is for a good reason, *non?*"

"Yes," I replied firmly. "Look, I'm not going to get in your way,

Inspecteur. And I certainly don't want to put myself in danger"—he scoffed at this; a quiet sound, but I heard it—"but you must admit I might be able to find out some interesting things because people will talk to me.

"In fact, tomorrow, Grand-père and Oncle Rafe and I have a private appointment at Maison Dior—with Monsieur Dior himself. If I have the opportunity, I'm going to find out everything I can about when Mesdames Lannet and Pineau worked there."

He heaved a sigh. "I suppose there is nothing I can do to dissuade you?"

"Not in the least. Rest assured, I will share with you anything I learn."

"I am quite certain you will," he replied. "Sadly, it appears my . . . what is it you said? . . . off-putting demeanor does *not* have such an effect on you, mademoiselle."

CHAPTER 11

I HAD MERVEILLE'S SUGGESTION IN MIND WHEN I DELIVERED MONsieur le Chat to the veterinarian—the same one Julia and Paul used for their precious Minette. Monsieur Héroux's office was located only three blocks from where we lived.

My feline monsieur had quieted a little during the car ride to the vet's office, emitting only an occasional growling sound or hiss. However, the minute I picked up the case to carry it inside the veterinary office, he began yowling and squalling as if he was being tortured. By this time, I was wondering if trapping him in the carrier had caused more harm than good. The violent bouncing, leaping, and crying couldn't be good for his overall health or the sores on his back end.

Even though I was hesitant to release the cat, the event turned out to be less traumatic than I had expected. Monsieur Héroux seemed completely nonplussed by the snarling and hissing coming from inside the carrier, even when I put the case down on the examination table and it began to rock and shudder.

"Ah. I see that we have a little bit of the live wire here, eh?" he said, giving me a smile.

Monsieur Héroux was younger than I had expected—not much older than me—and he seemed perfectly at ease with the idea of releasing a feral feline into the small examination room. Tall and wiry, the veterinarian wore a white utilitarian coat with a shirt and tie peeking out from beneath it. He had dark hair with a neat mustache about the height of a finger's width and steady, deep-set brown eyes that looked upon his new patient with interest.

"He's an alley cat," I explained. "His tail is broken—it's been broken for a while, I think, and it doesn't seem to bother him. But now he has some very bad sores on his hindquarters. I thought maybe he should be treated. I—I wouldn't want anything to happen to him."

Monsieur Héroux looked at me and smiled. "So you have captured *un chat de gouttière* and brought him into civilization, have you? It is very much like the lion tamer coaxing the formidable feline into the circus tent. You are either a very brave woman or a very foolish one." His smile grew warmer and our eyes caught. "I think perhaps you are a brave woman, *non?*"

"That remains to be seen. I think I might make my exit before you open the door of the carrier," I said with a laugh, waving my hand at the case. "No, no, I jest. You see, Monsieur le Chat de Gouttière saved my life a few weeks ago, and I have been feeding him treats occasionally since then. But when I noticed the sores on his back, I thought he might need some medical treatment."

"This cat has saved your life? But how is that possible . . . is it *mademoiselle*, I hope?"

"*Oui.* Mademoiselle Tabitha Knight," I said.

"And you are the friend of Madame Child, *non?*" he said, offhandedly unlatching the carrier.

To my surprise, my wild, tortured cat did not explode from within and tear about the small room. He tentatively extended one paw, placing it onto the steel examination table after a moment of hesitation.

"Yes. Madame Child gave me your name and the cat carrier as well."

"And how is it that Monsieur le Chat came to save your life, mademoiselle?" said Héroux. He was giving the cat absolutely no attention, a strategy of which I approved.

"I was riding my bicycle along the quai toward Pont au Change. A car came up behind me, trying to run me down, but the handsome cat with his poor broken tail drew my attention. I stopped, rather suddenly, to find out whether he was all right with his broken tail, and the car drove past me, knocking me off my bike instead of running me over."

Héroux's eyes widened with shock and concern. "But you are saying a car tried to run you down? Surely it was an accident."

By now, the cat in question had poked his pale pink nose out from inside the carrier. Apparently though he'd been given what he'd so vehemently desired until moments ago—freedom—he wasn't certain about it after all.

"No, he was trying to kill me. He was a murderer who'd already killed two people," I said bluntly, "and he was afraid I'd realized what he'd done. And so he was trying to . . . uh . . . frighten me, I suppose."

"Frighten you? *Putain de merde!*" exclaimed Héroux in horror and shock, and seeming not at all afraid to offend with strong language. (Since I had heard and at times used strong language, more than once in my life, I was not offended.) "But you are so fortunate to be alive. Escaping a killer! And now, *now* I understand. You are the friend of Madame Child!"

I gave him a small smile. "But you already knew that."

"No, no, it is that you're the one she told me about. The one who is always finding the dead bodies."

Good grief. My reputation was certainly getting around. But Héroux seemed more fascinated than repelled by that fact.

"Well, I've stumbled over a few of them," I admitted. Seven was more than a few. . . . "And I'm very grateful that he drew my attention—oh, look, he's come out." My voice dropped to a whisper.

"Ah, *oui*, it usually only takes a moment or two. We are very calm in here, *non?* And in this room, there is nowhere for him to hide. No beds or sofas or even shelves on which to perch. And so we will make friends and I think he might allow me to . . . yes, there we are, monsieur," he said, holding out a steady hand for the cat to sniff. "Does the handsome gentleman have a name, mademoiselle?"

"No," I replied, then wondered: Should I name him? It seemed odd for a street cat to have a name.

Was I going to put him back on the street?

To my surprise, the cat didn't hiss or snarl or even try to get away from Héroux. Either the feline knew he was safe here, or the doctor had such a way about him that the animal trusted him inherently.

I could understand that, and I admired the easy, efficient, and gentle way Héroux handled the skittish cat. His hands—no rings—were gentle and long-fingered with slender knuckles, a few scratches, and short, neat fingernails.

The examination didn't take long and was surprisingly devoid of hisses and claw-swipes. In fact, the cat seemed to acquiesce surprisingly easily. Maybe he understood why he was there; that I was trying to help him.

It was also the first chance I'd had to really take a look at him in close quarters. He *was* a handsome cat, even with the top third of his tail broken off. He looked like a model-sized tiger, only his coloring was black, gray, and white instead of amber, brown, and white. The gray was a pretty gray, too; almost bluish.

"I will keep *le pauvre* monsieur overnight," said Héroux. "The infection is not as bad as it could be, but it is not very good. If you had waited any longer to bring him in . . ." He tsked sadly. "Ah, but all will be well, and I shall take good care of him. Perhaps you can retrieve the little patient tomorrow afternoon, mademoiselle?"

"Yes," I replied, suddenly wondering how much an overnight stay at a veterinary office was going to cost me. Ah well. It was too late to worry about that now.

"And perhaps by then you will have decided on a name for Monsieur le Chat de Gouttière?" Héroux said with a smile.

I smiled back. "I will do my best."

"And perhaps you might consider joining me for a little glass *de vin*, once Monsieur is feeling better?" Héroux said with a little smile. "There is the cafe only across the *rue*." He made a little gesture.

"Indeed I might," I replied, smiling back.

As I was leaving the veterinary office, I noted that it was barely two o'clock in the afternoon. M. Héroux's establishment was very close to Maison de Verre, and so I decided to walk over and see whether my messieurs were there with M. Grandpierre, the decorator—or whether they were at home, shooting each other daggerlike looks.

When I arrived at what had only a month ago been a dark, dusty, and abandoned building, I was shocked by the change. The building's facade had always been dominated by a huge bow window that stretched two floors high, and when I saw it last, it had been dark and dingy with grime, and covered with fabric and boards on the inside.

Now it gleamed and glittered in the late afternoon light, obviously having been cleaned and polished. The restaurant's name, literally "House of Glass," had been inspired by this window—or perhaps the restaurant had inspired the window. I didn't know.

Five tall vertical panels were made from textured glass and they alternated with five others that were clear and smooth. This would allow only slices of view from the street, looking in. The window was still covered on the inside, so I couldn't see through it into the restaurant even in slices, but the shiny, sparkling windows with freshly painted panes would certainly be cause for any passerby to be curious about the interior and its imminent unveiling.

A very smart move on the part of my messieurs.

The front door, which was set into a neat, covered alcove, was accessed by a small pair of concrete steps that had only recently had a swastika imprinted on the tiny landing. It was now gone, as was the odor of urine I had noticed last time—someone's obvious feeling about this remnant of the Nazis and their takeover. I had a feeling that applying a new layer of concrete over the little porch was probably the first thing Oncle Rafe and Grand-père had done upon taking over.

Through the door's window—which had the design of a broad V with an inset M etched on it—I could see that lights were on inside, so I was certain my surmise was correct and that I would find my housemates therein.

The two previous times I had been at Maison de Verre, I had not entered through the front door for different reasons. This time I would, for the door was unlocked. I didn't hesitate to turn the knob and walk in.

The door opened directly into the main space of the restaurant. Someone had already placed a mat on the floor to catch the slush and snow that might accompany boots or shoes. Probably Oncle Rafe.

A few steps inside was the small counter, where the maitre d' would eventually act as a sort of gatekeeper for the patrons. It was newly fashioned from polished mahogany. A small gold lamp with a dark blue shade sat on it, as if ready for business.

The entire establishment was small and intimate, a narrow, deep rectangle fronted by the dominant bow window—currently obscured by what I recognized as fresh paper—and extending back into the kitchen area. The front two-thirds would be for diners, with tables scattered about and three solitary booths on the back wall. I automatically averted my eyes from the booths, for I had a not-very-pleasant memory related to one of them, but then I looked again. The old upholstery had already been removed from the seats, and the tables were polished, gleaming as if they were new. Perhaps they were.

I was startled by how much work had already been done on the restaurant without my knowledge. Not that Grand-père and Oncle Rafe had to tell me everything they were doing, but it seemed as if I should have known that they'd been so busy.

Or maybe they'd decided it would be better to make the changes before I knew about their plans because I hadn't had the most pleasant of experiences here at Maison de Verre. Maybe they wanted to remove anything that would prompt bad memories.

I was distracted from all of these thoughts and observations an instant later by something that had me sprinting across the room.

"Grand-père!" I cried, nearly leaping upon the base of the ladder that leaned against the far wall . . .

. . . The ladder that my eighty-year-old relative was standing on . . . *several feet above my head.*

"What on *earth* are you doing up there?" My heart was in my throat as I gripped the sides of the ladder so that it wouldn't suddenly eject him or go tumbling to the side.

"Ah, *ma mie!* What a nice—"

"Don't turn around!" I shrieked, beset by visions of my rickety grandfather hurtling to the ground. "Now come down here this minute!" I demanded, gripping the ladder even tighter. If I could have climbed up there and carried him down, I would have.

"No, no, no." He was ignoring my entreaties by not only *not* descending, but also turning to look around and down at me, which put his torso frighteningly far from the rungs. One of his feet pivoted into what appeared to be a dangerously unstable position. "I am waiting for Rafe, the blasted old crow, to bring me the fabric so I can—*Rafe, what is taking you so long?*" he bellowed.

I hadn't realized he had such great lung capacity. But more importantly . . .

"Oncle Rafe knows you're on the top of a ladder?" I couldn't believe it.

"But of course. I—"

"Eh, don't be so bloody impatient, *cher.* I told you it would take—Tabitha! How good of you to stop off to see our little project." Oncle Rafe was all smiles as he strolled into view, carrying several large swaths of fabric.

"What is he doing up there?" I demanded, pointing violently in Grand-père's direction.

"But we were trying to decide on the fabric for the walls, and I wanted to see what it would look like so high and far away, you see?" Rafe smiled at me with a disingenuousness I hadn't expected. After all, I'd seen the way he watched Grand-père when he was making his way up or down the stairs—or even lowering himself into a chair.

I drew in a deep breath, trying to keep from shouting again. "You let him climb the ladder?"

Rafe, who'd dropped his burden on a table, spread his hands and shrugged. "Have you ever tried to stop the old goat from doing something he wanted to do?"

I gritted my teeth. That was not an excuse, and I could hardly believe Oncle Rafe was treating the situation so cavalierly. "Grand-père, why don't you come down and allow me to go up and hold the fabric. That way you both can see how it looks, *non?*" It was a struggle, but I kept my voice smooth and casual.

"Ah, but of course, Tabi. That is an excellent idea. You see, your *oncle*—he does not like to be very high off the ground and so it fell to me . . ." The rest of his words were muffled as he began to descend, finally.

After a brief, surprised look at Oncle Rafe, who scoffed and rolled his eyes at my grandfather's comment, I watched Grand-père like a hawk. My breathing didn't start again until he stepped on the rung at my eye level, and it was all I could do to keep from bundling him in my arms and dragging him off the ladder to safety.

My *grand-père* is well over six feet tall, even slightly stooped with age, and I top out at five feet five, so gathering him up and forcing him away would have been a challenge; even so, I wanted to and nearly did. But he stepped all the way down quickly and with surprising spryness, and my hands fell to my sides.

I happened to look at Rafe at that moment, and I was gratified to see the flash of relief in his own eyes. Maybe he wasn't as cavalier about it as I'd thought. Still.

I draped the three large pieces of fabric around my neck to keep my hands free and clambered up the ladder. I have no fear of heights, and in fact, the sprawling apple tree in our backyard had been one of my favorite places to hide out. I'd go as far from the ground as possible, for none of my younger sisters were fans of climbing trees and I liked getting away from them. The only time I'd gotten in trouble was when I'd climbed up while still in my First Communion dress—the one my *grand-mère* had slaved over, with extensive embroidery and rows of lace, that was supposed to be passed on to my sisters.

Needless to say, it wasn't.

"All right, here we go," I said once I got to the top. It was a long way up here, which didn't bother me, but renewed my terror over the fact that Grand-père had been hanging out on the highest rungs *by himself* while Oncle Rafe fetched the fabric.

I hooked my feet around the sides of the ladder for stability and, leaning forward so *I* didn't fall, unwrapped one of the fabrics and held it against the wall with both hands. After a moment I did the same with a second, and then the third one.

They were all silk damask and all of rich, jewel colors: one was of a deepest garnet with black designs. Another was a lush sapphire with subtle silvery blue. And the third was black with elegant white designs.

"Ah, and now the blue one again, *chère*," called up Oncle Rafe. "It is the best, I think, *non*, Maurice?"

"No, no, that is not even an option," retorted Grand-père. "It is the red one we like best, *non*? Hold that one again, Tabi, please? *Le rouge.*"

"But the *red—ridicule*! It is like the lady's boudoir! We cannot have that here in la Maison de Verre. It will not do," Oncle Rafe snapped. "Can you not see? The blue—she is calm and soothing—"

"But *non*! It is *la rouge* that is soothing and warm, like the food, *non*? Listen to me, you old crow," Grand-père shouted over Rafe's equally thundering response, their voices echoing in the open room. "We do not want to *freeze* out the people! To make them feel cold like the icy winter or the frigid river! We want them to be warm and happy so they all order much food and much wine and they stay all night!"

"Ah, *oui*, to stay all night in your boudoir," snarled Rafe. "*Non!* I will not have—"

"How about this one," I said loudly, and unfurled the black-and-white piece again. It was my favorite, because it actually looked a bit like the glass of the window—the shadows and light, a chiaroscuro effect that would appear stunning next to the grandness of the window.

They both looked up at me and spoke in unison: "*NON!*"

Needless to say, a decision was *not* made on the wall covering for Maison de Verre. I hesitated to leave my two messieurs there alone; besides the danger of the ladder, there was also the possibility that they might come to blows.

Instead, I managed to convince them that their beloved Madame Child was waiting to hear my updates on the murder investigation, and that they should join us to discuss it. Aside from that, I remembered Julia's gleeful offer to make dinner for us for a week if I managed to capture my alley cat and remain unscathed. I couldn't wait to boast to her about how it had all went.

Sadly, I knew I wouldn't be able to actually take her up on a week's worth of dinners. I would feel too guilty for not cooking since it was the only contribution I made to the household. And it wouldn't be right to rely on Julia when she had her own monsieur to feed. But maybe for one or two nights . . .

The alacrity with which the gentlemen accepted my invitation suggested they, too, knew there was no reason to stay here and argue. I had hoped their meeting with M. Grandpierre had put to rest the enmity and arguments, but that was clearly not the case, for even as they accepted, they exchanged frigid, dagger-like glares.

"I'll telephone Julia when we get back and see if she wants to come here or if we should go there," I said as I bundled them into their Bentley, which was parked in the alley behind the restaurant. It was a short walk home—only five blocks and around the corner—but on a chilly day where there might be ice or slush, I fully supported them driving. I probably would insist they take their car even when there wasn't ice or slush.

I arrived at the private courtyard where we kept our vehicles just as the door into the house closed behind Oncle Rafe. Following in his path, I found Bet (or Blythe) in the kitchen.

Our two day maids, identical twins, were in their late forties or so. They wore the same dark blue dresses with crisp white aprons every day and had the same dark brown hair threaded with gray pulled back in neat twists. They even each had a mole at the temple on the same side. It was completely impossible to tell them apart, and although I wished I could refer to them by their names, I never did because I was afraid of making a mistake. Once I even tried to address one of them as Mademoiselle Blanc since it would have worked for either of the twins as they were both unmarried, but that idea sparked such abject horror that I never tried again.

Whichever one of Bet or Blythe was in the kitchen when I entered was scrubbing the countertops, and already the windows shined from her efforts. The faint scent of ammonia lingered in the air.

"Mademoiselle, you have a letter," she said, looking up with a smile and gesturing with her chin that I should look in the foyer.

I was mildly surprised, for today's postal mail had already arrived—including a familiar white envelope edged with blue and red markings and stamped *par avion*. It was a letter from my parents filled with anecdotes and updates about everyone back home. I loved hearing the news, but I didn't feel the slightest bit of homesickness. Paris was now my home, and I couldn't imagine ever going back to Michigan.

The letter waiting for me on the small table in the front room was in a distinctive blue-gray envelope with a brick-red stamp on it. The word TÉLÉGRAPHE was printed on the front, but I knew it wasn't a telegram in the way one normally thinks about telegrams—with Morse code tapping over the lines while someone on the receiving end jotted down the words and ending each phrase with "stop."

No, this little letter-card of distinctive blue was a message that had come through the pneumatic tube system that had been installed throughout Paris in the late 1800s. For forty-seven francs, you could send a *pneu*, as they were called, to anyone in the city to be delivered within two hours.

I'd never received one before since Grand-père and Oncle

Rafe had had a telephone installed at their home almost as soon as there was someone to call—long before my arrival. But for many people who didn't have telephones, it was a cost-effective and speedy way to communicate without having to travel to the person or to pay a courier to deliver it. It had long been part of the telegraph system, even though these types of communications were handwritten by the recipient like any other letter, and placed inside the blue envelope.

The *pneu* would be sent from a convenient pneumatics station and fly through the city inside a metal cylinder placed in a tube—then was either blown with a powerful puff of air along the tube from one station to another, or sucked by a strong vacuum. Once it arrived at the station closest to the delivery address, someone would conduct the message to the recipient.

I was mystified over who would be sending me a *pneu*. Most anyone I would normally communicate with—Julia, my tutoring clients, even Merveille—would use the telephone to contact me. Or, in Merveille's case, he might simply show up unannounced. Especially if he was annoyed with me.

I could hear Grand-père and Oncle Rafe getting settled up in the salon. Monsieur Wilde was more interested in their arrival than mine, mainly because Oncle Rafe was very liberal with the treats and affectionate petting whenever he returned home, so the little dog wasn't standing on the stairs barking at me. I was certain Madame X was surveying the ado with condescending green eyes, expecting her treat as well.

The message inside the little blue envelope was brief but clear, written in spindly feminine writing: *Mademoiselle Tabitha, please come to the shoe shop again tonight at closing. Half six. There are others who know more about Madame Lannet and Robert Illouz, if you are interested. X X X, Lisette Feydeau.*

Well, wasn't that interesting? I smirked a little as I tucked the letter into my pocket. As I had told Merveille, I had an advantage in talking to people about a murder because I wasn't with *les flics*. I was almost certain *he* hadn't gotten a message like that.

I called over to Julia's flat, not certain whether she would even be at home, for she often attended cooking demonstrations in the afternoon.

"Tabs! I've been simply *dying* to hear from you!" Her voice boomed and lilted over the line. "How did everything go? Did you see Merveille? Did you capture the cat?"

"Yes and yes. There isn't much to tell, really, but I do have a date—"

"*With Merveille?*" Julia shrieked.

I brought the telephone back to my ear. "No, no, with M. Héroux and—"

"Oh, he *is* very nice, isn't he?" Julia said at a lower volume. I could hear her smiling over the receiver. "He's a little young, though it won't matter to you, and he has nice hands and a good sense of humor."

She might have gone on to further discuss the veterinarian's attributes, but I interrupted to explain how I'd needed an excuse to get my messieurs away from ladders and volatile arguments by volunteering her a visit with them.

"Of *course*, Tabs! I'd *love* to see your darling gents. Let me just pull this out of the oven . . . here we go, you *charming* little monsieur"—I could hear clunks and shuffling about—"*Oh* my *goodness!* Aren't you just *perfection*, all gold and brown and *delectably* crispy—I'll be right over."

The phone line went dead.

I hung up, chuckling to myself, and went into the kitchen to ask Blythe (or Bet) to help me put together a little tea for the four of us.

I had learned the hard way that I had to ask them for what I needed, rather than trying to do it myself—at least when they were around. I'm not sure whether it was fear that I'd mess things up after they'd just cleaned, or because they were aware of my lack of skills in the kitchen.

Bet or Blythe shooed me out of the kitchen and assured me she'd send up a nice tea tray via the dumbwaiter.

To be clear, in the Saint-Léger and Fautrier household, "tea" actually meant *café*, often *au lait*, cognac or brandy and occasionally a Sauternes, and some little treats to eat—macaron, cheese, tiny croissants or other flaky pastries, and, sometimes, a bit of charcuterie. On occasion, we had caviar and crêpes with jam.

I just started up the stairs when the front door rattled in its frame from energetic knocking. "Yoohoo!" called Julia, opening the door.

Oscar Wilde came bounding to the top of the stairs so excitedly he went airborne over the first three of them. I'd seen him tumble head over tail down the entire flight once before upon Julia's arrival. He, like everyone else in the household, knew that the arrival of Julia Child meant *food* . . . gorgeous, incomparable food.

Sure enough, she was carrying a large cardboard box—which she must have set down in order to open the front door. I took it from her and found myself assaulted by the most delicious smells.

"Whoa, what is all this?" I said, barely able to keep from pawing through the tea towels she'd placed over the top of it.

"Oh, it's just a lovely little *blanquette de veau*," Julia trilled with a smile, scooping up the box from my grip. "Veal stew with onions and mushrooms—and I've already put some happy little boiled potatoes in there too. Just warm it up and serve! After all, you captured the cat, and I promised dinner. I'll just put this in the kitchen for later. Show me your arms," she said with a grin.

"Scratchless," I said, thrusting out my arms and pulling up the sleeves of my blouse to prove it. "I'll take that into the kitchen for Bet to put away. You go on up." I took the box and managed to peek at the stew. It was dark and thick, and it smelled *divine*. My mouth began to water.

Julia was on her way up the stairs. "Yoohoo! Gentlemen! It's me! Giving you fair warning to put away anything you don't want me to see!" She cackled.

As I went into the kitchen, I heard Oncle Rafe say, "Quick, Maurice, with the secret treasure! Hide it before she—*ah, Madame Child*! There you are, looking lovely as always."

Giggling, I gave the box to Bet or Blythe, then ascended to join the others.

Julia was ensconced on the sofa—a plump wine-red affair with a matching bolster on each end. She was holding a tiny sipping glass of cognac and leaning forward as if confiding in the two gentlemen.

"... *And* Tabitha has a *date!*" Julia crowed as I entered the room.

CHAPTER 12

*T*HREE PAIRS OF EYES SWIVELED TO ME, ALL GLEAMING WITH SALA-
cious curiosity.

I rolled my own eyes and went to open the door to the dumbwaiter. "Can't you find anything to talk about other than my dat-
ing life?" I grumbled as I brought the tray over to the large table
around which everyone was gathered.

"There's nothing nearly as interesting," Julia said.

"I think *murder* is more interesting," I retorted, beginning to
make a plate for Grand-père.

As I had expected, Bet or Blythe had created a wonderful
spread. There were tiny almond cookies from a patisserie around
the corner that Oncle Rafe favored, as well as creamy Brie and
crispy-crusted baguette, a small bowl of soft green olives, large
pungent caperberries, pickled artichoke hearts, and tiny spicy
red peppers. A saucer-sized lemon tea cake, just enough for us,
had been cut into four compact pieces. The cognac was already
here in the salon, but Bet (or Blythe) had included milk, sugar,
and a fresh pot of coffee.

"Speaking of murder, do you know anything about Frédéric
Outhier?" I said as I glared warningly at Oscar Wilde, who seemed
to think that if he put his tiny paws on my leg and looked at me
with soulful brown eyes in the cutest face ever, that I would give
him a crumb of cheese.

Drat it, he was right.

"Ah, *oui*, of course," said Grand-père, gesturing with his ever-present cigarette. "He is in the trade of glass—jars and bottles, you see. He owned a glass plant . . . and I believe he bought or took over the business of a distributor just before the war. It seems he somehow made it through, coming out and growing his share since then. What interest do you have in Frédéric Outhier, Tabi?"

"He is the one who gave the money to Madame Lannet to start her own atelier. As an investor, I mean. I was thinking about how, with her death and that of Madame Pineau, the atelier would need to close down."

"And therefore how would it affect Outhier's business," said Oncle Rafe, nodding. It wasn't a question; he was making a statement. "Or at least, how it would affect Outhier himself if he put up the money for it."

"*Exactement*," I replied, handing Rafe a cup of coffee.

"It is a strange bedfellow I think, for a glass business to invest in an atelier," mused Grand-père. "They have no connection, no . . . eh . . . intersection. Unlike Monsieur Broussac, who financed Christian Dior to start his own atelier—he is in textiles. You see, there is a logical connection, *non*? But with Outhier . . . there is no logic."

"Eh . . . perhaps the man only wishes to make money any way he can," said Rafe with an easy shrug. "Or perhaps he has a wife who likes the high fashion."

"You're thinking the motive for the murderer might be to ruin Outhier as well as Rose-Marie Lannet?" Julia said, adding a good dollop of cognac to her coffee. "That's brilliant. I was only thinking of a jealous lover or that someone broke in trying to steal something and got caught!" She gave a husky laugh.

"Well, I do think whoever did it *was* looking for something. After all, they came back the second night when all of the police were gone." I poured my own cup of *café*. "Anyhow, I was wondering if you could think of anyone in particular who might want to ruin Frédéric Outhier, Grand-père. Or someone who would benefit by him having business troubles."

"Ah, *oui*, of course. I will think on it, *ma mie*. And perhaps I will ask around, *non*?" He winked.

I smiled. Having a grandfather who could obtain knowledge about the financial situation—as well as other gossip—of nearly everyone in Paris was very helpful when investigating a murder.

"Still," commented Oncle Rafe, "it is a strange business in which to invest with no connection, *non*, Maurice? The haute couture, it is still very important here in Paris, and with the upper class, of course, and there are those clients, but the fashion industry itself is not so very strong since the war."

"Monsieur Block said the same thing," I replied. "Although haute couture lives on, the everyday fashion industry is struggling."

"And this Block, he is the shoemaker that we are to help, *non*?" Oncle Rafe said with a smile as he flipped open a silver case to withdraw one of his dark cigarettes. "We will go there tomorrow, then, with all of the pomp and circumstance—just before our appointment with Monsieur Dior."

"Yes, that would be very good," I replied. "As long as people see you going in and out. You don't have to buy shoes from him—"

"But we will, of course! I have heard of Godot & Block, and they are quite reputable with good quality. It is no problem to spread our attention among more than one designer," Rafe said as he lit his smoke. "They were, after all, closed down of their own volition during the Occupation. They refused to serve the Nazis and shut their doors instead of doing so."

"It must have been difficult for their business, but I'm glad the shoe shop reopened," I said, registering the hard, flat note in Oncle Rafe's voice.

"*Oui.* And we will be happy to help Monsieur Block reestablish his business after those years closed," Grand-père said, with a glance at Rafe.

"Do you have any other suspects, Tabs?" asked Julia. She must have sensed that the subject was a difficult one for my messieurs and sought to change it.

"Not really," I replied sadly. "I'm flat out of motives, too, other than the one about ruining Outhier as well as Maison Lannet."

"*I* think you ought to go for the jealous lover motive," Julia said with one of her cheery smiles as she forked up a piece of tea cake. "Oh my *goodness*." Her eyes popped wide. "This lemon cake is *divine*! It is . . . why, it's like a citrusy cloud that just *melts in your mouth*! Who made it?"

"Bet," I said.

"Or possibly Blythe," added Grand-père with a grin. He'd once confessed that he couldn't tell them apart, either, and just randomly used either name. Neither of them seemed to care. I could only suppose they were used to it.

"A jealous lover is as good a motive as any," said Oncle Rafe as he spewed out a long, easy stream of smoke. "Is there any rumor that Rose-Marie Lannet and Frédéric Outhier were lovers? Perhaps that explains why he made the investment in Maison Lannet. And perhaps Madame Outhier sought to remove her rival. . . . Or perhaps Madame Lannet's lover sought to remove his."

I looked at him in surprise. "I hadn't thought of that. I suppose I thought—well, I got the impression that Madame Lannet and Madame Pineau were . . . together."

"Ah, like Mademoiselle Chanel and her Madame Lucie?" said Grand-père with a laugh. "There is the rumor, you know, that they are lovers."

"No, no, no! *La femme* Chanel was sleeping with a Nazi and reporting to him about Parisians while the rest of us were—*egh!*" Oncle Rafe's face twisted as he made an emphatic gesture of a thumb grinding down upon the French people. "It is good that Chanel has not come back to Paris, although I hear the rumors that she might someday."

I glanced at Grand-père. The topic of those who collaborated with the Germans, and those who were part of the Resistance against the Nazi Occupation and the French Vichy government—who had capitulated far too easily to the Germans—was a volatile point for most every Parisian, but for Oncle Rafe, it was far more of a black-and-white line. He'd been very much a part of the Resistance, although neither of my gentlemen housemates were willing to give me many details about exactly what he'd done.

On the other hand, my grandfather had needed to straddle the line between actively collaborating with the Germans, outright resisting them, and doing the bare minimum in order to stay safe and alive. He funneled money and used his knowledge and power to assist the Resistance—and to spy for them—while appearing as if he was in cooperation with the Germans.

I knew that the two men had helped move Jedburgh soldiers in and through Paris before D-Day, and I suspected they might have done it in this very house, under the nose of some Nazi officer. But I hadn't asked for details.

Well, that's not true. I had—but every time I brought up the subject, Grand-père firmly changed it.

"We still cannot know all of those who helped the Germans, who washed their hands and closed their eyes to that which happened," Rafe went on in the short, edgy tone he always used when the topic came up. His expression had darkened and I wanted nothing more than to take his rough, knobby hand in mine and somehow comfort him, even though I knew that would do little to alleviate the painful and humiliating memories from that time. "Some of those who screamed the loudest about the collaborators were in fact secretly licking the arses of *les boches* in order to make a fortune."

"Eh, perhaps—although most of those in bed with the Nazis have paid their due," said Grand-père as I handed him the plate I'd made. "And, *cher*, you know there is the gray area sometimes. The line is not so clear between those who actively collaborated and those who did only what they had to do to survive. There are even those who say *I* traveled along the gray area."

"There is *no* gray area where I am concerned," Rafe said. "It is simple: one who took money from *les boches* collaborated with them. There is no other way to look at it." His eyes were hot with fury.

"Even if the money received from the Germans under the

guise of collaboration was used to help fund the Resistance?" Grand-père replied in a mild voice. "As Monsieur Dior did with his pay, and so did many others. Including myself at Banque Maine-Saint-Léger?"

"Dior . . . *oui,* oh, he was one who rode that fine line, working for Lelong and all the while making the designs for the Nazi women and collaborators' wives . . . no, he was not the only one," Rafe went on. "But it is only for Mademoiselle Dior that I do not clump Christian Dior in the category of collaborators and German arse-kissers. She paid the price, did she not, and her brother can carry the guilt for it."

"If you would otherwise clump Dior in that category of collaborator, then you must also put me there, Rafael," said Grand-père in a voice I'd never heard before. "For La Banque Maine-Saint-Léger touched a great amount of German marks. And we gave a large amount of them to the Resistance . . . not to mention passing on information to them."

The hair on the back of my neck lifted and I felt a little queasy. I didn't understand everything they were talking about, especially relating to Monsieur and his sister, the aforesaid Mademoiselle Dior, but I got the gist.

This was an entirely different disagreement than what color scheme to use for the decorations of the restaurant. The air in the salon had changed abruptly. I gave Julia a covert glance. She appeared as uneasy as I felt.

For a moment, I thought Oncle Rafe was going to rise and leave in anger. His jaw moved and he stabbed out his cigarette with a sharp, angry movement of finality.

The tension was so thick I could hardly breathe. Even Julia, who could nearly always find a way to lighten the mood, was silent and still.

Finally, Oncle Rafe said, "Of course I do not clump you in that category, Maurice—although you and I have had some disagreements not so very different than those between Dior and the brave Catherine. There is sometimes, as they say, no clear line. Sometimes one must do what is needed to survive . . . although the definition of 'survive' may change depending upon to whom one speaks." He gave a very small, wry smile and shrugged.

With that, the tension eased. It didn't quite snap, but I no longer feared a great argument—or, worse, a furious exit that might lead to something more serious.

Surely Grand-père and Oncle Rafe had had this conversation many times before. Perhaps it went the same way every time. Or perhaps it went worse when they were alone. Either way, I was relieved that the moment had passed.

In an effort to radically change the subject, I said brightly, "And in some other interesting news, I've received an invitation—"

"*The date!*" Julia was definitely jumping on the idea of a subject change. "Tell us about it, Tabs."

Although that wasn't what I'd been about to tell them, I capitulated. I knew the idea of me having a love life—any sort of love life—would be a great distraction and pleasure to my messieurs.

"I met a veterinarian today and he asked me for a drink tomorrow when I go to . . . uh . . . pick up the cat." I realized as I spoke that I hadn't actually told Grand-père and Oncle Rafe about my plans for Monsieur le Chat de Gouttière.

"*Le chat?*" Grand-père tilted his head.

"Well, you see . . . the gutter cat who saved my life back in December is sick and injured. I couldn't just leave him there, so I lured him into Julia's cat carrier and took him to the veterinarian," I explained swiftly.

Madame X—who until now had been arranged on the fireplace mantel with her sleek black tail curled around her equally sleek, black body—skewered me with her emerald eyes. Her tail dropped suddenly, the tip curling like a J, and it twitched like an angry snake. It seemed she knew precisely what I was talking about—and even what I was thinking.

"Oho! So you think you might be introducing another cat into the household?" Oncle Rafe said with a laugh. Apparently, he saw the writing on the wall as well. "And how do you think that will go with Madame X, Maurice?"

My grandfather was looking at me closely.

I felt my cheeks warm. "Well, I hadn't really thought—well, I couldn't just *leave* him there and let him get sicker and die, could I? After what he did for me?"

"You really ought to give the beast a name," Julia said. Not very helpfully, might I add.

I gave her a dirty look and she smiled complacently as she sipped her cognac. "He doesn't need a name if he's going back on the street," I said.

"But he is not, is he, Tabitha?" said Grand-père.

I couldn't tell by his tone or expression whether he was annoyed or irritated or merely curious.

"Well, I . . . I don't know. I . . ."

"Oh, let her bring him here, *cher*," said Oncle Rafe with a wave and a little laugh. "It'll do *la madame hautaine* good to have a bit of competition. We all know Monsieur Wilde does not provide it." He picked up the little dog, who'd been giving Julia the sad, brown, beady eyes of long-term starvation and abject neglect.

Grand-père sniffed and lit another cigarette. I still couldn't read his expression and that worried me. He'd been so generous and gracious since I'd arrived, the last thing I wanted was to slap him in the face with an out-of-line expectation.

"There is no doubt Madame X will quickly put a flea-ridden gutter cat into his place," he replied at last. "She suffers no fools"—he glanced pointedly at Oscar Wilde—"nor does she cede her space or authority. You may allow them to meet," he said quickly as my eyes lit up. "As long as he has been well-soaked in a flea bath," he added sharply. "*Thrice*. And then we will see how it is to go."

Madame X sat bolt upright and gave her master a shocked and affronted look. Then she gave a peremptory yowl, surprising me, for I'd never heard her make a sound except for a half-hearted hiss at Oscar Wilde, or her rough, grating purr.

"It will be all right, madame," Grand-père said.

She turned away and presented him with her backside, tail high, clearly furious.

"I could keep him upstairs," I said, and all three of my companions burst into derisive laughter. I shrugged. "It's worth a try."

When Oncle Rafe finished wiping the tears from his eyes, he said, "And what was in the *pneu* that arrived for you, *ma petite?*"

I was not surprised by his question—there was nothing that went on in this house that my messieurs missed, which was part of the reason I hadn't even *considered* trying to sneak in Monsieur le Chat de Gouttière. I explained what was in the letter from Lisette.

"Oh, drat!" Julia moaned. "If I didn't have some of Paul's colleagues coming for dinner tonight, I would *insist* on going with you. Speaking of which," she said, bolting to her feet. "*La cuisine* calls! I must to the stove and the chopping board. Dinner is at eight and there's much to do. Enjoy your *blanquette*, Monsieur Saint-Léger and Monsieur Fautrier."

And with that, she was gone in a rush of movement.

When I arrived at Godot & Block, I found Lisette sitting on one of the benches inside, waiting for Mathilde to finish dusting off the counter and shoe displays so she could close up.

"Ah, you came! That is wonderful!" cried Lisette when I walked inside. She rose to her feet and we exchanged quick kisses, one on each cheek. "And, *oui*, the hair, it looks very good. Very, very good," she said, stepping back to eyeball me closely. "*Oui*. I am *l'artiste magnifique.*" She didn't even try to sound humble.

"It's so much easier to do my hair with it being this short," I replied as Monsieur Block came out from the back. He was puffing on a cigarette even as he carried two swatches of fine leather and a wooden shoe form.

"Ah, it is you again, mademoiselle," he said, and automatically glanced down at my feet. "Bonjour."

I had learned my lesson and so I was wearing the dark red Mary Janes that had been made in this very shop. Fortunately, it had been dry today, so I wasn't going to ruin them in the name of vanity and ego.

"Yes," I replied with a smile. "And I believe you can expect Monsieur Saint-Léger and Monsieur Fautrier tomorrow. And so then tomorrow night, you can lay the trap by saying that they had come for their last fitting and they will soon pick up their shoes?"

"*Oui, oui,* that is very good," said Block. "And what are you doing tonight, the three of you?" He gave us a narrow, almost suspicious look, rather like a father might before his daughter went out at ten o'clock on a Friday night. Not that I had any experience with anything like that. . . .

"Oh, we are going to Lisette's to talk all about the tragedy at Maison Lannet," said Mathilde. "Mademoiselle Knight, she is investigating the case, too, instead of *les flics.*"

"Not *instead* of," I said quickly. "They are of course still investigating. I'm simply . . . curious about it."

Block looked at me in surprise, his eyes narrowing thoughtfully. Then he nodded. "*Oui. Les flics*—they are—*egh!* And Mathilde, she tells me it is you who discovered the dead woman last night, mademoiselle?"

"Yes," I admitted.

"Well, perhaps you will not come around here again soon, mademoiselle, if you are the one who keeps finding the bodies." He chuckled, but it sounded pained. "I would not want you to find one here, *non?* Unless it is that Philippe," he added with a flash of annoyance. With that, he turned and started to the back of the shop, calling over his shoulder, "Lock it up tight, Mathilde! And do not forget to turn off the lights!"

Mathilde did not forget to turn off the lights, and she locked the door behind us. "Eh, he was in such a foul mood today," she said as she linked arms with me on one side and with Lisette on the other. "I think he is more worried about the break-in than he lets on, even with your plan in mind. I think he will feel better when Monsieur Saint-Léger comes in tomorrow. He will come, won't he?"

"He will," I promised.

We stopped at a *cave* to get a bottle of table wine and a *tabac* for cigarettes for Lisette, and we were soon climbing the four flights, mostly in the dark, to the room.

Last night, I'd been a little distracted over the horror of finding Madame Pineau, as well as the fact that I was about to have many inches cut off my hair, and I had hardly noticed anything about Lisette's room.

Tonight I paid more attention to my surroundings, reminding myself that if I was going to be a detective, I should *always* be observing my surroundings, even if I was under stress or frightened. It was a good lesson, for I didn't remember much about the stairs we climbed, with its dark carpeting held in place by brass rods on each tread and the sconces that lit the way . . . but I noticed the sconces tonight because they went out when we were halfway up the stairs again. This time, Mathilde and I were prepared for the sudden darkness, and we didn't even pause on the steps.

Lisette's room was as I vaguely remembered from last night's debauch of my locks. It was a surprisingly spacious space with a sink and tiny counter where she plugged in a small electric burner. There were two large windows that would offer wonderful light on sunny days but tonight were covered by heavy drapes to keep out the chilly drafts.

A bed was tucked in the corner near a large built-in wardrobe. There was a screen blocking a small area of the space where presumably she changed clothing. A row of nylons dangled from a line hung over the radiator. A little vanity littered with cosmetics and other beauty products offered a mirror and chair. The walls were painted a dull gold that needed to be updated, and the battered wooden floor was covered by two large, dark rugs.

Lisette also had a small dining table with two chairs near the sink and electric burner, as well as a sofa and two chairs near a low table. As apartments went, it was a nice size and the furnishings were in good condition. As was the case with most every room rental, the bathroom was located down the hall and shared by those who lived there. I had read somewhere that fewer than fifteen percent of rooms in Paris had toilets en suite. This knowledge made me even more appreciative of my own luxurious living quarters.

Not long after our arrival, a bell buzzed in the room. I realized belatedly it was the front desk notifying Lisette that guests had arrived for her.

"It's not so very fun to be without a telephone," she told me, glugging a generous amount of red wine into something that looked like an old jam jar. She handed it to me. "Every time there is a telephone call for me, I must run down the stairs to the desk to take it. And Madame Villet, she complains when I have many calls, that I tie up her telephone line. But is it my fault? No of course it is not. If she would allow a telephone to be installed here, then I would not tie up the lines, would I?"

She left the room to greet her guests and Mathilde and I took up seats on the sofa.

"And how was your day at the shop today?" I asked. "Were there many people coming in again because of the news about Madame Pineau?"

"Oh, yes, of course," Mathilde replied, sipping her wine. "Today it was even more sensational because it was two times now that it has happened that a body is found at Maison Lannet. And of course, with Madame Pineau, well, there was all of the blood too."

I nodded. Yes, there was something about blood and gore that had people coming out of the woodwork like curious little ants to investigate. "And did any of the curious customers buy any shoes?"

Mathilde shrugged. "*Oui*, there were some. Many people came to gossip and only some made orders, but it was more than yesterday so, eh, it was good. And also many people expressed concern to Monsieur Block about his break-in, so that was good for him and for business."

"So Monsieur Block must have been pleased with all of that."

"Eh, *peut-être*. Monsieur Block, he has been in a very bad mood these last days, since the break-in, I think. He misses his wife, you see. It was her birthday only three days ago and he was very sad on that day."

"Where is she?"

"Oh, she has died—only two years ago. That is why he was so sad. She was Jewish, you see. She lived through the war because many friends in the city hid her, but . . . ah, her brothers and some cousins, they did not."

"I'm sorry for Monsieur Block," I said.

"I am too. Madame Block was always very kind to me—but even so, I did not want to date her son," she added with a little smile.

Before I could commiserate, she went on, "And it is Monsieur Block who has made *me* telephone the clients whose shoes have been ruined in order to explain the situation, and that if he cannot get the correct leather again, the orders will be canceled. The clients, they were not happy about it—it is because not only were their shoes ruined, but also some were clients of Maison Lannet.

"But I think, if the shoes were to be worn with the gowns from Lannet, then perhaps they should be pleased that the shoes are canceled too?" Mathilde said with an insouciant shrug and a clear disregard for business.

"Well, that is one way to look at it," I said, even as I felt a little interested prickle as my internal sprite sat bolt upright. "Who were these customers that were clients of both Monsieur Block and Maison Lannet?"

"Ah, there was La Comtesse Grenèche, and also Madame Joilliet, and there was Madame Outhier and—*qu'est-ce que c'est?*"

"Madame Outhier? That is the wife of the man who financed the starting up of Maison Lannet?"

Mathilde looked at me in surprise. "Why, I don't know. Is she? I only know that she is a recent and new customer of Monsieur Block. I think this is the first time she has made an order—and now she may not get her shoes after all. That Philippe Wathelet—he must be stewing in his own juices over losing Madame Outhier and Madame Joilliet to us!" She cackled.

Just then, the door to the room opened and Lisette and three other young women swarmed in. They were loud and energetic and chattering happily.

Introductions were made—the newcomers were Cerise, Yvonne, and Noëlle—and there was a flurry of more red wine being poured into olive and jam jars and distributed.

"Cerise and Yvonne are mannequins for Monsieur Dior," said Lisette, settling onto the floor on a pillow stolen from her bed, "and they also worked with Monsieur Lelong at his atelier during the war. Madame Lannet was there, too, you see. And so was Robert Illouz, the designer.

"They are going to get me a job with Dior," she added in a murmur to me, nodding at Cerise and Yvonne as more activity erupted between the guests over the sharing of a pack of cigarettes and lighting them, finding ashtrays, and finally joining us in comfortable seating around the low table. "And Noëlle, she also worked with me at Maison Lannet. She has already been hired by Dior since two weeks."

"It is your makeup," Noëlle said earnestly. "You only have to work a bit more at it to be perfect, and then Madame Raymonde will be certain to hire you. Once Cerise showed me how to do it, then it was very easy and it was the right look—the right look to go with the New Look, eh?—you see. That is what they expect."

"Oh, then you must show me now," said Lisette, springing to her feet.

I watched in dismay. Not because I wasn't interested in learning how mannequins did their makeup in a particular way in order to be hired—it was a concept that fascinated me by its very specificity—but because I had come in order to learn more about Mesdames Lannet and Pineau.

"First, you must make the outline of your eye," said Noëlle, sitting at the vanity table and taking up a little pot of Maybelline black mascara and a tiny makeup brush. "But I will need some water to wet the mascara and show you."

While Lisette hurried to comply, getting water from the sink in a small coffee cup, I turned to Cerise and Yvonne. They were watching what was to be the makeup demonstration, but that didn't mean I couldn't question them.

"Lisette said you knew Madame Lannet."

"Oh, yes! It is *très horrible* what was done to her!" said Yvonne. Like the other mannequins in the room—and presumably like every other one in Paris—she was tall and slender, but had definite curves at the waist and bust. Her hair was blond and she had very light blue eyes. She had the same wide-eyed, doll-like look as Bette Davis. "And Madame Pineau, too!" She shuddered.

"Do you have any idea who might have wanted to kill either of them?" I asked. "Or at least someone who didn't like them or had it in for them."

"Oh, but you would have to hate someone quite a lot to kill them, *non?*" said Yvonne. "Not only to dislike them or to have a disagreement."

"I think Robert Illouz," said Cerise, lighting a cigarette. She blew out a long stream of smoke as she gave a sly smile. She was dark haired with a dusky skin color and sparkling brown eyes. "He is the designer who loathes Rose-Marie Lannet like one loathed *les boches*. He is talented, *oui*, and not only in the haute couture," she added, her smile turning complacent with meaning. "And he has a very loose tongue in the pillow talk."

"You see, Tabitha?" Lisette called over from the vanity as she watched Noëlle in the mirror. Noëlle had outlined her eyes with the mascara, making them look very dark and almond-shaped. Now she was using a brown makeup pencil to draw long, very arched eyebrows. "I told you they would know."

"You think Robert Illouz might have killed Mesdames Lannet and Pineau?" I said.

"I think he hated Rose-Marie Lannet enough to want to kill her," said Cerise. "They were at Lelong together during the war, and when Dior left to make his own atelier, of course, Lannet went with him. Dior did not ask Robert Illouz to go as well—but he's hoping now, soon, to be hired—and for that—for being passed over in favor of Lannet, Robert was very angry. And then when Robert learned that Maison Lannet was to open, he was incensed.

"*He*, Robert Illouz, should be the next Dior! *He* should be the next Fath or the next Lanvin! *He* should take the place of

La Chanel! But this old woman who is only very average in her designs should not have someone give her a pot of gold to start up a house! How could Outhier be so blind! And so, and so, and so," she said with a flap of her cigarette hand. "He had much to say. And I . . . eh, I listened because, as I say, he is not only accomplished on the clothing designs, but also between the sheets."

I smothered a smile. One of the things about living in Paris that was far different from living in Michigan was how open the French were about sex. Back home, we *talked* about having sex. Here, everyone actually *did* it. And you couldn't walk down the street in Paris without seeing a couple kissing or making out, even in the winter when it was cold and they should have been cuddled up together inside.

"Is it possible Madame Lannet and Monsieur Outhier were having an affair, and that is why he decided to invest in her atelier?" I asked. "Could the killer be a jealous or rejected lover?"

"Lannet and Outhier?" Cerise and Yvonne burst into screams of laughter.

"Maybe *Madame* Outhier!" gasped Cerise from between whoops.

"But, *non, non,*" said a giggling Lisette from over at the mirror. "Everyone knew that Madame Lannet—she does not like the men in that way, you see."

I had suspected this, but it was good to have it confirmed. "And so she and Madame Pineau, were they . . . uh . . . together—as lovers?"

"Oh, yes, that is no secret to any of us," said Cerise with an unconcerned wave. "They were together always. Where one went, so did the other. What one did, so did the other."

"All right," I said. "So the only person you can think of who might want to kill Madame Lannet is Robert Illouz. Does Robert smoke?" I asked.

"But of course," Cerise replied. "Who does not?"

"What brand does he smoke, do you know?"

She shrugged. "That I cannot tell you. I pay no attention to that."

"Do you at least remember whether the cigarettes are dark or white?"

"Oh, well, they were probably white, I think," she replied with a shrug.

"Can you find out?"

She gave me a complacent smile as she exhaled from her own cigarette. "But of course."

I nodded. "And can you find out where he was on the nights of the murders? Last night, and the night before that."

She nodded again.

Another thought struck me. "So Robert knew that Frédéric Outhier invested in Rose-Marie Lannet's atelier. Was that common knowledge to everyone?"

"Oh yes," said Yvonne, her heavily made-up lashes going wide. "Everyone talked about it. How strange it was, and why he would do such a thing."

"Robert—he said that the only reason Outhier would have done such a stupid thing was that Lannet must have something over on him," Cerise commented. "It was a bad investment, he said. A losing proposition. It was stupid."

"Do *you* agree that Rose-Marie Lannet's designs were so bad it was a losing proposition for Outhier? Or was that only Robert Illouz's bruised pride talking?" I was sincerely curious, and these young women, literally enfolded and enrobed in haute couture, would certainly have an opinion. I had found Rose-Marie Lannet's gowns stunning, but what did I know?

"Oh, she has created some beautiful frocks and gowns," said Yvonne, refilling her jar with wine. "But she is not Dior or Lelong."

"Or Fath or even Balenciaga," added Cerise. "Or, to be honest, Illouz. Robert does, I think, have the right to be offended that she was chosen over him."

"Which does make one wonder why she was," I mused. "If Robert was right, perhaps she did have some leverage over Outhier. Did she know something damaging to him?"

"Mm, *oui*, it is possible." Cerise didn't seem concerned.

"Look!" Lisette exclaimed, turning away from the vanity

where she'd been peering into the mirror as she worked on her face. "Is it right?"

Cerise, Yvonne, and Noëlle swiveled to Lisette, giving her a critical once-over.

I could see that her eyes were not only darkly outlined as in Noëlle's demonstration, but that blue-gray eye shadow now covered the lids. Her brows were darker and more arched, longer than they were naturally. She wore pale pink lipstick that had been outlined with a very narrow maroon pencil. Lisette now reminded me of a gentle fawn, with her eyes so large they dominated her delicate features.

"*Très bien,*" said Yvonne, nodding.

"Ah, *oui,* that is very good," agreed Cerise. "But you ought to practice again. Mademoiselle Tabitha, come over here! It is now your turn!"

"But I'm not interested in being a mannequin," I said, rising reluctantly.

"*Non, non,* but you will allow Lisette to practice on you so that she gets it right!"

And that's how I ended up sitting helplessly on a stool for the second night in a row as Lisette fussed over me.

CHAPTER 13

*I*T WAS NEARLY NINE O'CLOCK BY THE TIME I EXTRICATED MYSELF from Lisette, her mannequin friends, and Mathilde.

I hardly recognized myself in the mirror as I replaced my hat. With my short, chic hair tousled and curling around my ears and leaving my long neck bare, and the makeup that made my eyes look big, dark, and sultry, I could easily have passed for a fashion model myself. I had learned all I could about Rose-Marie Lannet and Robert Illouz from Lisette and her friends, and I didn't want Grand-père and Oncle Rafe to worry about where I was.

I bid farewell to everyone and hurried down the stairs to the main floor, mindful that the lights would go out in twenty seconds.

The night air was crisp and still as I walked south on rue Clément Marot. It was well past dark by now, but there were regular streetlights to illuminate the way, not to mention the headlights of passing cars and buses. There was no breeze even though I was near the river, and the temperature was cold but not frigid. A few snowflakes danced about like nimble fairies; unthreatening and charming, lighting on my cheeks and cold nose and leaving the tiniest bit of moisture.

The shops were closed, their windows dark and doors locked, but the eateries and bars were still open for business. Streetlights offered plenty of illumination, and the sidewalks weren't deserted, nor were the streets empty. There were plenty of cars and pedestrians, for as late as ten o'clock was the ending of dinner for many Parisians. Some patrons were still lounging at table with their main courses just being served. Others sipped Sauternes, cognac, or some other digestif with their cigarettes, their meals having been cleared. Others were on their way home, fully sated. Still others were likely on their way to a dance club or music hall.

I'd parked three blocks and around a corner from Godot & Block, so I had to take Clément Marot to avenue Montaigne, then follow that to rue Jean Goujon where Godot & Block was located, in order to get back. I wasn't the least bit anxious about walking alone to my car. There were plenty of people around and it wasn't that late. Besides, it was in a safe, reputable part of the city.

I passed a couple walking two small fluffy dogs who barked at me as if I was intruding on their property. Nearly to avenue Montaigne, I found a couple canoodling in a little alcove. They seemed to really be getting into it, if the expressive noises coming from them were any indication.

Another couple strolled along, holding hands and laughing together, and two men walking very fast and speaking loudly cut curtly around them. There was a pedestrian who had a pale Afghan hound on a leash who'd paused to do his business next to the tire of a parked car. That reminded me to check the ground near my own Renault before I climbed in.

All in all, it was a pleasant if chilly evening to be outside, with a half-moon and a swath of stars draped with clouds passing by as smoothly as if they were on a train. I was suddenly, acutely aware that I was alone . . . and maybe a little lonely. It was the first time I had felt this way since arriving in the City of Light. All at once, I found myself looking forward to having a glass of wine with Monsieur Héroux tomorrow afternoon.

A traffic police agent in his white uniform—the white version being a new development for those working at night in order to make them more visible—suddenly blew his whistle, startling me from my reverie as he tweeted an insurgence of cars to *Stop!* while others turned left onto Montaigne from Clément Marot.

The scents of tobacco and coal smoke mingled with vehicle exhaust and roasted coffee at a cafe near the corner. A few tables tucked near the cafe were occupied by people with mittened hands curved around warm cups of *café* or glasses of *vin*. They wore hats and coats, and had blankets provided by the establishment spread over their laps. A man and woman sat very close to each other with their backs to the cafe so they could snuggle and watch the passersby as they smoked and drank.

I crossed avenue Montaigne then turned west, in the opposite direction of Maison Dior and its elegant, awning-covered entrance, and had gone two blocks when I noticed a sign hanging from a different establishment. It read WATHELET & COMPANY: FINE SHOES.

I slowed. This must be the shop belonging to Philippe Wathelet, the suspected perpetrator of the break-in and vandalism at Godot & Block.

I peered in the windows. I had no idea what I was looking for, but since Philippe Wathelet was apparently Monsieur Block's greatest rival and suspect, I didn't want to miss the chance.

What little I could see inside was sketchily illuminated by a streetlamp above my shoulder. The glare on the glass obstructed most of the view but when I cupped my hands, I could make out enough to see that the shop seemed neat and clean, closed up for the evening. The shoes displayed in the windows were similar in style to the ones I'd seen at Godot & Block. I wasn't expert enough to be able to assess their craftsmanship, but they looked fine to me despite Monsieur Block's criticisms.

Perhaps I'd convince Grand-père and Oncle Rafe to make a stop here at Wathelet & Company tomorrow before or after our meeting at Dior. I could question Monsieur Wathelet about his whereabouts on the night of the break-in and see if I sensed any guilt.

I continued on my way along avenue Montaigne—a wide, straight thoroughfare with random pedestrians and a steady stream of passing cars—and I'm not embarrassed to mention that I took a little detour on my route in order to continue far enough so that I came to Maison Lannet. I didn't expect to see anyone or anything around the building, but there was the old adage that the perpetrator always returned to the scene of the crime.

He'd done so last night and been interrupted. There was a chance he'd do the same tonight to finish what he'd started.

But the boutique was dark and silent. I scrutinized the windows for any sign of lights inside, but I saw none. Something white— a note or poster—fluttered at the door, and I wasn't about to miss the chance to assuage my curiosity. I took the walkway up to the entrance and read: THIS IS A CRIME SCENE. DO NOT ENTER. CLOSED UNTIL FURTHER NOTICE.

As if everyone in a ten-block radius didn't already know that. I shook my head, grinning a little. That was most definitely Merveille's touch. I didn't expect such a notice would keep the killer away, but I appreciated the *inspecteur*'s effort.

I was just about to turn and walk away when I caught a flash of light through the window. It came from deep inside, and at first I wasn't certain whether it *had* come from inside or whether it was the reflection of a car headlight driving past. I instinctively ducked back from the window at the front door so my shadow wouldn't be seen if I was right and there was someone inside, then carefully eased back to the edge of the window to peer inside.

Yes. There was definitely a flash of light in there. It seemed to be making its way down the stairs that led from the salon and the other areas, including Madame Lannet's office.

I knew immediately it wasn't Merveille or any of his men. They wouldn't be sneaking around with a flashlight; they'd have the lights turned on.

My heart began to thud and my stomach shifted greasily— partly because I hadn't eaten anything even though I had had a jar of wine at Lisette's. It *had* to be the killer in there! Who else would it be? And he was coming down from upstairs, probably still looking for whatever he'd been looking for on his two previous visits.

But what should I do?

I certainly wasn't going to go in there. But if I ran to call for a police agent, the person might get away.

The light inside flashed again as it reached the bottom of the stairs.

I surged back from the edge of the window so fast I bumped into one of the large concrete planters at the entrance. Ducking low, I hurried down the walk away from the door. Then, after hesitating for a moment, dashed back up to crouch in the shadowy nook behind the massive planter to the left of the doorway. If whoever it was came out the front door, I'd see him and I could follow. Unless he looked closely he wouldn't spot me.

But if he didn't come out this way . . .

I glanced to my right and saw that the building ended only a few yards away. The structure next to it was so close and the passage between the two edifices was so narrow that only a bicycle or a very slender cart would be able to navigate to the courtyard behind. If the intruder went out through the back, I'd miss him. As soon as I thought about it, I realized it was logical he *would* go out the back so no one would see him. It was also the same way he'd exited the two previous times.

After a glance at the entrance above my head, I bolted from the protective shadows and dashed to the end of the building and the narrow passageway. I flew around the corner into the depths of the tiny alley, aware that now my dark red Mary Janes were certainly going to be ruined. Between the snowy slush, mud, and whatever else was on the ground in this tight passage, there was no hope for them. But it would be worth it.

I hurried toward the back of the building, kicking up icy slush that soaked the backs of my stockings as I went. I didn't want to think about what else was in the slush I stirred up; the alley did not smell very pleasant. I should have worn boots, but who would have known I'd be lurking in a malodorous alley at nine o'clock at night?

I slowed as I passed the halfway point, which was marked by a chimney. It occurred to me that the intruder could come out from the back but then traverse this passage out to avenue Montaigne and be on his way.

I needed a place to hide if that happened, but it had to be somewhere I could see the back of the building so I'd know when he came out. The alley was empty of anything that would offer a place to hide. No garbage cans, and even the chimney that jutted out was too narrow to provide cover.

I strained my ears, listening for any sound of a door opening or closing. The only thing I heard was distant voices from passersby and the low rumble of vehicles punctuated by a loud, angry car horn. There was a quiet clang from somewhere, as if someone had closed a metal gate. A dog barked twice in the distance, then subsided.

By now I'd reached the back of the alley and peered around the corner. Everything was quiet and still. The courtyard was a long, slender triangular shape due to the position of the streets and the way they joined at an acute angle. I had come out at the narrower end, although not quite at the point. There were a few lights glowing from the windows overlooking the courtyard, but no signs of movement—not even a cat, which surprised me. Maybe the lack of garbage cans explained the absence of felines.

A few scraggly bushes dotted the barren, winter landscape. A bicycle leaning against a wall gleamed in the shifty moonlight. Some of the back doors had little stoops, and some opened out flat onto the ground. Here in the courtyard, there were garbage cans tucked randomly against some of the walls. A single bench sat in the middle and there was a pergola, I think it's called, where a rosebush or some vining plant would climb.

I went to the closest stoop, which offered some shadow in which to hide and gave me a good view of the back of Maison Lannet.

I had only just positioned myself, crouching in the dark, when the door of the boutique opened. *Whew.*

My heart thudded as a figure emerged, closing the door behind him. It was definitely a man if the attire was any indication: a flapping overcoat, a fedora, and trousers. He was of average height and build, but between the brim of his low hat and the anemic light, I couldn't make out his face.

I watched, holding my breath as he glanced around and un-hurriedly walked toward the narrow alleyway through which I'd recently come. I breathed another sigh of relief that I'd been smart enough not to be lurking there as he walked past.

I waited until he was well into the alley before I rose to follow. I darted toward the alley and had just reached it when someone grabbed me from behind.

CHAPTER 14

*T*HE HAND YANKED ME BACK AND I SLAMMED INTO A SOLID, LIVING being. It was probably just as well that the breath got knocked out of me, or I might have screamed.

I *wanted* to scream; I tried to scream—wouldn't anyone, if they'd just been grabbed in a dark alley?—but nothing came out but a sort of gasping, gurgling sound. I started to struggle wildly even as my vision dimmed and narrowed with terror.

"Mademoiselle Knight," someone murmured over the roaring in my ears. "Be still."

My stomach plummeted to my toes and I went still. *Merveille.* What in the *hell* was Merveille doing here?

"What in the hell are you thinking, grabbing me like that?" I gasped on a heave of breath, trying to keep my knees from giving way as I struggled with the rapid change from stark terror to bald relief to irritation. I pulled away from the warm, solid torso against which I'd sagged in that relief. He released my arm.

"The better question is what are *you* doing here, mademoiselle," he replied. His voice remained low, and he was still standing close enough for me to smell the wool blend of his coat and the faint aroma of mint along with some other subtle scent that might have been in his hair. I couldn't see his expression; that darned hat he wore so low on his brow cast a long shadow. All I could see was the square angle of his jaw and chin, and a hint of mouth. It was flat and unsmiling.

"We've got to follow him," I said, far too aware of how nice he smelled. My heart was beating very hard and I was still struggling to catch my breath without making it obvious that I was doing so.

"No, no, no." He caught my arm again, this time more gently but no less firmly. "It is taken care of. I have a man watching. I have instructed him to follow."

"But don't you want to know who it is?" I exclaimed in a quiet voice.

Apparently I was too loud for the *inspecteur*, for he hushed me and said in a calm voice, "But of course I already know who it is."

"Who is it?" I demanded.

"It is Frédéric Outhier."

I was so shocked that he'd answered me with actual, real information, I was momentarily speechless. But I quickly gathered my wits. "Frédéric Outhier is the killer? But . . . that doesn't make sense."

He didn't shush me this time, even though my voice had grown louder—but it was still relatively quiet. Presumably our quarry had put enough distance between us that Merveille wasn't worried about him hearing.

"Outhier is not the killer, mademoiselle."

"How do you know—"

"Mademoiselle Knight . . . perhaps we do not need to have such a conversation at this moment, and here," he said, then gestured for me to precede him into the narrow alley.

I had no choice but to start walking. As I did so, I mentally reviewed the details of what had happened, and realized Merveille must have been watching me sneak around in the alley and courtyard for some time. For how long and where exactly he had been while doing so, I wasn't certain—but it was long enough that he'd been able to come up behind me without me even realizing it. I felt my cheeks heat and I was very grateful for the darkness.

When we came out from the alley to the sidewalk on Montaigne, Merveille held out a hand to stop me. "Please, mademoiselle, wait here for one little minute."

I didn't argue. I guess I was still in a state of confusion.

Instead, I watched him walk to the building adjacent to Maison Lannet on the opposite side of the alley from which we'd come. A row of low bushes grew in front of the edifice. Merveille must have found what he was looking for—or not; I was guessing that the agent who'd been directed to follow Outhier had been secreted there, and now he was gone, as expected, on the man's trail.

The fact that his man might have been hiding so close to where I had been lurking in the shadows was almost hilarious. It was also embarrassing, because he'd probably seen me dashing around and skulking about and hadn't known what to make of me.

Merveille returned. "Now, mademoiselle . . ." His voice trailed off as if he wasn't at all certain what to do with me.

I straightened my shoulders and marshaled my thoughts into order. "Outhier isn't the killer? Then what was he doing here, sneaking around in the middle of the night?"

"Again, mademoiselle, the same question might be asked of you."

I barely caught myself from stamping my foot in frustration. Instead, I gritted my teeth and said very calmly and mostly truthfully, "I was simply walking to my car and saw a flash of light inside as I passed by. Obviously, I was curious."

"But of course. The curiosity."

This was one of the strangest interactions I'd ever had with Merveille. He was usually grim and brief, exuding irritation, and couldn't wait to get on with whatever he was about—which was usually out of my presence.

But in this case, I didn't get the impression that he was as impatient to be off as he usually was. And not only that, he'd actually answered a question I'd asked him without shutting me down or making ambiguous statements.

"And what is it that you were doing walking to your car in this area, mademoiselle? After nine at night? Alone?"

I started to tell him it was none of his business, but I caught myself in time. The truth was, I had some information he might find useful and I also was desperate to know why Merveille was certain Monsieur Outhier wasn't the killer, even though Outhier had been poking around the scene of the crime.

"I was leaving Lisette Feydeau's place. We were there with some other people who worked at Maison Lannet and knew Madame quite well," I said, not so subtly dangling the suggestion that he might learn something valuable from me. Then I drove the point home. "You might be interested in what I learned."

Merveille made a noise that sounded like the cross between a groan and a sigh of capitulation. "Ah. I suppose there is no help for it. But at least I should be allowed to fortify myself, *non*?"

I wasn't exactly certain what he meant until he continued. "There is a little brasserie just there, and their wine is good. There is not much on the menu besides cassoulet, but it is the best in the city. I believe I should not be required to listen to your tale on an empty stomach."

I blinked but recovered quickly. "I haven't eaten dinner either. Cassoulet sounds perfect."

"Very well then, mademoiselle. It is decided."

Ten minutes later, we were seated at a table thrust up against the front window of a cupboard-sized brasserie. A single candle in a red jar flickered between us on a surface so small the tablecloth was barely the size of a handkerchief. The lights inside the eatery were low and soft. None of them matched and they weren't the least bit fancy like those at Maison de Verre.

We were not the only patrons, but we were the latest arrivals. A fluffy black dog lay sprawled beneath a table in the corner crowded with six people. There were at least four bottles of wine on the table, and based on the jollity coming from those packed in around it, I assumed the bottles were empty—or soon to be.

A large gold birdcage hung from a floor stand in a different corner near the entrance, and inside was a live parrot swinging on a little bar. He gave an irritated squawk when we came in the door. There was one server—a young, slender man with a whip-like figure and an agreeable smile who obviously knew Merveille, for he greeted him as Étienne. He gestured us to seats at the front window.

It felt odd and yet strangely comfortable to sit alone with Merveille at a table. I had done so once before in my *grand-père*'s kitchen, where I had managed to cook the *inspecteur* a Croque Monsieur without embarrassing myself.

As I sat, I shrugged off my coat into the rustic, wooden chair behind me, letting its sleeves dangle, while Merveille removed his and hung it and his hat neatly on a coatrack. I took off my gloves, hesitated, then removed my own hat and set it on the windowsill. After all, now I didn't have to worry about my hair looking like I'd stuck my finger in an electrical outlet. I hoped. I itched to pull out my compact and sneak a peek, but I didn't.

As usual, Merveille's own dark hair was unnaturally neat and still combed ruthlessly in place despite him removing his hat. The very tips curled up—and likely went unnoticed by him, or they would not dare to be so impudent—at the nape of his neck and behind the ears. I suspected he was probably due for a haircut— or at least, *he* would think he was due for a haircut. I found the incongruous imperfection in an otherwise military-neat and aloof mien rather adorable.

He sat down and briskly ordered wine from the smiling waiter, glancing over to confirm that red was acceptable to me as well. I nodded, then nodded again in agreement when Merveille suggested the ashtray could be removed from the table. Neither of us would use it.

"I assume you're off duty now," I commented when the waiter left after pouring wine for both of us.

"*C'est vrai*, and most gratefully, mademoiselle. It has been a very long two days." He lifted his glass in a little salutary gesture before taking a sip.

I followed suit. The wine was excellent. All wine served in Paris was very good, worlds better than anything I'd had at home, but this was several steps above an average table wine. I made a little hum of appreciation and Merveille glanced up with an expression that verged on a smile.

"I've learned to appreciate excellent wine since living with Grand-père and Oncle Rafe," I said. "Back in Michigan we didn't appreciate a good vintage. We mostly stick with beer or vodka."

"Not gin? I thought that was the favorite of Americans," he said, pushing the basket of bread gently toward me in invitation. "Did they not make it in the bathtubs during the Prohibition?"

I made a face. "They did, but gin is not for me. I had a very bad experience with it once upon a time."

"Somehow that does not surprise me, Mademoiselle Knight." His voice was low but it had a tinge of the ironic. The corners of his eyes crinkled.

I resisted the urge to point out the incongruity of his continued formality while we were sitting at a tiny table with our knees nearly touching. I was beginning to wonder if he was so insistent on it because he knew it bothered me, or for some other reason. I considered what he would do if I addressed him as Étienne.

Smiling to myself as I imagined his chagrin, I took a piece of bread and edged the basket back toward him. When I glanced up, I discovered he was looking at me intently.

He realized his scrutiny had been noticed and made a little twirling gesture with his finger in my direction. "Your eyes; they are different, *non?*"

I couldn't tell if this was a good "different" or not. It was certainly much more eye makeup than I usually wore, but it wasn't garish by any means. "This is the way the mannequins do their makeup. We were practicing."

His brows rose. "And you are seeking to be a mannequin at a *maison de couture?*"

I laughed. "No, of course not. Lisette—Mademoiselle Feydeau—was practicing for herself."

"Ah." He seemed mystified and I decided not to enlighten him.

"So . . . back to our previous conversation. How do you know Frédéric Outhier is not the killer?" I asked.

"Because, mademoiselle, he has an alibi for the time of Madame Lannet's murder," replied the *inspecteur.* "He was at a dinner with business associates."

I found myself watching his dark, long-fingered hand as it reached for the bread and I realized all at once what I could no longer deny: I was attracted to him. *Really* attracted to him. So much so that I felt a little flutter in my stomach as I eyed those deft fingers, remembering how warm and strong they'd been over mine, how close he'd been, when he was taking my fingerprints last month.

Oh my God.

I was hung up on an aloof, acerbic man who was *engaged*. What a disaster.

I could *never* tell Julia.

I took a gulp of wine and focused on my own bread. The last thing I needed was for Merveille to catch me mooning at him. He was so dratted observant, he'd suss out my unfortunate infatuation in an instant.

"So if Outhier isn't the killer, then what was he doing sneaking around Maison Lannet?" I asked.

"That, mademoiselle, is an excellent question—to which I am certain you must have a supposition. Ah, *merci beaucoup*, Geoffrey." He looked up with a grateful smile as the waiter placed large, shallow bowls in front of each of us.

The bowls brimmed with a sort of thick, meaty stew beneath a crunchy, buttery, golden crust. The very scent of it made my mouth begin to water and my stomach rumble. Fat white beans, slices of plump sausage, chunks of tender meat—lamb, I thought— and crispy leg of duck mingled with carrots in a rich, dark broth speckled with aromatic herbs and pieces of tomato.

I didn't reply to Merveille's prodding at first; I had taken up my first spoonful of cassoulet and was in the throes of pleasure as I tasted the beauty of the beans that were infused with the essence of heavenly broth. The pieces of lamb and duck were so tender they practically fell apart on my spoon. I remembered Julia saying it took days to make a good cassoulet, and even though I knew very little about cooking, I could tell just by the layers of flavor that it was true.

I glanced up to discover that Merveille was applying himself to his own meal with great gusto and efficiency, and I wondered whether this was typical for him: to go all day, working very hard without stopping to eat until late at night. My father often came home ravenous when he was working on a difficult case, for he wouldn't take the time to eat during the day. But I knew that today, at least, in Merveille's case, he'd had at least one croissant since morning—courtesy of Julia.

"Well, then, mademoiselle?" He glanced up after a few moments and our eyes met. "What do you think?"

I tore my eyes away and managed to swallow without choking. "This is one of the best things I've ever eaten—but don't tell Julia I said that!"

Now he did smile, his eyes crinkling and the corners of his mouth curving up. It was brief but genuine, gone so quickly I couldn't fully appreciate it, as he gestured to his bowl with his spoon. "I will not, and although I share your opinion—as I said, this is the best cassoulet in the city—I was referring to Outhier. Surely you have a theory as to what he was doing at Maison Lannet."

I didn't even try to hide my skepticism as I eyed him. Why was he asking me for my theories? Was it some kind of test? Was he teasing me? Or did he just want me to talk so he could enjoy his stew?

But he had *asked* me to join him; he hadn't needed to do so. And since he seemed particularly amiable tonight, I thought I might as well take advantage of the situation and see what information I could glean from *him*.

"Well, if you're certain he isn't the killer, the only thing I can think of is that, since he gave Madame Lannet the money to start her business, maybe he thought he should get back what he could if the business was going to close down."

"If he was an investor or a part owner, some of the profits would belong to him, wouldn't they? So he sneaked in to get— even steal, maybe—what he could, before ... I don't know, I suppose before the banks and creditors come and demand their share? And he probably had a key, so he didn't have to break in."

"That is what I think as well," Merveille said, once again surprising me with his candidness. "That he was after something and probably it is money. But I will find out. My agent will see where he goes tonight, and tomorrow I will have a little interview with Monsieur Outhier."

"Do you think the same person killed both Madame Lannet and Madame Pineau?" I asked. I suddenly realized I had been more focused on why someone would want to kill the couturier, and not why someone would kill the vendeuse.

I had assumed it was the same person, but maybe that wasn't the case. Was I completely missing the point? Perhaps Madame Pineau had been the original target, but Madame Lannet had gotten in the way first?

I felt bad. Here I had been, focusing mostly on Rose-Marie Lannet, hardly giving any attention to Gabrielle Pineau, as if she were merely an afterthought. I realized I didn't know anything about her but her name and the fact that she was Rose-Marie Lannet's lover.

"It is likely that it's the same person, but one cannot rule out the possibility that there are two killers," he replied.

"Does Frédéric Outhier have an alibi for the night of Madame Pineau's death also?" I asked, grinning.

The corners of his eyes crinkled again. "That I do not know, but I will certainly find out during our little meeting tomorrow."

"Why kill both of them?" I said. "I think whoever it was came back the next night to get something—maybe that metal tool he dropped, or maybe something else—and Madame Pineau startled him, so he had to take care of her too.

"But maybe I'm wrong, and he always planned to get rid of both of them, and that was why he had to come back the next night because I came into the boutique before Madame Pineau returned." I gave a little shiver. If I was going with that theory, I could just as easily have been a casualty as well as Madame Pineau.

Merveille was not about to allow me to brush past that. "Indeed, mademoiselle. Once again, you have been made known to a killer—he has seen you, don't forget."

"I don't know if he's actually *seen* me," I reminded him. "He— or she; it *could* have been a woman—was hiding behind the door when I came in and they struck me from behind. It's not as if we came face-to-face. But," I said quickly when I read his expression, "I will be careful. I've no desire to repeat what happened in the catacombs." I suppressed a shudder.

Merveille made a sound of disbelief, but refrained from commenting.

"What about the little bit of material that got caught on the desk?" I asked. "Surely that's a clue to the killer. And the tiny key—did you find out what it belonged to?"

"Ah, sadly—for your purposes, at least, mademoiselle—the few threads that got caught on the desk belonged to Gabrielle Pineau. There is a cut on her leg and a tear in her skirt. The fabric of her skirt matches the threads that were left behind. So, there is no help there, eh?"

He seemed almost pleased to deliver this information to me.

I hid my disappointment over the dead-end clue and realized that my surmise must have been right: Gabrielle Pineau had been sitting at the desk in Madame Lannet's office when she heard something and she hurried off to find out what it was. The pushed-back chair and cut on her leg fit the scenario.

"What about the key?" I asked.

He shrugged. "It belonged to a small lockbox."

I waited a beat or two, then realized he wasn't going to tell me what was in the lockbox. The man was *so* annoying! He only gave me information when it was meant to stymie me or disprove my theories.

He glanced up as if to check my reaction and I gave him a dark look. "The fact that you won't tell me what was in the lockbox suggests that it's important," I said.

His brows lifted and the crinkles flashed at the corners of his eyes. "*Oui*, mademoiselle, perhaps that is true . . . or perhaps you are simply making another baseless deduction. And so now, what is it you can tell me from your gossiping this evening?" He'd made short work of his stew and now swiped a hunk of bread through the last dredges of the meaty broth.

I chose not to take umbrage at his characterizing my visit with Lisette and her friends as gossip, because I didn't get the sense he was using the term in a derogatory manner. After all, a detective *relied* on gossip to get the job done. Instead, I said, "Do you know who Robert Illouz is?"

"The jealous junior designer at Lelong and who is now trying to woo himself to Dior? But of course. He was not at all pleased Rose-Marie Lannet was chosen for Outhier's investment instead of himself."

I wasn't surprised he had that information, but I was a little disappointed not to be the one startling him with the news. "According to Lisette's—I mean Mademoiselle Feydeau's—friend Cerise, Illouz was angry enough to do Madame Lannet harm. He thought he should be the one to start his own atelier and not her."

"Mm, *oui*. I have heard this too." He settled back in his seat and sipped his wine.

Very often, a person would light up a cigarette or cigar at this time of the meal, but it was clear Merveille not only didn't smoke when he was on duty, he didn't partake at all. I'd dated my share of men who smoked, and while it didn't bother me that they smelled and tasted of cigarettes—practically everyone did—I found it different and attractive that Merveille did not.

Oh boy. I had it *bad*.

As if reading my mind, Geoffrey came over to offer an ashtray. "Mademoiselle?" asked Merveille.

"No, thank you," I said, and Geoffrey melted back into the shadows. "I don't smoke."

"*Non?*"

I shrugged and grimaced. "I had a bad experience with cigarettes once too. Not at the same time as the gin."

His eyes crinkled *so* attractively at the corners when he was amused. "You have had bad experiences with gin *and* with cigarettes? And anything else?"

I shrugged again, this time smiling a little. "I've since learned that moderation is a better choice."

"Except when it comes to the curiosity, *non?*"

I rolled my eyes, shaking my head at his droll humor. "Illouz even said that he thought Madame Lannet must have had something to hold over Outhier in order to induce him to invest in her atelier."

"And you have met this Illouz?" The teasing was gone from his face. The intense *inspecteur* had returned.

"No. But a friend of Lisette's is quite . . . ah . . . *close* to Illouz." My cheeks heated and I was mortified. Sex was such a common and open subject in France that people spoke of affairs and liaisons like they did the weather. I didn't know why I was reacting this way.

Actually, I suppose I did. It was a good thing he couldn't read my mind.

"Mm," he said again.

"It's the opinion of some of the mannequins that Illouz is more talented than Lannet, and so there must be a reason Outhier chose *her* to invest in, rather than Robert Illouz."

"But that may only be the opinions, and perhaps there are others who have the opposite opinion. Art and fashion and beauty—they are in the eye of the beholder, *non?*"

"Yes, that's true. And Madame Lannet seemed to have many clients. I recognized a lot of their names—they're famous people. Joilliet and Comtesse Brigitte and others."

"And now none of them will get their frocks and gowns." He sounded as if he were musing more to himself than to me. "And is that important?"

"And shoes too, perhaps," I said.

"*Comment?*"

"Oh, you don't know about that. Right. There was a break-in at Godot & Block, the shoe boutique just behind the courtyard from Maison Lannet. Someone came in the front door, jimmying the locks—"

"And how do you know this, mademoiselle? The break-in and the jimmying?" His eyes were intent and thoughtful and not as cold and gray as usual. "No one has mentioned this from the interviews we have done in the area."

I explained how I knew Clarice and that her sister had asked for my help—and that Monsieur Block did not trust *les flics* and so he would not talk about it to them. This latter bit of information I stumbled over a little since I didn't want to go in the direction of the fact that policemen had been collaborators with the Nazis.

"And so of course, I thought perhaps the break-in at Godot & Block was related to the murder of Rose-Marie Lannet since it was on the same night and they are across from each other in the same courtyard . . . but the intruder obviously came in the front door and not the back door from the courtyard. I could see markings around the keyhole so it was obvious he came in that way, picking the lock.

"And all of the destruction was in the front of the shop as well. There were several pairs of custom shoes that were destroyed so that Monsieur Block will need to try and make them again—if he can find the leather."

Merveille made a sound of interest, but remained silent.

"I only just found out tonight that Madame Outhier had ordered shoes from Godot & Block as well as gowns from Maison Lannet. And there are other clients too who are the same between the two establishments," I added.

"Frocks and gowns and shoes, destroyed and orders canceled, perhaps not to be reinstated. *Intéressant.*"

The waiter approached at that moment and I realized the loud table of six was getting ready to clear out. There was only one more table with patrons besides us and they were finishing their coffee. It was near closing time, although no one was rushing anyone out the door.

Merveille looked at me. "*Café*, mademoiselle? Cognac?"

"Oh, no, I'm fine," I said.

He gave a curt shake of his head and Geoffrey scuttled off into the back of the brasserie.

"Monsieur Block thinks Philippe Wathelet is the one who broke in to his shop," I explained. "He's a competitor—a shoe-maker. Because the destruction of the shoes was purposeful and of the sort another shoemaker would know to do." At his curious look, I explained further about how only one shoe in a pair was destroyed so that the whole pair would need to be remade because the leather wouldn't match, and how Philippe was apparently angry that Block had taken on some of his clients.

Merveille listened intently as he finished his wine. When I finished, he nodded thoughtfully. "That is all quite interesting." He looked at me. "Is there anything else?"

I hesitated. "I suppose you know that there is no chance Madame Lannet and Monsieur Outhier were lovers and that's why he set her up in the atelier."

"*Oui.*"

"And that Lannet and Pineau were . . . close."

He nodded again.

I shrugged. "That's everything I can think of."

"Very well. Ah, and I think that Geoffrey is preparing to turn off the lights." He glanced over at the waiter, who stood in the corner, hands folded over his middle, waiting patiently.

The parrot, who until now had been quiet except for that single squawk when we came in, offered a comment that sounded suspiciously like "*Va-t-en!*"—"Go away!"

Chuckling, I reached for my pocketbook and withdrew my wallet. "*L'addition, s'il vous plaît,* monsieur," I said to Geoffrey.

"Ah, no, mademoiselle, it is finished," said Merveille, rising.

I frowned, standing as well. I hadn't seen a bill and I hadn't seen him settle anything. Besides, I'd certainly intended to pay for my own expenses. After all, it wasn't a date. "But—"

"Geoffrey will not present a bill to me," he explained, coming around the table toward me. "He is as stubborn as someone else I know."

My heart surged into my throat as he came close, then I realized Merveille was only getting my coat from the chair in order to help me into it. I allowed him to do so as quickly and efficiently as possible, then put some space between us when I collected my hat and gloves.

We left the brasserie, and I noticed for the first time the name of the place, which was etched on the door: Le Cage au Perro-quet. The Parrot Cage. How very fitting.

"Why won't he give you a bill?" I asked as we started down the street. "Do you have a running tab or something?" I wondered if Merveille lived nearby and ate there often and so had established credit with the place.

The sidewalks were mostly empty now, and there were fewer cars rumbling past. Everything was quieter, and I realized it was well past ten and moving closer to eleven. The moon was still shrouded by clouds and there was a haze in the air from some moisture that was neither snow nor rain nor sleet. It made the glow from the streetlights look soft and fuzzy and dampened my face. It felt good on my hot cheeks.

"And where did you park, mademoiselle? Or did you take the Métro?"

I told him and he nodded, making it clear he meant to escort me to my car. After another minute, he said, "I once did something for Geoffrey and his family—they own Le Cage à Perroquet—and so they will not allow me to pay. That is all."

Of course I wanted to know what he'd done for them, but I decided, for once, not to pry.

I kept my distance from him as we walked along, but every so often my arm brushed against his when one of us stepped around a puddle or pile of slush. I was acutely aware of it every time that happened, and I was becoming frustrated with myself over this heightened sensitivity. I wasn't a young schoolgirl with her first crush, for Pete's sake!

"Thank you for dinner," I said when we got to the block where I was parked. "It was very good."

"Thank you for joining me, mademoiselle," he replied with a slight bow.

I was self-conscious and feeling very awkward, so I didn't belabor our bonsoirs. I opened the door to my car and slipped in as quickly as I could.

"I hope you catch the killer soon," I said; then, with a little wave, shut the door.

He waved back, then turned to walk away.

My heart was thudding and my cheeks were hot as I drove off. I had no idea when or if I would see him again, but I was glad I had a date with Monsieur Héroux tomorrow. I needed something to get my mind off the attractive and implacable—and unavailable—*inspecteur*.

CHAPTER 15

I HAD NOT INTENDED TO TELL JULIA ANYTHING ABOUT MY ENCOUNTER with Merveille, but that resolve lasted for all of five minutes.

"Oh, Tabs! You're just in time to learn how to make crêpes!" Julia greeted me as I poked my head into her kitchen.

It was late the next morning; I had gone to a tutoring appointment while Julia was at class. The kitchen was filled with the fresh scent of spinach and chopped onions.

"I tried that once," I confessed, eyeing with trepidation the pale batter that sat in a large bowl. "They turned out either very mushy or burned to a crisp."

I also remembered how much time it took to make them. They were so thin it took forever to pour each of them and cook the batter, and I'd stood, frustrated, at the stove for over an hour, just trying to use up all of the batter, making one miserable crêpe at a time. I eventually ended up throwing half of it out, and we ate cold ham and cheese for dinner that night.

Sigh.

"Well, we can fix that right up," Julia said with a grin, shoving an apron at me. "Arm yourself, dearie! We're making two *gâteaux de crêpes à la Florentine*—and you can take one home for your messieurs for dinner tonight!"

A gâteau—wasn't that a sort of cake?—sounded very complicated. And the bowl of batter looked really big.

We were going to be here forever.

Fortunately, I would have to leave just after noon in order to get ready for the appointment at Dior.

I was putting on the apron—reluctantly, to be honest, because I was not the least bit confident in my ability to learn to make the French type of pancake—when I casually said, "I had the most delicious cassoulet last night at a cute little brasserie. With Merveille."

I'm not sure why I spilled the beans on that so quickly and openly. Maybe I was hoping it would distract Julia from teaching me how to make crêpes. She could do it much more quickly and easily on her own, while I filled her in on what happened last night.

The initial result was just as I had hoped and expected: she spun, holding the bowl of thin pancake batter, her eyes wide. The batter sloshed, coming close to the rim, but it didn't spill out.

"*Tabitha!* Cassoulet? I just *adore* cassoulet! Such a delicious and hearty meal—very peasantlike, you know, and everyone everywhere makes it differently. I think of it as French baked beans. And you were *with Merveille?* Were you tête-à-tête? How *ever* did that happen?"

She set the bowl of batter safely down on the tiny counter near the equally tiny stove. I had no idea how Julia managed to create so many delectable, complicated dishes in the minuscule space her landlady called a kitchen, but she did. There was no doubt—Julia Child was some sort of wizard chef, fired by determination and love for her craft.

She was so tall that everything—the stove, the counter, the table—was too low for her, so she was always bent over her workspace, which made *me* feel uncomfortable for her. But she was used to it, I supposed. I hoped that someday she would have a kitchen that was specially designed for her, with countertops the proper height and plenty of space to store her myriad of copper pots and pans, utensils, vessels, and gadgets.

Now, in this itty-bitty kitchen, she had everything imaginable hung on the walls, including shelves to contain everything from dishes to spices to gadgets to the myriad of utensils she collected. This left very little working space, so she often used the table. The lack of hot running water hadn't stopped her either, for she and Paul had figured out how to fit a tub of water over a gas geyser to keep hot water available.

As Julia clattered three little frying pans onto the stove, I explained how I'd encountered Merveille while I was lurking about Maison Lannet.

"That must have been embarrassing," Julia said, bending and squinting at the burners as she lit one under each of the pans. "Him watching you skulk about."

"No kidding," I replied, wondering how she was going to use three pans at once.

"Here," Julia said, thrusting a small measuring cup at me.

"What's this for?" I took it and noted it was about a fourth-cup measure.

"That's for you to pour *la pâte à crêpes*," she said with a grin.

"Oh, Julia, I don't know . . . I'm not very good at making crêpes—"

"You'll be fine. Now, one of the secrets of *pâte à crêpes* is that you have to let it sit in the icebox or somewhere cool for at least two hours after you first make it. Don't stint on that time, Tabs, if you want your crêpes to be marvelously light and thin—and as delicate as a man's ego." She laughed heartily.

"Oh," I said, remembering that my crêpe batter had been mixed and used pretty much immediately. That might have contributed to my lack of success.

"All right, come on over here and let's get to work. You can tell me all about your date with Merveille."

"It wasn't a date."

"Did he pay for dinner?" she asked, giving me an arch look.

"No," I said truthfully.

Julia—who, as usual was moving like a whirling dervish—came to an abrupt halt and this time she *did* slosh some *pâte à crêpe* on the floor. "Are you saying *you* paid for your own dinner with Merveille?"

"Well, not precisely," I replied, crouching to wipe up the spill.

"Explain!" she demanded in a voice that brooked no prevarication. I explained, grinning, and she rolled her eyes. "Semantics, Tabs. Semantics. Now, focus on this pan for a minute."

She drew my attention to the little seven-inch pan on the left side of the stove. "This is yours. I'll handle two at a time—the ones on the right—and you do that one, okay? Now, you're going to brush the bottom of the pan with oil—*just* a little bit there, Tabs, don't *pour* it in like a glug of wine, just brush it like the lightest of kisses. You don't want it *swimming* in oil."

She demonstrated with her two pans as I watched. The heat on the three burners was turned up pretty high.

"Now fill that little measuring cup I gave you with the batter and—wait!"

I halted from where I was about to dump the batter into the pan.

"It's got to be smoking, you see. The oil in the bottom of the pan. You're waiting for just a little bit of smoke so you know the pan's hot enough—see? All right, now take the pan *off* the burner—watch me, Tabs—and pour just that one-fourth-cup measure of batter into the pan and give it a good *swirl.*"

I watched as she demonstrated and I saw how the batter immediately spread and clung to the pan in a perfect circle. There were no runny spots on top—unlike when I made pancakes at home or when I'd tried to make crêpes here.

"Now put the pan back on the stove—just for a minute, see?" She filled her small measuring cup again and pulled the other of her oiled pans, which was smoking, off the heat, then dumped in another measure of batter. She swirled the pan, then set it back down on the burner. "See? I can be two-fisted when it comes to making crêpes." She laughed. "These first ones are just tests to make sure the heat and the batter are correct, okay? So don't worry if it doesn't turn out perfectly."

My pan was smoking and I pulled it off the burner and, holding it with one hand, poured in a fourth cup of batter and gave it a gentle swirl. It was a *miracle* how the *pâte* spread in a perfect circle!

"Get ready to flip them," Julia said, drawing my attention

from the beauty of my crêpe to her pans. "It only takes a minute or so to cook."

"Like an omelette," I said. Maybe I *was* learning something from Julia.

"Exactly! It's very similar. You pour the ingredients into a greased pan—eggs or batter—swirl it around on the pan when it's off the burner, then return it to the high heat once it's set. Now since it's been cooking for a minute, you're going to—watch me!—jerk the pan a little. Give it a good, hard yank or two—Mademoiselle Crêpe gets loose, all on her own. See? Yes, that's it, give her a nice firm shake. . . ."

To my astonishment, the crêpe moved around in my pan just like it was doing in hers! And it smelled really good. My mouth began to water, as it often did in Julia's *cuisine.*

"Check underneath—use that spatula—and if she's nice and brown . . . ahh, look at that gorgeous beauty—oh yes, it's ready. Even the first one is perfect today! Now, quick, before it over-cooks!—you can use the spatula to flip it, or I find it easier to just use my fingers, Tabs—just take it from the edge closest to you and just pull it up and flip her over—*et voilà!*"

I used the spatula to flip it. She'd finished flipping both of hers, using her fingers of course, before I managed to turn mine over . . . but since mine was the same golden brown as hers, I felt very accomplished.

"All right, it's time to take our pretty little mademoiselle off the heat," she said, hardly before I'd finished admiring my delicate brown circle.

"But it's not done," I said, using the spatula to look under. "It's only got spots; not completely brown."

"Oh, that's all right, dearie—it's done. That spotty part—that's the insides or the underneath. We don't show that part—it's kind of like her slip! We know it's there and it keeps things moving smoothly, but she never shows it." She chuckled as she brushed oil over the bottom of one of her pans again.

"Where do I put it—oh, I see."

She'd laid hers on a little rack off to the side.

"We'll let them cool for a minute, then start to stack them off to the side to use for the *gâteau*," she explained, already pouring batter into one of her pans again. "Don't forget to brush the pan with oil again, Tabs. You have to do that every time."

"Oh," I said. Another thing I hadn't known the last time I tried to make crêpes. It really was useful to have a friend who knew how to do things teaching me how to cook.

We got into a rhythm—Julia managing two pans and me managing one—and began to turn out perfect crêpe after perfect crêpe. I became so comfortable with the process that I was able to tell her about my conversation with Merveille at dinner.

"It wasn't a date, but it was informative," I told her, and explained about the false clue of the torn fabric belonging to Madame Pineau and that Merveille wouldn't tell me what was in the box the key went to.

"So you don't have any real suspects now that Outhier is out of the picture," Julia said, expertly turning her crêpes, two at a time, with a smooth, practiced thrust and jerk of each pan so the pancake went airborne, flipped, then settled back perfectly into the pan.

"I wish I could talk to Robert Illouz," I said. "He's the only other person who seems to have a reason to want Madame Lannet dead."

"He seems kind of an obvious suspect," Julia said, brushing oil over a pan. "Unless there's someone else with a motive that you haven't figured out yet."

"Yeah," I replied sadly. "And I have no idea how to find that out."

"Oh, that reminds me," Julia said. "I talked to Charmaine earlier today. She's decided to go to London to find a dress for the wedding, so your translation skills are no longer needed."

"Oh, that's good," I replied. I wouldn't have minded going with Charmaine to another appointment, but I thought she might have better luck in London anyway.

"And . . . on another topic," Julia said, giving me a sidelong look, "that was a tense conversation between your messieurs yesterday. Is everything all right with them?"

I was pouring the batter into my pan as I nodded. "Yes, I think so. It's such a difficult topic—collaborators versus resisters and all of the gradations in between. What's the difference between barely accommodating the Germans—so you don't get killed or starve—and going a step further and collaborating with them? I was talking to Lisette when she was cutting my hair the other night, and she told me about all the women whose heads got shaved—whether they'd actually been collaborators or not. Whether they'd had a *choice* or not."

"I can't imagine how awful it must have been to just have another country come in and take over your city," Julia said with a little shudder. "And for them to suddenly have control over *everything*—the food, the shops, the money, the law—even some of them living in your own *home*."

"It had to have been nightmarish. Horrific. I think most people did what they had to do to survive—in order to be able to eat and to live, they had to cooperate at least to some extent with the Germans. But then there were those who actively collaborated with them and, I guess, made money by working with them. Made a profit, I mean."

I shrugged, giving her a sad look. "I wasn't living here, so I can't really have an opinion about what was right and what was wrong, or who was out of line and who wasn't. I think most people probably did the best they could and tried to have as little to do with the Germans as possible, but they didn't have much choice. And they didn't know whether the Allies would win the war!"

"And some resisted—strongly and overtly," Julia said. "And that was your *oncle* Rafe."

I nodded, wishing I knew more about what Rafe had done. "And Catherine Dior, Christian Dior's sister. *He* kept working for Lelong, designing clothes for the very people she was resisting against—the Germans *and* the French mucky-mucks who actively consorted with them. Lelong said that it was the only way to keep haute couture here in Paris—otherwise, they would have moved all of the designers to Berlin! He says he worked with the Germans in order to save Parisian fashion. And because Dior did the work, he had money and resources that he could use to secretly help his sister and her cohorts."

"Like your *grand-père* did."

I nodded. "Yes, that's what I understand. Technically, they were seen as collaborators, but they did, I think, the bare minimum in order to stay safe—and alive. It's a very complicated matter."

"There are still people being tried in courts for their participation," Julia said soberly. "It's like a witch hunt."

"And others whose sentences are being commuted, if it was found they didn't *actively* collaborate. Some people were even falsely accused by people who were trying to hide their *own* guilty activity!"

"Pointing fingers at someone else so no one looks too closely at your sins," Julia said soberly. "Finding a scapegoat so you go scot-free."

"Yes. It's all really ugly and terrible, and I don't see Parisians getting past those memories for a long time." I shook my head.

As I'd had cause to reflect before, I'd lived far across the ocean from the war. I worked to help build bomber planes, but they were for a conflict that was ugly and terrible and frightening— but also so far away it only affected me superficially . . . at least in comparison to the people in France.

I was grateful for that distance, but also, while living here in Paris and being constantly reminded of how terrible it had been here, I felt slightly ashamed because I hadn't really been so deeply affected. Not as the people here had.

Julia sighed. Her normal cheery demeanor had faded into one of thoughtfulness and regret. We worked in silence for a few more minutes.

By now, we had created two stacks of crêpes and the batter was almost gone.

Julia edged me out of the way. "You finish the last bit of the batter while I make the *la Sauce Mornay.* Unless you'd rather make the sauce while I supervis—"

"No *thank you,*" I said with a laugh. "I'm finally getting the crêpes down; I don't need to add anything else to my reper-toire."

She laughed heartily. "Somehow I thought you'd say that. But a béchamel sauce is *so* easy, Tabs!"

"Maybe next time," I replied, flipping my crêpe expertly. I had enough batter for four or five more pancakes. It had only taken twenty minutes to do over fifty crêpes! I was just pouring my last measure of batter into the pan when a thought struck me.

"Robert Illouz said that Madame Lannet must have had some-thing over on Outhier to get him to finance her atelier," I said.

"Do you mean like blackmail?" Julia dumped some grated cheese into the large pot where she was making the sauce. With her other hand she was stirring spinach, garlic, and onion in butter in another large pan. It smelled like heaven. "You're say-ing maybe Lannet blackmailed Outhier into giving her the money to start the business?"

"Yes. At least, that's what Illouz thinks—or at least, that's what he *said.* That might be a big assumption, but I can't help but won-der if it's *possible* that she knew something about him—Outhier, I mean—or how he ran his business.

"Didn't Oncle Rafe say something about his glass distributor-ship making it through the war? Maybe Madame Lannet knew Outhier was a collaborator—an *active* collaborator—and that's how his business was so successful. Maybe the extent of his col-laboration was unknown and kept secret during the war—and after."

"And she blackmailed him into giving her money so she could go off on her own?" Julia sampled the sauce with a small, clean spoon and moaned appreciatively. "*This* is glorious, Tabs." She took another sample and moaned again. "Mmm. Yes. This is per-fect. Honestly, a good béchamel is a *must* for every cook, Tab-itha. Anyway, as for the blackmail thought—that might be a little bit of a jump because we've only got Illouz's rantings to suggest it, but if it's true, it's definitely possible."

"People have been executed—or beaten and tortured and jailed—when found guilty of active collaboration. And the same even if they weren't found guilty in a court of law, but were just accused."

Julia nodded soberly. "There were—and probably still are—definitely vigilantes who took matters into their own hands."

"Right. And staying free and alive might have been worth it to Frédéric Outhier to give her the money if she kept her mouth shut—and maybe he even helped to make sure she got clients too."

"Then he got tired of giving her money and decided to kill her?" said Julia as she poured half the creamy pale sauce into the pan with the spinach and onions. My mouth was watering.

"Outhier didn't kill her—according to Merveille. But if she knew something about Outhier, maybe she knew something about someone *else* and tried to blackmail *them*. That's what I'm thinking. Once a blackmailer, always a blackmailer. Or maybe I'm completely barking up the wrong tree." I sighed.

"Or maybe it was just that Robert Illouz was jealous of Rose-Marie Lannet and he's spreading lies about her to draw suspicion away from himself. He's really the only suspect, isn't he? Now, sit, Tabs. We've got to get these gâteaux put together."

I sighed again and took my seat. It wasn't my job to be investigating these murders, but I was invested in them because I'd been the one to find the bodies of Rose-Marie Lannet and Gabrielle Pineau. I felt like it was the least I could do, that I owed it to them and their memories to do anything I could to help bring their killer to justice. Besides, I knew I was capable of getting information Merveille could not—or couldn't get very easily.

I was definitely looking for reasons to excuse my continued interest and involvement in the case. Fortunately, I didn't need to give any excuses to Julia. She was already right there with me.

"To put these little babies together, all we have to do is layer the crêpes with the filling I made. One by one," Julia told me. "You do one and I'll do one. Make sure to hide the slip—put the spotted side face down."

It was easy, now that the tedious work of making the crêpes

was done. I didn't really even have to watch Julia—I just put a crêpe into a dish and then spooned some of the spinach-onion-béchamel mixture over it, then covered it with another crêpe, and so on.

They made a nice little mound. At the end, when we'd run out of crêpes, Julia poured the rest of the sauce over each gâteau.

"And there you have it! Just put that little darling into the ice-box until later tonight when you get home from Dior. Heat her up, and *voilà*! Dinner is served."

"Julia, you're the *best*!" I said, giving her a big hug. "I don't know what I'd do without you."

"Starve, probably," she said with a wink and a hearty laugh. "Now, you get off to your appointment at Dior—and I want to hear everything about it!"

I brought the *crêpe gâteau* home with me and slipped it into the icebox, then ran upstairs to get ready for the visit to Dior.

I knew I was going to have to wear my most fashionable day-wear outfit, which was a gray-blue skirt and jacket made of fine wool shot with just a little bit of black. The hem was higher than Monsieur Dior would approve of, since he'd dropped hems to about mid-calf—and they changed slightly every year—but there wasn't anything I could do about that. I paired the suit with a cream silk blouse and a colorful blue and yellow scarf, also silk, tucked around my neck and into the unbuttoned dé-colletage of the blouse.

I knew I had chosen perfectly when I came into the salon and Grand-père and Oncle Rafe both beamed at me, nodding in ap-proval. With my short, tousled hair clinging to the nape of my neck and curling sleekly around my ears, and the large square earrings that looked like sapphire and diamond brooches clipped to my earlobes, I thought I looked very French.

Maison Dior was located at 30 avenue Montaigne, near the top of the avenue and at the opposite end of where Montaigne joined rue Jean Goujon in an acute angle—and far up the block from Maison Lannet.

I don't know why, but my palms felt damp and sweaty and my stomach fluttered a little as we approached the entrance to the storied atelier. It felt almost as if we were entering a church or some other hallowed space—and, I suppose, for some people who worshipped fashion and elegance, it probably was akin to that.

While I was experiencing all of these strange emotions, I noticed that Grand-père and Oncle Rafe were relaxed and casual, and when the front door opened for us, they ushered me in as if they owned the place.

"Ah, Madame Raymonde!" said Grand-père, greeting an attractive, stylish woman in a sleek suit that looked more like Chanel than Dior with kisses on each cheek. "You look stunningly beautiful as always. I trust you are keeping our dear Christian organized and working hard, *non*? And not allowing him to flit off on too many flights of fancy?"

She laughed. "But of course; always one must keep the good monsieur's feet nailed to the ground, *non*? That is my job, of course." Next, she surged into Oncle Rafe's embrace with smiling ease, and they exchanged kisses as well. "And who is this lovely young woman?"

Grand-père proudly introduced me.

I smiled and shook Madame Raymonde's hand, then she stepped forward and we exchanged cheek kisses. It was still a little strange to me to kiss someone I'd only just met, even as briefly as we did, but I didn't mind. She also smelled delicious and I wondered whether it was one of Monsieur Dior's perfumes that she wore—Miss Dior, perhaps.

"You had better not let the Master see this lovely girl," said another woman as she approached. "Or he will snatch her away and put her to work in *la cabine* as a mannequin!"

"Ah, Madame Bricard! The most unfailingly stylish and elegant woman I have ever known," said Grand-père with a smile. I could tell he was proud as a peacock to be showing me off, and I was so glad I'd not only dressed the way I had, but also that my hairstyle was so much more chic now.

Madame Bricard greeted both Grand-père and Oncle Rafe in

the same way Madame Raymonde had done—with warm embraces and kisses—but when she came to me, instead of bringing me in for a little buss on each cheek, she held me off at a distance. I was a little nervous as she looked over me, obviously assessing my choice of attire, as well as makeup and hair.

"*Magnifique,*" she said at last, giving Grand-père a warm smile. "She is very much your granddaughter, and she will look extremely well in one of the Master's creations. The only problem will be which one!"

We all laughed—me a little nervously after being so scrutinized and gushed over, even though I well knew such exclamations were mostly exaggerations in the form of compliments to my grandfather—and then the two mesdames insisted on showing us upstairs to the salon.

If I had been impressed by Maison Lannet's elegant viewing room, I was bound to be awestruck by the salon at Dior. The ceilings were high, so *very* high and airy, and the walls were a soft, pearly gray with ornate, concave crown molding in the same hue. The rugs and the drapes over tall, slender windows matched the same elegant gray, but the curtain blinds that lowered between the drapes were in a subtle pattern of grays, blues, and cream.

There was a marble fireplace with an ornate mantel topped by a six-foot-tall, arched mirror framed in gold. A massive crystal chandelier hung over the center of the salon where gilt bamboo chairs and settees—both upholstered in the same gray—were arranged around a small open area of floor where, I assumed, the mannequins would walk. Freestanding ashtrays and tiny tables dotted the viewing area. Lilacs spilled from huge urns in every corner and the fact that I could smell them indicated that they were, in fact, real and not silk. I could only imagine the expense of getting fresh lilacs in February.

Needless to say, the entire space was an expression of cool elegance and financial extravagance. It was fresh and new and beautiful and I was in awe.

"Do you know, *ma mie,* that the formula for this signature gray color of Dior is a carefully guarded secret?" Grand-père said to me as we settled into our seats. We were the only ones in the room. "This particular gray that is used everywhere—here in the salon and on the shopping bags and in the boutique and even on his stationery. It is proprietary to Dior and will not be seen anywhere else."

"And you might ask your *grand-père* how he knows this, *chérie*," said Oncle Rafe with a grin, taking the chair on the other side of me.

I looked at my grandfather. "Did you attempt to get Monsieur Grandpierre to give you the formula of the Dior gray for Maison de Verre?" I was laughing by now—but keeping it at a low volume because I still felt like I ought be hushed, as if I was in a church, even though we were the only people in the room.

"Maurice and I might have agreed on that color, at least, had Grandpierre allowed it," Oncle Rafe said with an affectionate smile at my *grand-père*.

A young woman came in pushing a glass-and-brass cart of wine-glasses and a bottle of champagne in a gold-plated ice bucket. Oncle Rafe reviewed the label of the vintage and nodded with a pleased smile.

"And you will permit me to open it for you, mademoiselle? And then you may have the honor of pouring."

The young woman was more than happy to allow him to open the bottle. I would have felt the same way. You never knew what direction and with how much force a champagne cork was going to be released. One time, a cork had escaped me and it left a mark on the wall of Grand-père's salon.

Madame Raymonde came in a moment later. Her polite expression seemed a little tighter than before. "Monsieur Saint-Léger and Monsieur Fautrier . . . I know this was meant to be a private showing, but . . . is it possible that another client might join us today?"

"But of course it is all right," said Grand-père, waving an easy hand. "It was so kind of Monsieur Dior to see us anyhow, even after most of the *passages* have ended."

"Ah, *merci beaucoup, messieurs*," said Madame Raymonde. "I

very much appreciate it. I assure you, the Master will consult with you privately after. He is finishing up a meeting with a possible new assistant and will be awaiting you in his office." She explained that it would be only another five minutes before the viewing would begin, then excused herself, presumably to collect the other attendee.

"Dior not only revolutionized the haute couture, he also put on the most dramatic and theatrical performance of a fashion *passage* when he revealed his first collection three years ago," Grand-père told me as he lit a cigarette. "After that, it changed the way everyone did it—although no one quite does it like Dior."

"We were here for that first show," said Oncle Rafe as he handed the open champagne bottle to the young woman. "Sitting right there." He pointed to chairs two rows back and to the right. "The place was crowded—you would not believe it!—shoulder to shoulder, elbow to elbow; everyone was so close, you see, there was hardly any room at all. People had been buying invitations on the black market even!" He glanced at Grand-père. "Not that we would know anything about that, eh, Maurice?"

Grand-père chuckled. "Not at all. We were in the first round of invitations, of course. But just before the showing started, some young rascals snatched a ladder from down the street and put it right up to that window there." He pointed. "They were trying to sneak inside—or at least, to sneak a look!"

Oncle Rafe nodded, his eyes gleaming with appreciation for such audacity. "Then at once, the *aboyeuse* announced the name and number, and a young woman came out, walking so very fast and with great purpose—so very different from any other show, where they come slowly and cautiously. *She* walked like so, with the hips and the"—he made a motion that was supposed to be, I think, a provocative sort of rear-end movement—"and she turned so quickly, making a great spin with her skirts that she knocked over ashtrays and brushed against the fashion editors sitting in the front row, bumping their pencils and perhaps even stepping on their toes!"

"Ah, *oui*, those skirts! No one had seen such skirts for years until then—and this one was stiff and pleated and when she spun, it was like a windmill! A helicopter blade! Everyone was immediately, madly entranced by the New Look," said Grandpère, accepting a glass of champagne. "What a day that was. The only thing that made it not so perfect was that then I had no one for whom I could buy one of those magnificent creations."

He reached over and patted my gloved hand with his, and I felt my eyes sting with emotion. "And now . . . now I have the most beautiful and interesting woman in the world sitting next to me—sitting next to *us*, eh, Rafe?—and you will soon be clothed in Dior, *ma chère* Tabi."

In an effort to hide my emotion, I took a sip from my own champagne. Before I had the chance to decide how to respond without sounding too sappy or soggy, Madame Raymonde returned. She was accompanied by a man and woman, both well-dressed and exuding wealth; probably in their late forties.

I recognized the man right away.

It was Frédéric Outhier.

CHAPTER 16

*T*HE VIEWING OF MONSIEUR DIOR'S COLLECTION BEGAN ALMOST immediately. The Outhiers—for it was, indeed, both Monsieur and Madame Outhier who were joining us—had just settled into their chairs near ours and poured their own champagne when a little bell tinkled to get our attention.

"*Le premier numéro*—Mozart," said a smooth but powerful voice.

I was still so shocked and elated by the sudden appearance of the Outhiers that I barely noticed when the first mannequin appeared from behind a heavy gray curtain and strode into the room. I wasn't certain what to make of this new development—them showing up at Dior only a few days after their favorite fashion house was forced to close—but even so, I was determined to take any opportunity to speak with them. What great luck that they should be here at the same time I was!

But now I was faced with an even more difficult decision than which evening gown I should choose: how I was going to go about finding out what I could regarding the deaths of Mesdames Lannet and Pineau and any connection the Outhiers might have with them. I couldn't just begin interrogating them. And even if I could, I wasn't certain what I should *say* or ask.

And what good would it do anyway, I thought with a sigh that was meant to be an admonishment to my internal sprite. Merveille had already cleared Monsieur Outhier from being the killer.

I frowned and sipped my champagne. This was the perfect opportunity but I was afraid I was going to waste it.

"And what do you think of this, eh, Tabi? It is named for the composer Mozart. It is like the music, is it not . . . something elusive and ethereal and yet something we cannot touch but still enjoy . . . and so much more, *non?*" Grand-père's murmur in my ear, his breath warm and smelling of tobacco, snapped my attention back to the viewing.

I had been so distracted, contemplating the Outhiers out of the corner of my eyes, that I'd nearly missed the first piece. The mannequin had already walked past us, turned, and was striding back.

I caught my breath. What a travesty that I had been so distracted I'd not given my full attention to what seemed like a glittering, shining spill of champagne-colored material, rippling and flowing in many layers of tulle down the back and train. The fabric sparkled and danced like the vintage we were currently drinking.

The Mozart evening gown was strapless, with a fitted bodice made from the sparkling material that flowed in layers over a smooth silk skirt. The layers were open in the front to reveal the simple skirt, but cascaded down the back, each layer ending with a ruffle and gorgeous beading and embroidery along the edges. I didn't know the terms for all of the details—I could only guess that the fabric was tulle because of how light and airy it was.

"It's stunning," I whispered to my grandfather as the mannequin paced out of the room between the slit in the opening of the curtains. "I've never seen anything so beautiful."

"You would be lovely in that gown," Grand-père said, patting my hand. "I cannot imagine anything more suited to your coloring and figure."

I wasn't about to argue. I might be terrified to walk around in a gown like that, let alone eat or drink while wearing it, but I would actually feel like a goddess if I wore Mozart.

"*Numéro Deux*—Debussy," announced the voice. It seemed

that this particular collection by Dior was themed by music composer.

I gave a little gasp of pleasure when I recognized Cerise as the second mannequin. She was wearing a gown—the Debussy—that was less full and frothy than the rich and warm champagne dress, but it was no less magnificent. In fact, my eyes bulged as she came close enough for me to see the details.

Unlike the Mozart, this gown had a slim-fitting skirt with a flowing train. It sparkled blues and lavenders, and the dress—again, strapless and with little poufs of grayish netting dancing along the décolletage—was completely encrusted with glittering sequins in every shade of blue and violet. If I were to imagine a mermaid's tail or a close-up of a fish with gems or sequins for its scales, that's how I would visualize it. A narrow, dark blue sash of tulle was fitted around the waist and its length fell to one side in a free-flowing swath, and was the only part of the gown that didn't shine with sequins.

I couldn't begin to comprehend how much time had been spent sewing on what had to be hundreds of thousands—possibly even millions—of sequins! I was beginning to understand how a single gown could cost tens of thousands of francs. And it must be *heavy*! How could Cerise even *walk* in it?

But she strode confidently in front of us, the Debussy's train brushing over the tips of my shoes as she passed by. I could hardly look away from the hypnotic glitter of the sequins, but when I did, she caught my eye and gave me the slightest wink. She was close enough that I could smell the perfume she wore—probably another Dior scent—and feel the stir of the air as she flew past. I noticed the swath from the belt fluttering and the sequined train undulating behind her.

The third mannequin was Noëlle, who also gave me a wink as she glided past in the same no-nonsense, nose-in-the-air stride as the others. It was definitely a characteristic of the Dior viewing, this purposeful, provocative walk. She wore a design called Chopin.

This dress was not the least bit glittery and sparkly. In fact, it was black and white and very simple but dramatic in the way the two colors were blocked together. A seemingly basic black cocktail-length dress, fitted from the strapless bodice over the waist to a full skirt to mid-calf. Over it was a large and flowing white sort of cape that settled and draped, instead of at the shoulders, at the waist. Two large white wings or swaths of material flowed out from the hips like curtains being flung wide, and shifted and fluttered with each movement.

By the time Yvonne, the last of the mannequins I'd met at Lisette's, appeared, I was overwhelmed by not only the stunning beauty and uniqueness of each gown—how would I ever choose?— but also the desperation that I should not lose my chance to speak to the Outhiers. The *passage* would be ending and they would surely take their leave. It was frustrating to sit there and know that a chance was slipping away.

"Ah, and this one, *chérie*? What do you think of it? It is not so very . . . eh . . . bright and sparkling, *non*?" murmured Oncle Rafe.

I agreed with him. I think he sensed, perhaps better than Grand-père, that I would feel overwhelmed in a gown that sparkled and glittered and flowed like a light show. This final gown, the Francis Poulenc (named after a composer friend of Monsieur Dior's, I was later to learn), was stunning in its simplicity and elegance.

It looked as if someone had taken a dozen or more huge seashells—clam shells—and used them to make a gown. The fabric was sharply pleated all over, and each section—or clam, for lack of a better term—was connected in cascading layers to create a beautiful dress. The bodice was one such "clam" shape, with the rounded edge for a subtle upside-down C-arc for the bustline. The fabric was pleated, but it wasn't stiff, and it flowed and shifted and shined with every movement of the mannequin, each section fluttering, draping, rippling on its own.

"It's elegant and yet understated," I said. I wished I knew what kind of material it was.

Oncle Rafe smiled and nodded at me. "And it would become

you. All of the others—ah, they are magnificent and glorious, and you would be lovely in any of them, *chérie*—but one gets the sense that with those, the dress is wearing the woman, *non?* With the Francis Poulenc, it is more that the woman, *she* wears *it.*"

I agreed. He had put into words my exact thoughts, far more eloquently than I could.

The next task would be to convince Grand-père of my preference for the simplicity instead of the bright, sparkling gowns like Mozart, the frothy champagne piece. Having already witnessed the result of differing opinions over decor, I could only imagine how that was going to go.

The show was finished. I had to force myself to remain politely and patiently seated—for I wanted to spring to my feet and try to start a conversation with Monsieur and Madame Outhier. I couldn't just leap up and abandon Grand-père and Oncle Rafe. They were in deep conversation about which gown would be the best for me, speaking in front of me as I sat between them.

I wasn't the least bit put off by the fact that *they* were discussing it, not me. In fact, I not only trusted their opinions—even if they differed—but I *wanted* them to choose. After all, they were paying for it. And what did I know about haute couture? Every single gown that had been shown was magnificent and would be the most gorgeous and special piece of clothing I'd ever worn—or, probably, would ever wear. Yes, the last gown—the clamshell one—was probably the one I would choose, but if Grand-père wanted me in Mozart, then I would be in Mozart, and I would love and be grateful for every moment of it.

The Outhiers had risen and were speaking to Madame Raymonde. The discussion happening around me between Grand-père and Oncle Rafe was beginning to become a bit tense—as expected. No one was raising his voice, but each of them clearly had an opinion.

"Grand-père, will you excuse me? I seem to need the ladies' room," I said.

"But of course, *ma mie,*" he said, glancing at me with a smile.

"And I will continue to explain to Rafael here that you will be magnificent in the Mozart."

I exchanged a brief, sympathetic look with Oncle Rafe, then rose and slipped away from where they were sitting and started walking casually toward the Outhiers. I wasn't certain what I was going to do or how I was going to get the attention of either of them, but I trusted that something would present itself.

"Psst!"

A hiss caught my attention and I turned to see Cerise peeking out from behind the gray curtain that led to the *cabine*.

Glancing at the couple who was my quarry—they were still talking to Madame Raymonde—I went over to speak to Cerise.

"Come inside," she said, opening the curtain and gesturing me through.

I hesitated, then she said, "But I have some things to tell you! It is about Robert Illouz and more. He is *here*, you know! He is meeting with the Master!"

Illouz was *here*? With one more look back at the Outhiers, I put aside my previous intentions and slipped through the opening created by a break in the curtains.

The *cabine* was abuzz with activity and crammed full of people, dresses, clothing racks, and a long countertop strewn with make-up, perfumes, and boxes upon boxes of jewelry, shoes, hats, stockings, gloves, and other accessories. Mirrors glinted everywhere. The scents of perfume I'd smelled out in the salon were stronger in this room, and I saw bottles of Miss Dior cluttering the counters.

The mannequins were in various stages of undress. Cerise was no longer wearing the sequin-laden Debussy; surely she'd been helped out of it by one of the many dressers who were hanging gowns, boxing up shoes or jewelry, and folding undergarments and stockings. That reminded me—I'd need help dressing if I ended up with a Dior. What a bother haute couture could be!

"Bonjour, Tabitha!" cried Yvonne when she saw me. "I did not know you were going to be here today!" She was standing there in a fitted corset that was a sort of bra and girdle combination, and stockings, reminding me that although Dior's fashions and style were incredibly beautiful and eye-catching, they were also maneuvering feminine dress backward toward the turn of the century wasp waists and long skirts.

Ugh. It looked supremely uncomfortable. I'd have to wear one of those fitted foundation garments beneath whichever Dior gown I ended up wearing. Couldn't Dior have taken us back to the twenties, where everything was rather loose?

"Have you spoken to Illouz? What did you find out?" I said to Cerise. I had positioned myself at the seam of the curtains and held one side so it was parted enough for me to see the Outhiers. "He is here, you say?"

"Yes, I have! He is meeting with the Master about being hired as his assistant! But you wanted to know about his cigarettes, *non*?" Cerise said.

"Yes." I gave her my full attention even though I kept hold of the curtain.

"He smokes the Le Phénix Vie!" Cerise said in a low, excited voice. "Do you think *he* is the killer?"

I was a little shocked that she should exhibit such enthusiasm over the fact that her lover—and potential colleague here at Maison Dior—might be a murderer. "It is very possible. Do you know where he was on the night Rose-Marie Lannet was killed? And the next night, when Gabrielle Pineau was stabbed?"

"*Oh*. Oh . . . why, he was with me, of course, on the first night," said Cerise, looking stunned—perhaps even disappointed—at the thought. "We had dinner, and then . . . well, of course you know." She gave me a sly look.

"Yes, I know," I replied, feeling a jolt of my own disappointment. So that eliminated my only other possible suspect if he had an alibi. Investigative work was so frustrating! "And so you were together—the whole time. From when until when?" I asked, attempting to be as thorough as Merveille would be.

"I finished here . . . oh, it was after six. It was a long day, you see, because there were photographs to be taken because the first ones—the film, it was ruined for the magazine. I don't remember which one it was. *Harper's Bazaar? Vogue?* It is all such a blur. But so they had to come back and do them again. And so I think . . . eh, it was maybe half past six when I left. And then we met at seven for dinner—"

"You didn't meet Illouz until seven?" I jumped on that detail. "Madame Lannet was dead by six o'clock."

"Oh!" Cerise's eyes widened and she clapped a hand to her mouth. "Oh, if that is the case, then he *could* have done it!"

I nodded. Yes, Illouz could have killed Madame Lannet. But that seemed too easy . . . too simple. He'd been so overt with his complaints about her, it made him such an obvious suspect. Just as Julia had pointed out.

Still. This wasn't an Agatha Christie or Raymond Chandler novel with wild and often unbelievable plot twists. My father had told me often enough that in real life the most obvious suspect was usually the killer.

"I would really like to speak to him myself," I said, looking out through the curtain.

"But I don't know how . . . *ah*, but perhaps there is a way," Cerise said, her eyes lighting up again. "Tonight, we will go to a little oyster bar with the jazz music, and you could come there too, *non?* And then you can speak to him yourself. Of course I won't tell him about you. Only that you are the granddaughter of Maurice Saint-Léger."

"Yes! That would be perfect." As a young and hopeful couturier, it would be in Robert Illouz's interest to meet as many potential clients as possible, which would give me the chance to question him.

As Cerise was telling me where to meet them and at what time, I saw Madame Outhier separating herself from the conversation with her husband and Madame Raymonde. *"Merci,"* I said a little abruptly to Cerise. "And where is the ladies' lounge?" I suspected that might be the reason Madame Outhier was excusing herself, and if so, maybe I could intercept her there.

My instincts were correct. Cerise told me where the ladies' room was, and that was exactly where Madame Outhier seemed to be going. I followed the waft of cigarette smoke that trailed her, contemplating my options for starting up a conversation.

The ladies' lounge was as elegant and well-appointed as every other part of Maison Dior. The signature gray continued into this space, but in here the flowers were soft pink peonies and white hydrangeas. The counter was topped by a row of silver-framed mirrors opposite two stalls with ornate wooden doors painted a slightly darker shade of gray. Of course, the interior smelled like a Dior perfume, as if someone had recently come through and sprayed it.

I took my time at the mirror, arranging my hair and freshening my lipstick until Madame Outhier emerged.

This was my first close look at her, and my impression was of a woman who wore tension and indignation like a fur coat. Her features were neither beautiful nor homely, but her makeup, hair, and clothing were stylish, expensive, and neat. She had very thick dark eyebrows that were even longer than the ones the mannequins drew onto their faces. They sat in heavy arcs on her large, unlined forehead. Her lipstick had been completely wiped or chewed off, it seemed, leaving just a dark red line around the outer edges of her mouth.

"Bonjour," I said with a friendly smile. Since she would have seen me during the *passage*, I knew she would recognize me. "What a stunning collection of gowns from Monsieur Dior. I can hardly decide on my favorite! Is Dior your preferred couturier?"

Madame Outhier dried her hands with a hand towel—also gray, and embroidered with the name Dior—and frowned at me in the mirror. "Not at all," she replied. "But I will have no choice now, will I?"

"But what do you mean?"

She had set her hat and handbag on the counter and was using the long, pointed end of a comb to pick through her hair, lifting it from where it had gone flat beneath her hat. "But my husband is the patron of Maison Lannet. Surely you heard what has happened there." She gave me a pointed look through her reflection, those heavy brows drawing together.

"Oh, *oui*," I replied. "What a tragedy! Two women dead—*murdered*, even—and now I suppose the atelier will have to close down with no designer to head it up. Is that why you've come now to Dior?"

"Of course," she said with an air of impatience, and I knew I was fumbling this opportunity by speaking so clumsily and obviously.

I either needed to think of something clever to say, or something audacious that would startle her into speaking. I opted for audacious, since I couldn't think of anything clever. "You're Madame Outhier, aren't you? And it was your husband who invested in Maison Lannet. I suppose he is very upset to be out of so much money, *non*? Just as she's unveiled her first collection."

She tossed the comb into her purse and I thought she'd snatch everything up and stalk out of the room. Instead, she looked at me coolly—still via the mirror—and pulled out a cigarette case.

"Not only is my husband out of money from the investment, but I am now divested of the wardrobe I expected. As are the friends I referred to Lannet instead of Dior. It is an untenable situation."

She lit the cigarette and blew out an angry stream of tobacco-scented smoke. "What am I to do? Dior—he is magnificent, there is no argument there—but overpriced. Lannet . . . ah, well, she was very, very good—nearly as talented as Dior—but she knew better than to charge me at those prices. Or *any* prices. She created an entire line only for me. And now—*peh!* There is nothing. But without me and Frédéric, she would have been nothing but a latent, rotting, miserable traitor. And now she is dead, and *I* am to be unclothed this season."

I was so shocked by this speech that I froze for a moment, our eyes holding in the glass. "Traitor? Do you mean a collaborator?"

Madame Outhier spewed out another stream of smoke. She seemed more than willing to confide—or complain—to a stranger. I wondered how long she'd been simmering and stewing. "But of course. She worked at Lelong, did she not?" Madame Outhier set her smoking cigarette roughly in the slit of an ashtray.

"But so did Dior," I said weakly. "And Lelong collaborated with the Germans only in order to protect the fashion industry of Paris—to keep the designers here."

Madame Outhier had retrieved a lipstick from the depths of her handbag and was now slashing a wine-red color over her pale lips. "*Ça ne fait rien.* As he would say, if one asks. Of course he would say that. But ask Rose-Marie Lannet how she knew that my husband was making a contract with the Germans. Oh . . . one cannot do that—*la vache* is dead."

So Madame Lannet had known Monsieur Outhier was working closely with the Germans. *Had* she indeed blackmailed Frédéric Outhier into investing in her studio?

Since audacity seemed to be working, I tried again. "Are you saying that Rose-Marie Lannet blackmailed your husband into investing in her business?"

She shoved the cap onto her lipstick with an angry click. "Of course not. It was my husband who told her that *she* would be better off if no one knew what she had done during the war. And so an agreement was made for her to design clothing exclusive to me, and Frédéric would help pay for her to set up shop and ensured she would be classified by the Chambre Syndicale. *I* could not wear the designs from someone who was not *le haute couture*, could I? Lannet had the talent. She only needed the classification by the Chamber Syndicale."

I stared at her, stunned wordless by so many elements of this speech. So the Outhiers had leveraged Rose-Marie Lannet into making clothing for Madame Outhier at cost—or perhaps even less than that!—not the other way around.

"Why are you telling me all of this?" I said quietly.

She replaced the hat on her head and once more looked at me through the mirror. "Because it no longer matters, does it? Lannet is dead and the designs and clothing are gone with her. I tried to find—my husband, as he most often does, has made a mess of things, and now I will be forced to wear basic couture or to spend a fortune on Dior or Fath or Balmain. And so many of the designs are already sold." She nearly spat the words. "Frédéric thought by bringing me here today I would feel so much better. That he could soothe my feelings over all of this. *Peh.* He is a fool, my husband. I should never have married him."

She turned and stalked from the lounge without even a bonjour. When I turned back after watching her leave, I saw that she'd left her cigarette smoking in the ashtray.

It was a Le Phénix Vie.

CHAPTER 17

WHEN I RETURNED FROM THE LADIES' LOUNGE, STILL REELING from Madame Outhier's outburst, I saw that she and her husband were no longer in the salon. However, Grand-père and Oncle Rafe were in animated and jovial conversation with Madame Raymonde and Madame Bricard.

"Ah, and there she is," said Grand-père, beaming at me. "Perhaps we can arrange for her measurements to be taken now?"

Apparently, a decision about my Dior gown had been made. I glanced covertly at Oncle Rafe, but he wasn't looking at me, darn it!

"The Master himself will want to meet the lovely mademoiselle first," replied Madame Raymonde. "If you please, Monsieur Saint-Léger and Monsieur Fautrier."

And so, I met Christian Dior.

He was a man of average height in his early forties, dressed in a long white coat and carrying a baton that I was later to find out was used for him to point out problems with designs or *modèles*. Smiling, courtly, with a kind, roundish face and a head of hair that was very much thinning on top, he didn't have the sort of imposing personality I had expected from an *artiste*, a celebrated couturier. Instead, he was warm and courteous with an air of humility.

"Mademoiselle, I will wait with bated breath to see you in my creations," he said, bowing over my hand and kissing the back of it. My hand was still gloved, of course, but I appreciated the gesture.

"Your designs are incredible," I said with great emotion. "I'd be honored to wear one of them. Do you have an opinion as to which one might be the most suitable and becoming to me?"

"But you have already decided, *non*, Maurice?" he said. There was a twinkle in his eye. "Or are the two of you at odds and ends over this as well?"

Grand-père gave a rusty chuckle. "I see Victor Grandpierre has been telling tales."

"But surely he would not," replied Dior with a smile that indicated he surely had. "Although Victor, he does warn me that the formula for the Dior gray . . . it is perhaps some one little thing that you and Rafael might agree on. Nonetheless, you will not have it at *any* cost." He wagged his finger in admonishment, still smiling.

Oncle Rafe laughed heartily. "Ah, Maurice, you have been caught out! Now, Christian, if you would—you are the Master. Make the decision for us. Then none will hold it against the other, *non*? When the Master speaks, there is no response other than 'but of course.'"

"Ah, you are very kind! I have a very little idea, then, if you will." Dior turned his attention back to me, and the next thing I knew, I was being led away from my messieurs to a small room walled with eight mirrors, giving it an octagonal shape.

It wasn't the *cabine*, where the mannequins had been. It was obviously the room where measurements were taken of the clients. I knew that every haute couture establishment was required to do at least three fittings for each piece ordered by a client. A specific dressmaker's form would be made with my measurements for the seamstress—for there would be only one assigned to make my gown; she would sew the entire dress by hand, by herself! If I selected a gown with beading, embroidery, or other details like that, a different person would do that close handiwork once the dress was made.

I would return to Maison Dior for the actual fittings—starting with a version made from toile, which would then be unassembled to use for cutting the actual fabric for my gown—but the dressmaker's form would ensure there would be no problems in the meanwhile. It was a very complicated process.

This little room, meant obviously for fittings and measuring, was just as elegant and well-appointed with the unprepossessing gray as every other space in Maison Dior. It was, however, the smallest chamber I'd seen in all of the building.

A short, pudgy woman in her forties with a tape measure hanging over her shoulders and a pincushion on her wrist was waiting. She wore a simple black uniform and no gloves. She eyed me closely as Monsieur Dior guided me onto a small platform in the middle of the room.

The woman murmured something and Dior glanced at her, smiled, and nodded. I couldn't hear what they said. All I knew was that I felt unusually uncomfortable under their serious regard.

"And what do you think, mademoiselle?" said Dior. "Did you have a favorite of the gowns? Which one do you want to wear?"

"I loved them all. Every single one of them. The Mozart is stunning. And the Debussy . . . like the night sky! I also loved the clam—I mean to say, the gown you designed for Francis Poulenc."

He was watching me closely—both as I spoke, but also as I was directed by the woman to turn, to lift my arms, to stand tall, etc., as measurements were taken. "I see you do have a preference."

I hesitated, then once again opted for audacity. "Monsieur, you are so very talented. I would be honored to wear any of your beautiful designs. But I think the simple yet stunning Francis Poulenc would suit me the best."

"And you are afraid of causing the rift between your *grand-père* and Fautrier, are you?"

I didn't dare shrug, as Madame was measuring the length of my spine from shoulder to hip.

"I see it," Dior said with a nod. "And I think you have made a fine choice. Perhaps we will choose a slightly creamier color for the taffeta, *non*, to bring out the flecks of green in your eyes?

And it will make your skin appear more golden and warm. *Oui.* I will handle it with Maurice, if you will allow it."

I thanked him profusely and he left, closing the door behind him. I was about to step off the platform, but the woman stopped me. "No, mademoiselle, we are not finished yet, if you please. I must ask if you will remove your suit and blouse. It is difficult to get the measurements with clothing on. I only began while the Master was here, but now, if you could strip to your underthings."

As I did so, the door to the chamber opened. I stifled a shriek—who wanted a random person coming in while they were standing around in their skivvies?—but it turned out to be Yvonne. I managed not to feel self-conscious standing half-dressed in front of a woman who was almost ten years younger than me, and with much longer legs. After all, only a few minutes ago, I had seen *her* in the *cabine* in her corset and stockings.

"Oh, Tabitha, thank goodness you *are* here! Hélène, this is Mademoiselle Knight—the one who wants to know about Madame Lannet."

"So this is the one. The one who is finding all of the bodies? The one who is helping *les flics?*" Madame Hélène paused in her measuring to give me yet another once-over.

Considering the fact that I was covered with goose bumps and standing there half-clothed in front of two other fully attired women, I think I handled the scrutiny pretty well.

"I don't really *like* finding bodies," I said. "And so I would like to identify the killer so that there won't *be* any more of them. Do you know something about Rose-Marie Lannet that might help me? Do you know why someone would want to kill her or Gabrielle Pineau?"

"I don't know about that," she said with a sniff. Her eyes narrowed on me, then she leaned forward to wrap the tape measure around my waist from behind. I resisted the urge to suck in my tummy, for the dress had to fit right, and I didn't want to be holding my breath every time I wore it. Besides, wasn't that what those boned, corset-like contraptions were for?

"Tell her what you were telling me, Hélène," urged Yvonne as the woman released the tape from my waist and made a note of the measurement. "That you weren't surprised someone did away with Madame Lannet."

The older woman cut her a sharp look, then sighed. "It is only that I worked with Madame Lannet when we were at Lelong. I am the fitter, and I was often with her, taking the measurements as I do now, you see." She hesitated, then shrugged. "They were the German wives, of course, who came for the dresses and the fittings during the war. And the wives and mistresses of the Parisians who collaborated with them or curried their favor. They were the only ones who had any money to buy haute couture— or any clothes—during the war, you see?"

I nodded. I was still standing there in my underwear but I didn't want to break the spell. The hair was standing up all over my body, but it wasn't only because I was chilly. I think I must have sensed I was about to learn something important, finally.

"And so they would talk—you see?—during the appointments with Lannet. I would be there as the fitter. It was private, and we were alone, and these were people who . . . people who were powerful. And they knew things.

"And Madame Lannet . . . she was the type of person who, I think, had a—a short vision. Who could not look far into the future, but only for the moment. You see? She did only what could benefit her at the time. She certainly did not care what would happen to France after the Germans came in. She wanted only to be famous. To make beautiful clothes. To be rich.

"And so she talked. And listened. And I think . . . I am certain she passed on information." These last words came out in a gust of breath, as if Madame Hélène had to push it out before changing her mind.

"You mean she was a spy? For who? The Resistance?"

Madame Hélène burst out laughing. It wasn't with hilarity. It was with disgust. "No, no, no . . . for the Germans. She heard things. She listened. Don't forget that the Master's sister worked for the Resistance." At my sharp intake of breath, she gave me a knowing look. "You see? And there were others, too, of course. Lannet used what she learned for her own gain." One eyebrow—

a naked one, not overdrawn or exaggerated with pencil—winged upward. "And then the Germans were driven out at last and here she was. . . ." She spread her hands, wide and empty, the tape measure dangling from one of them.

"And she was never arrested or identified as a collaborator?" I suddenly felt lightheaded and woozy.

If Madame Lannet had been passing information to the Germans about the Resistance—including the movements of people like Catherine Dior—was it possible Monsieur Dior had found out? Had Madame Pineau actually been correct when she accused him of being the killer?

I didn't believe that for a minute.

Did I?

I stood there in stunned silence, and after a grunt of irritation, Madame Hélène went back to work taking the last of my measurements. I couldn't think of anything else to say. I glanced at Yvonne, who was watching me with an "I-told-you-so" look.

"What about Gabrielle Pineau?" I said when I was finally dismissed from the little dais. I couldn't wait to get my clothes on. "Was she involved with the—uh—passing of information too?"

"That I do not know. They were close, of course, Lannet and Pineau, but I do not know whether Pineau did those things. She was not in the fittings, you see. She would not have the access." Madame Hélène gave me a tight smile. "I don't know who killed Rose-Marie Lannet, but I am glad she is dead. Who knows how many people died because of her? If you could have seen Mademoiselle Dior when she came back from Ravensbrück . . ." Her nose turned pink and she blinked rapidly, turning away as she whispered, "Her brother did not even recognize her."

I closed my eyes briefly. I felt even more sick. I could only imagine what Catherine Dior and others had endured. I knew about the horrors of what happened in the concentration camps. I'd seen photographs and read the stories.

When I finally composed myself, I realized I had to ask a difficult question. I had to know. "Did Monsieur Dior know about Madame Lannet and her spying?"

Madame Hélène had gathered up her tape measure and notebook. "I think, mademoiselle, that if the Master had known—or even suspected—he never would have brought her here."

I tended to agree. How could Dior have worked with a woman day in and day out, always wondering whether she had been the one who betrayed his sister and her colleagues? "Who else knew about her collaboration and spying?"

She shook her head. "I don't believe anyone knew, mademoiselle, except perhaps those to whom she spoke and passed on the information. The Germans and the other collaborators. I know only because I was there, in those fittings, and I kept my mouth shut." She sent a glare at Yvonne, who had sobered during the talk of concentration camps. "But I think that if people did know, Lannet would never have been able to open an atelier. She would long have been arrested and jailed. Or worse."

I was thinking about what Madame Outhier had said in the ladies' room.

She seemed to know about Madame Lannet's secret interactions with the Germans. But even so, even if other clients of Maison Lannet were aware of the collaboration, why kill Lannet? If they were blackmailing the couturier into creating their frocks and gowns and suits at low or no cost, there would be no reason to do away with the golden goose, would there? They were all keeping each other's secrets. Why upset the apple cart?

It didn't make any sense.

I was fully dressed by now and Madame Hélène stood impatiently at the door. She could hardly wait to get rid of me.

"Thank you for telling me all of this," I told her.

"I have told you nothing," she snapped, and stalked out of the room.

As I watched her stride down the corridor away from me, I scrambled to understand.

Madame Hélène had protected her suspicions for so long, perhaps she felt she was complicit as well. But to accuse, to tell . . . especially when she was not certain . . . that was yet another difficulty. And what would her friends and anyone else who'd been terrorized by the Nazis say if she only came forward now, five years after the war? Could they not accuse her as well of hiding information? Of protecting?

As I'd said to Julia: there was no simple answer. No black and white. Most everyone tried to do the best they could.

Maybe Madame Hélène's best was simply trying to survive.

We took our leave from Maison Dior. Grand-père did not seem to have his feathers ruffled, so I could only suppose that Monsieur Dior had deftly handled the decision of which gown I would wear.

As promised, we stopped into Godot & Block so that Grand-père and Oncle Rafe could make a scene with their arrival and start the plan to help Monsieur Block set his trap.

Monsieur Block came out from the workshop in the back and thanked them profusely for their help. He glanced down at my shoes and I was relieved that he would see not my clunky American shoes but the pair of shiny black pumps I'd worn. But my *grand-père* had seen his regard and insisted that I should be measured for some shoes as well.

Mathilde was giddy and all smiles with my two messieurs, and they were as charming and courtly as usual, making her blush when they bowed over her hand and told her how beautiful and lively she was. When I mentioned I was going to meet Cerise and Illouz at the oyster bar, she decided she would bring Lisette and Noëlle and come as well.

By the time we left avenue Montaigne, it was after four o'clock. I was supposed to be meeting M. Héroux at five thirty to pick up my hero cat . . . and to have a glass of wine. I felt a little flutter of interest. I needed to redirect my attraction to Merveille, and the veterinarian could be a possible distraction.

As Oncle Rafe navigated the Bentley the few blocks from the Right Bank over the river to our neighborhood, I got the idea that if things went well with our "glass of wine," I might ask M. Héroux whether he would like to go with me to the oyster bar tonight. I was supposed to meet—or, rather, to accidentally on purpose run into—Cerise and Robert Illouz at seven. Even

though Mathilde had decided to come, it would be more believ-
able if I were at a place like that with a date rather than by myself. If Robert Illouz *was* the killer, I certainly didn't want to
make him suspicious.

I still found it amusing and a little frightening that Cerise didn't
seem bothered by the fact that she might be sleeping with a
murderer. Not only was she not bothered, she was intrigued. At
least she was willing to have me question him.

Yes, Robert Illouz could be the killer. He was the obvious
choice. He had loathed Madame Lannet. He smoked Le Phénix
Vie cigarettes.

. . . And so did Madame Outhier.

There'd been no smudge of lipstick on the cigarette she'd left
smoldering in the ashtray in the lounge, which made me realize
that a woman could definitely have a smoke without leaving
makeup on it. But I could think of no reason she would have
killed Madame Lannet and Madame Pineau.

I heated up the *gâteau à la Florentine* and made certain my
messieurs had a nice bottle of white Bordeaux and a sliced pear
to go with their dinner, then I went upstairs to freshen up for my
date. As I was reapplying my makeup—eschewing the heavy eye
liner from yesterday's mannequin lesson—I reminded myself
that I needed a name for my heroic alley cat. In following the
tradition of my messieurs, I thought I ought to choose a name of
some person or character.

Someone who was cunning and sneaky but not malignant or
evil. Someone who was at home on the mean streets, as Raymond Chandler would say. Someone who was brash and heroic
and a fighter.

And then all at once, it hit me. I knew exactly what to name him.

I grinned at myself in the mirror, gave my hair one last gentle
tousle at the temples and guided a short curl around my ear.
Then I set my capulet in place. The bronze-brown hat didn't
have netting, but it was adorned with a bit of braided trim and
beading around the edges of its kidney shape—just perfect for a
casual evening out. My frock was the color of a rich Bordeaux,

printed with tiny yellow flowers and featuring a belted waist. The hat and dress looked good together.

I kissed my messieurs goodbye and warned them it could be a late night.

"And you will be with the veterinarian, then?" said Grand-père. "And he is a nice man, is he?"

"Julia thinks so," I said, then explained my plan for the evening—a drink with Monsieur Héroux and then the oyster bar, where I intended to interview my remaining suspect. I also filled them in on what I'd learned from Madame Outhier and Madame Hélène.

"What? And this is true? Madame Lannet—she was feeding the information to *les boches*?" Oncle Rafe's face darkened. He said a very vulgar word that I will not repeat, but I cannot say I blamed him.

"I have no proof, but I also have no reason to disbelieve Madame Hélène," I told him. "She has no reason to lie, especially after all this time."

"And so someone found out about this and they have killed her," Oncle Rafe said, as if the matter was settled. His expression was still dark.

"Yes, it is possible. But I don't have any idea who that might be. Madame Hélène said she didn't think anyone else knew."

"*Ça ne fait rien.* Someone else found out about it," said Grand-père, nodding at Rafe. "Only just now. And they had their revenge."

I shrugged. It was as good a theory as any, but it was frustrating because I had no idea who might have found out and how. Someone else who had also worked at Lelong—and might have seen the same things Madame Hélène had seen? Someone who worked at Dior now, or even . . . *someone who'd gone to Maison Lannet.* Without knowing about Madame Lannet's past.

That was definitely a thread worth pursuing. I could ask the others tonight if they could think of anyone who might fit the bill.

"And, now what about this *cat* you will be bringing back to invade Madame's sanctuary?" Grand-père said suddenly. He had demolished a large portion of the gâteau and was now enjoying a cigarette and the last of his wine.

"I'm not sure when I'll bring Monsieur le Chat de Gouttière back here. I certainly can't tow him about with me on my investigations."

He and Oncle Rafe laughed. "But he has already saved your life once, *chérie*!" Oncle Rafe reminded me.

"Well, I am certain Madame X will not be upset to find this beast is a day late in his arrival. And make certain he has had *two* flea baths, Tabi! At least two," said Grand-père.

"Three would be better," said Oncle Rafe, giving me a pointed look. "Monsieur Wilde does not want the fleas either, and I suspect he will get much closer to Monsieur le Chat than Madame X will. And do you have a name for this beast yet?"

I grinned and told them. They heartily approved, and I left them chuckling over this.

I had decided to drive myself to Monsieur Héroux's office so that I could put my cat in his carrier in the car until I could bring him home to introduce him to his new housemates. Or, I could leave him at the office while we had wine and went to the oyster bar, then come back and pick him up.

But when I arrived at Monsieur Héroux's office, I found him very agitated.

"Oh, mademoiselle . . . I don't know how to tell you this," he said, taking my gloved hands in his warm, slender ones. He had soft brown eyes that were brimming with concern and sorrow.

I knew the worst had happened.

CHAPTER 18

"**I**S HE . . . IS MY CAT DEAD?" I SAID, MY HEART SINKING. I HADN'T realized how attached I'd become to that mongrel alley cat.

"Oh, no, no, mademoiselle . . . it is not that. He is in fine health. Very fine health. In fact, I had given him the second flea bath as you asked, and then he slipped out of my gloves—they were rubber, of course, to protect from the claws—but very slippery. He slipped away and went on top of one of the cabinets.

"I did not worry so much then—it is not unusual for the felines, for they do not like the baths, of course—but then suddenly there was a commotion in the waiting room and I went out to see. It was an emergency with a poor little dog who'd been attacked by another bigger dog. And so I rushed out to get to him, and my assistant, he—we . . . ah, mademoiselle, I am so sorry, but the door was left open. And your *monsieur le chat . . .* he saw himself out."

"Oh," I said with a relieved laugh. "So he has made his escape, has he?"

"He will not come back," Héroux said mournfully. "I have asked him politely several times. I have even explained that if he does not come back, that if I have lost her cat, then there is no chance the lovely mademoiselle will have a drink with me." He gave me an endearing smile, his mustache curving upward on the ends.

I smiled back and said, "I am certainly still going to have the drink with you, Monsieur Héroux."

His smile was one of relief and amusement. "Ah, that is good, for otherwise I would have had to find a ladder to climb up there and bring him down. And then there would be the scratches on my arms and my face, and then you would not be seen with me in public anyway, *non?*"

I laughed again. Frenchmen were such charmers . . . unless they were police *inspecteurs.*

"And so where is the escapee?" I asked.

"He is perched in the tree, just across there, mademoiselle, if you can see?"

He gestured to the window in the examination room and opened it for me. Despite the cold, I stuck my head out and looked up. And yes, there was my hero cat, sitting on a branch just across from and above the window. He did not appear the least bit pleased or relieved to see me.

"But you've fixed his tail!" I exclaimed when I saw the way the cat was twitching it. The inch or two that used to hang, half-detached from the end of the tail, was missing. A little white bandage was wrapped around the tip, looking like a flag of surrender as the cat whipped it back and forth. I did not think for one minute it actually *was* representative of surrender, however.

"Ah, *oui,* but of course, mademoiselle," he said. "I could not allow the risk of the infection to return. It has all been treated—the sores you saw, and the infection—but the end of the tail . . . that needed to be closed up, you see?"

I could only imagine how that had gone over with the cat. No wonder he'd seized his first chance for freedom. First the indignity of a cat carrier, then likely a cauterization on the open wound of his tail (which hopefully he'd been asleep for), and then two flea baths . . . I didn't blame him.

"Thank you for fixing him up," I replied. "I'm so glad he's healthy now. And if he doesn't want to live a life of luxury"—I cast this last part loudly out the window toward the cat—"then so be it. Shall I settle my bill and then shall we have that glass of wine?"

"*Oui,* mademoiselle. But there is one thing I must ask of you first, if you don't mind."

I tilted my chin in question and waited.

"Please do not call me Monsieur Héroux. My name is Jean-Luc."

Well, I thought, hiding a smile. What a change from Merveille!

Jean-Luc and I had a lovely glass of *vin rouge* at a little cafe around the corner from his veterinary office, and not very far from Maison de Verre. I told him about my messieurs' plans for the restaurant, and he was very interested, for, apparently, he went down that street quite often as he lived in a flat above his veterinary office.

"I have to walk the dog, you see," he said with a boyish grin. "Actually, it is the plural. Dogs. Five of them."

"Five dogs?" I exclaimed.

"It is, as one says, a hazard of the profession. It is difficult to say no to any of the animals who wish to adopt me. My mother—she did not quite understand how it was that I always had to bring home the dogs or the cats in the street. It was the gutter rat with the injured paw that made her draw the line and insist I go to veterinary school instead of creating a zoo in her house."

I snickered. By then, between the wine and our easy conversation, I was feeling comfortable enough with Jean-Luc to ask if he might be willing to come along to the oyster bar as my cover. His eyes lit up when I asked, then he became curious.

"Your *cover?* Is this because you are investigating another dead body? A murder?" He didn't seem appalled; he seemed interested.

And so I went on to explain the situation. After all, Julia had already told him about me finding bodies.

"And you have no clues to the killer," he said as he helped me on with my coat. He smelled like tobacco and something astringent or chemical that I suspected was due to his medical work. "Such as the ashes from the cigarette or the footprints?"

"Ah, you sound like Hastings," I said, referring to the assistant of Agatha Christie's Hercule Poirot. Hastings was always more enamored of the idea of fingerprints and dropped matchbooks and cigarette ash, while Poirot focused on the psychology of the killer and things like motive and opportunity.

I had to admit, I still tended to be more like Hastings than Poirot—seizing upon the tangible clues—but that was something I was determined to change. Tangible clues could be important, but so was the personality of the killer—as well as the victim. At least, if Poirot could be believed.

"And who is this Hastings?" Jean-Luc offered me his arm as we left the cafe.

I explained, then finished, "He is like the Watson to Sherlock Holmes."

"And you are the Sherlock Holmes, then, mademoiselle?" he said teasingly.

"Not even close. And my name is Tabitha. Of course you should call me Tabitha," I said, realizing I'd never made the offer to him. "And to answer your question, there are a few clues. I think the term for them is trace evidence. Whoever did it smokes Le Phénix Vie cigarettes, and it has to be someone the victims knew because they turned their back on them. At least, Madame Lannet did. And she had him in her office. And then there was the metal tube he or she dropped." I'd almost forgotten about that. Merveille had never told me what it was, and I had forgotten to ask whether he'd found out.

"A metal tube?"

We were strolling down the street to go back to Jean-Luc's office, where I'd parked my car. It was just as the sun was setting, and the streetlights were coming on. Tonight, the air was cold and still, and our breaths came in little white puffs as we walked; although his was bigger because he was smoking a cigarette. Every time we passed someone with a dog, Jean-Luc paused to first greet the animal, then say bonsoir to its owner. I found his unabashed love for animals charming and amusing in the way he spoke to them.

I described the small metal tube to him and ended by saying, "I don't know what it is, so I'm not sure how helpful it is."

"But I have a little idea," he said, stopping at the front door to his office. "It reminds me of something I have, the way you describe it. If you would like to come inside for one moment and I will show you?"

I followed him inside and through the tiny waiting room, past the office and the examination room. I could hear the sounds of wild barking and mournful yowls coming from the back of the building.

"That is the overnight guests," he said with a smile over his shoulder. "They are often complaining of their accommodations, even though I try to make them as comfortable as possible."

Jean-Luc brought me into a room that turned out to be a small surgery. There were drawers filled with tools: scalpels, forceps, scissors, needles, bandages, thread . . .

"And what do you think of this, Mademoiselle Tabitha?" He withdrew something silver and metal, holding it up between his thumb and a long, slender finger.

It looked very much like the little tube I'd found at Maison Lannet. I took it from him and examined it. "Yes," I said. "The inside was hollow like this, and it moves a little—"

"It is to make a hole, you see," he said. "I use it to remove the cysts or perhaps small thorns or other problems on the animals. Take care, mademoiselle. It is very sharp." He took it from me and stood it vertically over a piece of bandage. Then he pushed on the top of the metal tube, and I realized how it worked: the inside was a hollow, spherical blade that went down inside its sheath and made a cut on the surface below. When he lifted it from the bandage, there was a small hole about the diameter of a pea left in the cloth.

I stared at the hole, then at the tool, thoughtful. Someone had dropped that. Someone who used it to make incisions or holes . . . in skin, yes, or *fabric*. . . .

"Thank you," I said. "That is very helpful, Jean-Luc."

"Now," he said with a grin, "shall we go to the oyster bar and interrogate this suspect of yours?"

He had just finished turning off the lights and was sliding the key into the door to lock it behind us when we heard the shrill *brrrrring* of the telephone inside. I heard the sound he made under his breath—one of dismay and regret.

"Forgive me, Tabitha, but I must answer that call. If someone is telephoning so late, it is likely important."

"Of course you must," I said, walking back inside with him.

When he returned, Jean-Luc had already removed his coat and hat—which told me everything I needed to know.

"I hope it's nothing serious," I said.

"Alas, it might very well be." His expression was grave. "There is a dog who has some terrible pain in the belly and the owner, she thinks he has eaten her stocking."

"Oh no!" I exclaimed. "The poor thing."

"*Oui.* The stockings, they are very smooth and sexy, but they do not do so well in the belly for *les chiens, non?* I have already telephoned my assistant to come in, and I will have to prepare for the surgery."

He was regretful, but I could tell he was focused on and worried about his incoming patient, so I wished him luck and said bonsoir.

As I was coming out, the poor woman with the injured dog was rushing up the walk, tears streaming from her eyes as she carried a pet who was barely larger than Monsieur Wilde.

I held the door for them, and when I got outside, I looked up into the tree where my cat was sitting and said, "Do you see the devotion of a pet owner? You could have that, you know. And a warm bed and plenty of food . . . not to mention an actual *name.*"

He gave me a chilly look and didn't bother to move, so I wished him a bonsoir and set off walking to my car. It was getting late and I was supposed to meet Cerise and Robert Illouz at seven.

The oyster bar was three blocks north of avenue Montaigne, but I had to park closer to Montaigne. It was just past six thirty and I wondered if I might encounter Mathilde coming from Godot & Block to meet the others who were going, and so I decided to walk a little out of my way to see if she was still at the shoe shop, then we could all go together and I would still be "under cover."

The lights were still on in the shop and when I peeked in through the window, I saw Mathilde just putting on her coat. I tried the door and found that it was still unlocked even though the sign had been turned to FERMÉ.

"Oh, Tabitha! It is you!" Mathilde clapped a hand to her chest, her eyes wide. "You startled me."

"Let's walk over to the oyster bar together," I said.

"Oh, yes, that is good. I am meeting Lisette at the corner in just a little moment. I will tell Monsieur Block that I am leaving. He will have to lock up."

While I was waiting, I looked around the shop. I'd been in there a short while earlier, but I was killing time. I picked up a pair of wingtip shoes that were made from two different colors of leather stitched together. They laced up the front.

The hair on the back of my neck rose very slowly as I stared at the shoe. My skin prickled as a wave of thoughts rushed through my brain and my body caught up with my thoughts.

Mathilde breezed in from the back, clapping her hat on her head as she came forward. "Are you ready to go, Tabitha?" Her lipstick was fresh and red and she held a pocketbook in her hand.

"Not yet," I replied slowly. My heart was pounding, but I also felt surprisingly calm. "I'll be right back."

I took off my coat and gloves—I don't really know why, but it felt right to be so unencumbered—and left my pocketbook on a bench with them.

I walked into the back where the shop was and found Monsieur Block at his workbench. He was smoking a cigarette and wore a heavy, beaten-up leather apron. He was working on a piece of shoe leather fitted over the form of a foot.

Monsieur Block looked up when I got close, and he must have read my expression, for his face fell and whatever he was about to say died on his lips. He grabbed a wicked-looking tool with a bulbous wooden handle and a long metal point. An awl, I think it's called, and he brandished it as he came toward me from behind the workbench. His expression had turned to one of fury and desperation.

I stepped back, my heart pounding, and felt the wall behind me. My mouth dried up and my knees wobbled. I was trapped and he was far too close, pointing that terrible tool at me. "Monsieur Block—"

"You have been sneaking around, poking about. I should have done something sooner. I should have . . . I should have . . ."

I was watching him closely. His hand trembled a little, and I thought I saw more fear than fury in his eyes. "But you're not a killer, Monsieur Block, are you? Truly?"

"Ah, you will see what I can do if I must," he replied, angling the awl toward my sternum. He was only inches away and I could feel the heat of his emotions emanating from him. "A man sometimes must do the worst, you see, mademoiselle?"

"Yes, I see, monsieur. But . . . you have already done that. You don't wish to do anything more again, do you?" My heart pounded in my ears as I tried not to look at that deadly spike. One good thrust, and I was done for.

He made a choked sort of sound, then all at once, his hand fell away. The awl tumbled to the worktable and he stepped back. "*Non.* I will not. I will not . . . make it any worse."

I breathed easier and stepped away so the wall wasn't behind me any longer. The sound of his heavy breathing filled the air for a moment, and I heard Mathilde moving about in the front room. Thank goodness she hadn't come back here during our standoff.

"When did you find out that Rose-Marie Lannet was a collaborator?" I asked. My voice was calm and low. "That she fed information to the Germans?"

His shoulders lifted, then settled back into place. A great, painful sorrow filled his eyes and my heart gave a little pang. But then the sorrow was swiftly replaced by anger. This time, it was not directed at me, and for some reason, I was no longer afraid of Monsieur Block, even though he'd threatened me only moments ago.

"It was only a week ago," he said finally. He heaved a long, heavy breath. "One week after my Esther's birthday."

I nodded. During my flash of insight when everything fell into place, I realized something like that must have happened. Just as Grand-père had said: *Someone had only just found out.*

"How did you find out? Did you overhear someone talking? Or did someone mention it or tell you, not knowing that your wife was a Jew—not knowing what it would have meant to you to know that a woman you knew, a woman you did business with, had sent many Jews to their death?"

His eyes glistened with tears. "She was talking about it! In the courtyard. The two of them—Lannet and Pineau. I heard them from my window; it was open because I was smoking. It was night and they did not see me." He heaved another sigh and I saw that his hands were trembling. "They were talking, and Pineau, she was telling Lannet that she ought not to be so proud of her work, and that woman—that damnable *traitor*—she laughed and said it didn't matter, it was so long ago, and no one would tell and that she ought not to worry so . . . and they were forgiving collaborators every day, you see." His voice broke. He shook his head wearily.

"I tried to forget about it. Pineau was right. It was years ago. The war was over, you see? God will judge them, I told myself.

"But how was God judging Rose-Marie Lannet when she had a new *maison de couture* and it was very busy and successful, and I am only trying to struggle along? And my wife is gone, and her family and friends? How could that be that the likes of Rose-Marie Lannet, a *traitor!*—should be so happy and carefree?

"And I thought about how my Esther . . . she was never the same again after her brothers and cousins were taken. How she lived through the war, but at the end, she was still broken. She was still sad, every day. Guilty for living when so many had died. And I could not . . . I could not . . . let it go from my head."

His fingers were shaking so hard when he put down his cigarette that it nearly fell out of the ashtray.

"Tabitha? Are you ready to—is everything all right? Monsieur?"

I turned to Mathilde. "Please telephone the *police judiciare.*
Ask them to send Inspecteur Merveille."

Mathilde froze and made a squeaky sort of shocked sound,
then, gaping over her shoulder, turned and fled to the front of
the shop.

Monsieur Block made no attempt to move or to stop her—or
me, for that matter.

"I'm very sorry for what happened to your wife and her family," I said, stopping just short of patting his hand even though
my heart was bleeding for him. After all, he *had* held me at the
point of a deadly spike. "It was horrific and unforgivable. I understand why you could have such strong feelings about . . . about
it all."

He drew in a ragged breath and tears streamed down his
cheeks and onto his unshaven jaw. "It has been hell these days
since then. Since I . . . I've never hurt anyone before, mademoiselle. Believe me. I never laid a finger on a woman in my whole
life. But her . . ." He shook his head. "I was afraid someone
would know. I was afraid *you* would figure it out. Mathilde said
you were very smart—smarter than *les flics,* those stupid men.
And you did. And I . . . I think that I must be glad for that,
mademoiselle. It has been . . . it has been like being in my own
prison, inside my head, these last days. I am glad you came to
me. And I am sorry for . . . for that moment." His gaze trailed to
the awl, sitting innocently next to the shoe whose leather would
be punctured with the sharp tip, then lifted to mine. "I would
not have hurt you."

"I believe you," I said. "But the break-in here at the shop . . .
you did that yourself, didn't you?"

He nodded. "I was so . . . so *angry!* I was so angry and I couldn't
control the anger. And when I came back here after . . . after I
had . . . done that to Lannet, I could not contain myself. There

were all of these shoes that I was making for them—the Outhiers, the Joilliets, the others. And I knew then that they had been laughing with each other, passing the information back and forth, celebrating it all—when my Esther had to rely on our friends to hide her away from the Germans. And so I could not . . . I could not give them my *shoes*. I could not give them that part of me, of my heart and my soul . . . these shoes that I make with love and attention. They did not deserve them. They did not deserve to wear them on their damned evil, traitorous feet. And so I was angry, I was *wild* with it. And I ruined them so I did not have to sell them to those traitors! And then . . . well . . . and then I knew it would be best to make it look as if someone had broken in, you see. So no one would suspect me of anything. And so I did."

He fell silent, panting quietly. His hands were steadier now and he lit another cigarette.

"How did you find out about the Outhiers and the others?" I asked, although I had a theory about that. "How did you learn that they were also involved with Madame Lannet's spying and passing of information?"

"She told me. Lannet. I confronted her in her office that night . . . I couldn't wait any longer. I couldn't hold it back anymore. I had to talk to her. I had to know whether what I thought I'd heard was true!

"She told me only that I should take advantage of it with the Outhiers and the others. That I should take their money and be happy about it. That the war was long over and there was no sense in dwelling on things that happened then. She had not the smallest regret in her about it all.

"And that is why . . . that is why when she dismissed me, dismissed my questions and concerns, and walked out of the office . . . I followed her. I—I could not see. My eyes—they turned red, I think. It was all I could see, was red. Dark, dark, red. And I couldn't breathe.

"And then I saw the lace. It was sitting there, draped over a dress form." He was speaking quietly, almost dreamily. His eyes had gone vacant and he reached out as if to pluck again that lace from the dress form. "I took it and I went after her, into the other room, and I . . ."

He gave a little shudder and dropped his unsmoked cigarette into the ashtray. "I couldn't watch. I was glad she was facing away from me. I came up behind her while she was standing there, picking up the perfume bottles. I saw her in the mirror when I slipped the lace over her head . . . and then I closed my eyes . . . I closed them and I pulled the lace, so tight, so tight my arms shook and I couldn't breathe . . . I pulled until I felt her stop moving."

My breathing was unsteady too. I had to resist the urge again to reach over and offer comfort to a killer. What a strange moment.

He closed his eyes, then opened them and looked at me. They were bloodshot now. Bloodshot and weary. "And that night in the office . . . I didn't mean to hurt you . . . I was only . . . I could hardly believe what I'd done, and I thought I could make it look like a robbery there too, you see. I was in the office, looking for something to steal and things to turn over, you see, when I heard you. I didn't mean to push you so hard."

"And Madame Pineau? Did you go back the next night because you dropped your tool, and you were hoping to find it before we did?" I reached over onto the work counter and picked up a small metal tube, very much like the one that had been dropped in the corridor at Maison Lannet. I held it up to show him.

"*Non!*" His eyes widened. "I did not hurt Pineau. I swear it. I did not touch her! I did not go back after . . . after that night. I could not. I *could . . . not.*"

I looked down at the cigarette burning in the ashtray. It was a Gauloise.

CHAPTER 19

MONSIEUR BLOCK AND I WERE SITTING IN THE FRONT OF THE shoe shop when Merveille arrived with two of his agents. I had sent Mathilde on to the oyster bar, cautioning her not to say anything about what had transpired. I realized it was a long shot to think she might keep silent after the shock and excitement, but I hoped she kept her mouth shut.

"Bonsoir, Inspecteur," I said, rising, when they came in.

"Mademoiselle Knight," he said, looking from me to the crumpled, sagging man sitting next to me. "How may I help you?"

"Monsieur Block has something he would like to tell you."

Merveille glanced at me, comprehension in his eyes, then turned his attention to the shoemaker. "Monsieur?" he said with quiet gravity.

I sat back down and allowed Block to grip my hand while he told Merveille what happened. I could offer at least that much comfort to him. My heart ached for Monsieur Block and for everyone who'd gone through such hell in the war, and who were continuously and unexpectedly reminded of the evils that had happened.

Did I understand why Block had done what he'd done? Yes. Did I condone it? Absolutely not. Yet . . . I could . . . I could see how it had happened. How he'd felt trapped and desperate for a justice that seemed as if it would never come. How he'd felt useless and helpless, and enraged.

I hoped that, somehow, Block was able to find peace with what had happened and what he'd done.

I didn't wait around. Once Block made his initial confession, he released my hand—his grip had been very painful—and as I flexed my fingers, I stood to collect my hat, coat, and pocketbook.

Merveille took a seat across from Block to continue the interview in a calm and sober manner. But he glanced up when I went over to murmur to one of the agents that I was leaving, but that I had more information for the *inspecteur*. Our eyes met and I felt an unwelcome stab of awareness. Merveille gave me a spare nod of acknowledgment and perhaps even gratitude, then returned his attention to Block.

The chill wintry air felt good on my hot cheeks. I was a little shaky after the emotion of Monsieur Block's confession, and I was overwhelmed by a feeling of sadness and despondency. A good man's life had been ruined by his actions—actions that were prompted by love and despair and loneliness.

I believed Monsieur Block when he said he hadn't killed Gabrielle Pineau, even before I saw the brand of his cigarette. Why would he lie about that when he had been so forthcoming about everything else?

No . . . there had been two killers all along, and I had a feeling I knew who the second one was. But I wouldn't be sure until I spoke with Robert Illouz.

The oyster bar was loud and crowded and reeked of cigarette smoke and the pungency of saline. A jazz trio was arranged in a corner and the moody music fought hard to be heard over the raucous laughter and conversation.

Surprisingly, after everything had happened, I was only forty minutes late from the time I was supposed to meet Cerise. In Paris, when one is having a meal and drinks with friends, forty minutes is a mere fraction of time and would hardly be considered late.

My new friends were crowded around a table that would normally seat only four people. With my arrival, there were seven of us: Cerise and Illouz, Noëlle, Yvonne, Lisette, and Mathilde. The air around them was clouded with cigarette smoke. The table was littered with glasses in varying stages of emptiness. There was a narrow bowl in the center filled with oyster shells.

"Bonjour, Tabitha!"

Cerise introduced me to Illouz and I was ushered into a seat wedged between him and Noëlle. I gave Cerise a grateful look that she'd put me next to my target. And when I glanced at Mathilde she made a gesture in front of her lips that looked like she was buttoning them. Good. She hadn't told anyone what happened at the shoe shop.

I'd hardly been seated before someone was pushing a glass of wine into my hand and shoving a basket of bread toward me. That was fine with me—I was hungry.

As I broke off a hunk of bread, I studied Illouz without being obvious. He wasn't what I'd call an obviously attractive man, but he had an air about him that was somehow rife with sex appeal. With a hooked nose and thick, dark hair that fell in a Byronic swath over his high forehead, he looked very Mediterranean. His eyes were dark and fathomless and he came across as a person very in control of himself and filled with confidence and bravado.

"I heard that you were at Dior today," I said. We were shoulder to shoulder and I hardly needed to raise my voice to be heard over the dull roar around us.

He blew the smoke from his cigarette in the opposite direction before responding to me, the remnants of fresh tobacco on his breath. "*Oui*. And I have heard that you are investigating the murders of Lannet and Pineau."

Well. So much for a cover. I managed to keep a blank expression even though I wanted to kick Cerise. On the opposite side of Illouz, she was leaning on the table, her elbow dangerously close to an ashtray, looking over at us. She gave me a wink and I could do nothing but ignore her.

"I found Madame Lannet's and Madame Pineau's bodies," I

said evenly. "It's natural I should want to find out who would do such a thing."

"*Natural?*" Illouz laughed. "*C'est ridicule.* To try and hunt down a bloody killer? Most women would turn and run the other way, screaming. Did you scream when you found them?"

"I did not." I was still feeling audacious, and since he was being just as bold, bordering on rude—and more than a little annoying; forget the sex appeal I'd thought I'd sensed—I looked him straight in the eye and said, "Did you kill Gabrielle Pineau?"

"*Pineau?*" The cigarette dangled precariously from where it stuck to his bottom lip as his mouth opened in shock. "Did I kill *Pineau?* Why in the hell would I kill *her?* Of course I did not." He rescued the cigarette and knocked off its ash into the vessel next to Cerise's elbow. She was practically leaning on his arm, her eyes misty and a little drunk as she watched us. "I thought you suspected me of killing Lannet. That I would have been hard put to deny, because I despised the woman, but this? *Peh!*"

I nodded. I believed him—partly because of the bald shock and incredulity on his face. It was as if I had insulted him by suggesting he'd killed Gabrielle Pineau, a lowly vendeuse, instead of the head of a *maison de haute couture.*

"Can you think of any reason why someone would have killed Madame Pineau? Or who might have done it?"

He shrugged. "But, *non,* of course not. Why would anyone care? It was Lannet who deserved it. I'm sorry for the woman, Pineau—she was stabbed, I hear—but who would kill *her?* I do not know."

I nodded once more, and suddenly I was overwhelmed by a wave of weariness. I'd confirmed my suspicions. I'd identified a killer—and now I was certain I'd pinpointed a second one—but I was still despondent over Monsieur Block's situation.

Perhaps it was wrong of me to feel so sympathetic toward a murderer—a man who'd killed with his own hands—but I didn't seem to be able to shake the feeling.

I just wanted to go home.

CHAPTER 20

"*T*ABITHA! YOU HAVE *GOT* TO EAT THIS! CAN I BRING IT OVER *RIGHT* now?" Julia's voice trilled over the phone. "Paul has an exhibition and won't be home for *hours* and *someone* has to eat this right away!"

It was late in the afternoon, nearly evening, the next day. I had been very busy since morning and had hardly seen my messieurs, so I hadn't had the chance to tell them what had happened last night with Monsieur Block.

I'd had two tutoring appointments that were just far enough apart that it didn't make sense for me to come home in between, so instead I went shopping, and then I'd stopped by Jean-Luc's office to see how the emergency surgery had gone the night before. I was also looking for my wayward gutter cat, but he didn't seem to be in the vicinity of the veterinary office.

Jean-Luc had been very pleased to see me and told me the surgery had been successful—and that there had been an entire silk stocking in the poor little dog's intestines. But, unfortunately, he was extremely busy with a mother cat who was having a difficult time birthing her kittens. We agreed to have a drink again soon, and he promised to keep trying to convince my cat to come home. When I left his office, I realized I was genuinely looking forward to seeing Jean-Luc again.

I had absolutely *not* taken the opportunity to stop by the *police judiciaire* to speak with Merveille.

He knew where I lived and he knew I had information for him. And I felt he owed me at least an acknowledgment that I'd helped identify Rose-Marie Lannet's killer. Regardless, I was not going to be chasing him down for any reason.

Still. By the time I got home from my busy day, I found that not only were my messieurs gone to another design and decor consultation at Maison de Verre, but there was no message that the *inspecteur* had called or stopped by.

I felt a little too much like a woman waiting for the man she'd gone out with to telephone or contact her after the date, and I definitely didn't like that feeling—especially when it came to the *inspecteur*. Since no one was around to bother me or require my assistance, I decided to take a long soak in the bathtub, accompanied by a cup of coffee and a novel about strangers on a train—apparently it was a thriller—that had just come out by a new author named Patricia Highsmith. And so if Merveille *did* happen to stop by, it wouldn't be like I was waiting around for him.

A third of the book later (it was gripping!), I dragged my pruney self from the tub because I had to start thinking about making dinner. By the time I joined my returned messieurs in the salon and there was still no word from Merveille, I was beginning to wonder whether the police agent had forgotten to give him my message.

So when Julia called and insisted we eat whatever delicious dish she had made, I latched on to that idea immediately. It would be a nice distraction, I wouldn't need to cook tonight . . . and then I could fill her in at the same time as I told Grand-père and Oncle Rafe what had happened last night. The three of them, at least, would appreciate my brilliance.

Barely two minutes after Julia had clattered the telephone down on the other end, there was a knock on the front door. Accompanied by Oscar Wilde's wild barking, I hurried down, still a little flushed and wrinkled from my bath—but at least I was decently clothed.

I flung open the door, and there was Merveille.

"Oh." I stepped back in surprise. "It's you." I immediately

wanted to smack myself for the most inane comment. "*Inspecteur*, come in, if you please."

He gave me an understandably strange look. "You were perhaps expecting someone else?"

"Yes—Madame Child. Look, there she is, coming across the . . ."

But he had turned, and, seeing Julia carrying a large cardboard box, hurried out to help her.

Under the cacophony of Monsieur Wilde's crazed barking, the three of us met in the foyer. I took Merveille's coat and hat and went to hang them up.

"You go on upstairs," Julia said when I returned. "I have to put this in the oven for just another few minutes. I'll send up dishes in the dumbwaiter—you know I know where everything is, Tabs. Inspecteur, would you like to have some dinner as well? I'm certain you've been working very hard and some very long hours these past few days."

I rolled my eyes as Julia openly and brazenly put into practice the first two rules of her technique to manage a man: feed him and flatter him. I knew she wasn't planning to implement the third rule (fornicate with him) because she thought she was doing me a favor by leaving that one—or at least some form of it—to me.

"*Oui*, Madame Child. I would be most grateful."

My messieurs—as well as Oscar Wilde—greeted Merveille like an old friend. As soon as it was ascertained that the *inspecteur* was off duty, Oncle Rafe pressed a robust glass of Médoc into his hand and urged him to take a seat. Someone, probably Grandpère, took pity on us and gave the annoying, yip-yapping dog a tiny biscuit from the glass jar kept within reach of his chair.

I resisted the urge to check my hair in the mirror and bemoan my lack of makeup. It didn't matter a bit what I looked like. If Merveille was here, it was on business, and it shouldn't matter whether I was stylishly groomed or still flushed and wrinkled from an overly indulgent bath. At least I'd been liberal with the bubble bath, so I probably smelled like lily of the valley and lavender.

"What is it we are eating tonight, Madame Child?" asked Grand-père eagerly when Julia came up the stairs a few minutes later.

"It is cassoulet," she said. "It is getting warm again in the oven right now. Tabitha told me she had tried some the other day"—she studiously avoided my eyes and thank goodness her tone was innocent of innuendo—"and that put me in the mood to make it myself. Chef Bugnard had given me some *confit de canard*, which was a good start because duck in cassoulet is a *must* in my opinion. And so I began slaving *dans la cuisine* yesterday. It takes at least a day, sometimes two or three, to make a good cassoulet, you see," she said as I went over to the dumbwaiter to unload the dishes she'd stacked inside, "because the beans have to soak, and you *have* to let the pork shoulder roast until it's tender and swimming in its own juices. And then you're obliged to cook up some bacon to add to it, with *all* of the *gorgeous, sparkling* fat pooling on top of it. It's really quite magnificent! Cassoulet is really a peasant dish—ah, but you already know that," she said, blushing a little when she realized she was lecturing Frenchmen about French food, peasant-ish or not.

"Anyhow, having the duck confit already given to me was a *godsend*, so I soaked the beans last night and I've been cooking the pork shoulder and the sausage *all day*. And now . . . !"

"And so what brings you for such a visit, Inspecteur Merveille? And at dinnertime, too, *non*?" Grand-père's eyes twinkled.

Merveille actually winced, just a little. So he *was* human!

"Ah," said the *inspecteur*, "well, I have some information for Mademoiselle Knight, you see."

"Is it about the murders?" Julia demanded. "Tabitha, what happened last night at the oyster bar? Did you talk to Illouz?"

Everyone looked at me, including Merveille.

"Nothing really happened at the oyster bar," I said. "It was what happened before that." I waited for Merveille to take up the story, but he merely raised his brows at me as if to suggest I continue.

Great. How in the heck was I going to explain my brilliance to everyone with those cool gray eyes watching me? I gritted my teeth and thought, *Checkmate, Inspecteur.*

"Well," I said lightly, "I figured out who killed Madame Lannet and so I called the 36 to let Inspecteur Merveille know about it. He came and arrested the culprit last night."

"Well, *who was it?*" Julia demanded.

"Monsieur Block," I said, and my messieurs and Julia exploded with surprised protestations.

"*C'est vrai?*"

"But why?"

"The *shoemaker?*" This last was from Julia, who'd never met Monsieur Block but certainly knew about him and the break-in at his shop.

I explained quickly and succinctly, and, for Oncle Rafe's sake, tried not to dwell too much on the painful reasons Monsieur Block had felt compelled to attack Madame Lannet. "He admitted to it immediately. Almost immediately," I said, remembering the awl. But what my *grand-père* and *oncle*—not to mention the *inspecteur*—didn't know wouldn't hurt them. "I think he was . . . relieved that it was over. That someone had found out."

I glanced at Merveille and he gave a little nod. His eyes were not nearly as cool and remote as they usually were. I attributed that to the fact that he was contemplating the fact that he would soon be eating Julia's cooking.

"How ever did you figure that out?" Julia demanded. "Who in the world would have thought it was *him?* I never would have! I was going for the discarded or jealous lover theory!"

"I didn't even consider Monsieur Block until I was at Jean—I mean Monsieur Héroux's office to pick up the alley cat. I had been telling him about the metal thing I found at Maison Lannet after the killer ran away, and he thought he might know what it was." I described the tool and explained how it was used to cut spherical holes in fabric . . . or, which was when I'd had my epiphany, *leather.*

"I was waiting for Mathilde to get ready to leave for the oyster bar, and I was looking at a pair of shoes that laced up the front.

And when I saw the holes for the laces in the shoes, it all fell into place." I shrugged. "I don't know why, but it just made sense.

"And there were a few other things that added up—like the fact that there had been a break-in in his shop, but he didn't want to tell the police about it. That was because *he'd* staged the break-in and he didn't want them poking around asking questions. And so he pretended—well, I'm not sure if it was complete pretense," I said with a quick glance at Merveille, "that he didn't trust *les flics.*"

"And so the shoemaker that we were to be helping—he is a killer, two times over?" Grand-père said, lighting a cigarette. He didn't look utterly shocked or surprised by this development; just mildly curious. I suppose that sort of acceptance of strange and unexpected things comes with age and experience.

"No," I said, giving Merveille a pointed look. "He strangled Madame Lannet. He didn't kill Madame Pineau."

"*Oui*, mademoiselle," said Merveille. "And we have arrested Madame Outhier this morning, you see. I thought you would want to know this, and that is why I came here."

I caught myself before my mouth fell open. So he'd already known? "*Merci,*" I said.

But how had Merveille figured it out? He hadn't been there when Madame Outhier was ranting at me about her stupid husband and the traitorous Madame Lannet—and smoking Le Phénix Vie cigarettes! I had intended to tell Merveille all of that, hoping he'd come to the same conclusion I had.

"She, of course, attempted to deny it," Merveille said. He adjusted his suit coat and settled into the corner of the sofa with his wine. I tried not to think about how good he looked, as casual and relaxed as I'd ever seen him. "But there was blood on the sleeve of her coat, you see, and there is no good explanation for how it got there. And of course the cigarettes of the killer were the same brand. But it was Monsieur Outhier who unintentionally settled it, mademoiselle," he said.

"How?"

"I did tell you that Frédéric Outhier had an alibi for the night of Madame Lannet's murder, *non?* We had not established whether he had one for the second night, for at the time, I was working under the strong probability that there was only one killer, you see."

"Of course. Everyone assumed it was the same person. But I did wonder, a little . . . because the murders were so different," I mused. "One was done violently, face-to-face, with so much blood—the stabbing with the scissors.

"And the other . . . Monsieur Block even said he could not look at Madame Lannet while . . . while it was going on. He was not someone who enjoyed the violence, I think," I said, feeling the weight of everyone's gaze on me. "He was angry and he lashed out, but even in his rage, he kept himself distanced from what he was doing. And he was miserable and even regretful after. Madame Outhier . . . she was still seething, still angry. She seems like someone who didn't regret her actions at all."

"I think not," Merveille agreed.

"But, Inspecteur, what did Monsieur Outhier say or do that clinched it for you that *she* was the killer?" asked Julia. "And not her husband?"

"When we asked Monsieur Outhier about his alibi for the night of Rose-Marie Lannet's death, he had a good one that we confirmed. He and his wife were together at a dinner with many friends in Le Marais—so, they were far away from the location and with many witnesses. And so my agent, unfortunately, did not spend the time right away checking on the second night's alibi. It was only when I spoke to Madame Outhier and asked for her whereabouts on the second night that she suggested she was with her husband."

"But her husband had already told you something different, hadn't he?" I said. "And she hadn't had the chance to coordinate with him. She probably never thought anyone would suspect her, so why have an alibi prepared?"

Merveille gave me a tolerant look. "Yes, mademoiselle, it was something like that."

"But why would this woman do such a thing? Kill that other

poor, poor woman?" said Julia. "Madame Pineau seemed like a nice person—even though she did accuse Monsieur Dior."

I glanced at Merveille. He made a quiet gesture for me to proceed. He wanted to hear my thoughts, and I was ready to share them.

"When I spoke to Madame Outhier at Dior," I began, "my strongest impression of her was that she was an angry, seething sort of person. That she expected things to go her way, and when they didn't, woe betide the person who got in her way.

"Even during our short conversation, she didn't hide the fact that she was furious that Madame Lannet had been killed because she had an arrangement with Maison Lannet to get all of her clothing at the cost of material or even gratis—but it was still haute couture, so Madame Outhier would be well-dressed in expensive clothing that cost her a fraction of such clothing from any other couturier.

"This was due to a mutual arrangement where Madame Outhier and her husband kept Lannet's work as a collaborator secret in exchange for the clothing. And Monsieur Outhier had had his own dealings with the Germans, and he preferred to keep that quiet as well. This mutuality benefited Madame Lannet because with Outhier's support and sponsorship, she was able to establish herself as a peer of the likes of Dior and Fath and Balmain.

"But when Madame Lannet was killed, the dirt-cheap but beautifully designed wardrobe went up in smoke. Maison Lannet was no more and the clothing would never get made without the supervision of the couturier. Perhaps if the house had been established for longer, there would be assistant designers who could have taken over, and more experienced seamstresses . . . but in this case, Maison Lannet was too young and new. This was their very first collection. Nothing more would happen.

"Madame Outhier was furious about this, and angry with her husband for the mistake—even though it wasn't his fault—and simply angry over everything. But during her ranting, she said one thing that caught my attention. She said something like,

'Lannet is dead and the designs and clothing are gone with her. I tried to find' . . . and then she stopped herself suddenly and began to complain about her husband instead."

"She tried to find the designs?" said Oncle Rafe, leaning forward. His eyes gleamed with interest. "Is that what she was about to say?"

I nodded, beaming. "Yes, I think that's what she meant to say, but then she caught herself. She went to Maison Lannet on the night after Madame Lannet was killed. It was very likely the Outhiers would have a key, considering their unique arrangement. They might even have been paying the lease for the building. And there was no sign of a break-in that night, so whoever it was had to have access to the place, even after the police had come through and locked it up.

"Madame Pineau was found dead in the workshop . . . where the drawings of the designs would logically have been kept as the seamstresses worked on them. I suspect that Madame Outhier confronted Madame Pineau and demanded the designs be given to her. She probably thought she could take them somewhere else and have them made.

"But Gabrielle Pineau wasn't about to give them up. They were the work of her beloved Rose-Marie, and she wasn't going to surrender them to someone else. Especially someone like Madame Outhier, who clearly had no respect for someone like her. And so Madame Outhier lost her temper and lashed out at Madame Pineau—with a pair of scissors. She was angry because she wanted the designs, but she also knew she needed to silence Madame Pineau. After all, she knew the Outhiers' secrets as well, and with Madame Lannet gone, she had no reason to keep silent any longer. And so Madame Outhier had likely gone to Maison Lannet intending to kill Pineau, whether or not she got the designs."

During this speech, I was watching everyone, but I was mostly paying attention to Merveille's reaction. There was no sign of skepticism on his face. He seemed interested and attentive as he listened.

I took advantage of what I hoped was a receptive mood and said, "I would guess the designs were locked up somewhere, and wherever it was, was what that little key unlocked—the key that was taped beneath the desk. Madame Pineau had hidden away Lannet's designs in a safe or lockbox after the police finished their initial search, probably for that very reason."

An almost imperceptible nod was all Merveille gave me, but it was enough.

"And Monsieur Outhier went back the next night to look for the designs, likely under her urgings. Did he know what she had done, Inspecteur?"

Merveille shook his head. "*Non.* It has become clear during my conversations with him. He did not understand until it was too late when he realized he'd given an alibi for himself but one that exposed his wife. He said he'd been at a club with gentlemen friends . . . and he was. She of course was not with him, even though she claimed they were together."

I had said all I wanted to say, and I was feeling quite pleased with myself. I listened as Merveille answered a few more questions from Grand-père and Oncle Rafe about the details of Monsieur Block and his arrest. I hoped that Merveille was as affected by the shoemaker's story as I had been, but it was difficult to tell with him.

Oncle Rafe stood and refilled wineglasses, and I changed the subject and asked, "Did you decide on a color scheme and fabric pattern for the restaurant? When you came home today after meeting with Monsieur Grandpierre, you were actually speaking to each other. Did a miracle occur and you've made a decision?" I glanced at Merveille, who seemed intrigued, and I explained, "They are reopening Maison de Verre, and neither can agree with the other about how it should be decorated."

My messieurs exchanged looks and Oncle Rafe shrugged. "We have come to an agreement, I suppose. I have been given permission to oversee the choices for the restaurant, while your *grand-père* is to undertake a complete redecoration of the house, here. This house," he added for clarity, flashing an unhappy look at my grandfather.

"And the only reason *mon cher* Rafael agreed to that is because he does not think anyone will ever see the salon after I am finished with it," said Grand-père with far too much glee.

"But *I* will see it," Oncle Rafe said glumly. "I will have to see it and live in it, day after day. The flowers. The lace. The fuss. And in the bedchambers too." He gave a little shudder and Julia and I exchanged amused looks.

An absolutely *gorgeous* smell was beginning to waft up the stairs. My mouth began to water, and I glanced at Julia. "The cassoulet smells *divine*."

"Oh!" She popped up out of her seat. "I almost forgot about it. Monsieur Saint-Léger, could I impose upon you for some fresh sage and parsley from your greenhouse?"

"*Bien sûr*, Madame Child," he replied, and began to rise from his chair.

"I'll get it, Grand-père," I said quickly, but he flapped an imperious hand at me.

"*Non, non, ma mie*, I will do it. You do not know where to cut the herbs and it is better for me to tend to my *bèbès* than someone who does not have the green thumb." He was out of the chair and moving to the door that led to the little greenhouse built over the portico, as if to forestall any argument on my part.

"*Merci*, Monsieur Saint-Léger. Please take your time," Julia said as she started for the stairs, casting a quick glance at Oncle Rafe as she did so.

"Ah, now then," he said, also rising. "Monsieur Wilde, he needs to have the moment in the courtyard, too, I think. Come along now, *mon petit monstre*," he said, scooping up the little dog who'd sprung to full alert as everyone stood, quivering with interest in case there was to be food in the vicinity.

"I can take him, Oncle," I offered, but once again I was waved back into my chair.

"*Non, non, chérie*," he said. "Monsieur Wilde gets too distracted sometimes with the birds and the squirrels and forgets what he is about. It is best if I am there to watch him."

With a sinking feeling that I understood too well what was happening, I sank back into my chair and tried not to look mortified that my friend and housemates had just engineered a private tête-à-tête between me and Merveille. I hoped he, at least, had no idea what had just transpired.

"And how is *monsieur le chat de gouttière?*" asked Merveille as the door closed behind Grand-père's exit to his greenhouse. "As I do not observe any scratches, I must conclude he was safely delivered to the veterinarian."

"Oh, yes, and he has been fixed up very well by Monsieur Héroux," I said.

"Ah, I am glad to hear that. And where is he now?" He looked around the room. "But surely Madame X wouldn't allow an interloper in her house."

"She won't have to find out—at least in the near future. Monsieur le Chat has let himself out of the doctor's office and is back living on the streets and alleys. He seems to have no interest in becoming domesticated."

Merveille nodded gravely. "Then I suppose it is just as well you have not gone so far as to give him a name, mademoiselle."

"Ah, but I did," I replied, smiling. "I've given him the perfect name."

"You've given the gutter cat a name? What is it then, mademoiselle?" said Merveille.

"Lupin," I replied, and the corners of his eyes crinkled with appreciation as he nodded.

"Ah. The gentleman thief who lives in the darkest and most dangerous streets, but yet will help those in need. *Très bien*, mademoiselle, and *touché*."

"Not that it matters, since he has no interest in becoming domesticated," I said. "But at least he's been healed and his tail has been stitched up and tended to."

"*Oui, très bien*." He sipped his wine, then—just as I was trying to formulate something interesting to say—he went on. "It was very kind of you to treat Monsieur Block as you did, even considering the situation. And it was quite astute—your conclusions and deductions about both him and Madame Outhier. I presume the latter is what you wished to speak to me about. Of your suspicions of her."

"Yes," was all I could say.

"It seems your curiosity served you well in this case, at least," he went on, still sitting there so casually in the corner of the sofa. "However, I am confident the same conclusions would have been drawn by myself and the agents relative to Monsieur Block—especially as it became clear there were two killers ... but the fact that you were able to obtain information not readily available to ... eh ... *les flics*"—his tone was ironic—"ensured that it happened more expediently. That enabled us to put this matter to rest sooner rather than later."

I could hardly believe what I was hearing. Merveille was not only acknowledging my contribution, but also ... *thanking* me? "At least this time I didn't almost get killed," I said with a nervous laugh.

"Ah, yes, mademoiselle, that is indeed a good thing. If Monsieur Block had been a different sort of man, however, that might not have been the case." The gray of his eyes had frosted over again. Surely he didn't know about what happened with the awl. . . . "Please do not take my comments here as any sort of suggestion that you ought to continue interfering in murder investigations. You were lucky this time—"

"And the previous two times," I reminded him, feeling a little stung now that he seemed to be taking back his compliments of a minute ago.

"Those were even luckier events, when you *were* in danger from a murderous person," Merveille replied coolly. "Even the cat with the nine lives eventually runs out of them, mademoiselle."

I managed to keep my smile in place, although it cooled a little. "At least you acknowledge that I was able to get some information that was not forthcoming to you."

"Again, mademoiselle, I do not deny that. But hunting killers can be dangerous. I know that ... your *grand-père* would not want anything to happen to you."

Something fluttered in my belly at the way he said those words in his deep, rich, grave tone, those ocean-cool eyes on me, but I ignored it. Instead, I said, "Was I right about the designs being locked away with that little key taped beneath the desk?"

"*Oui*, mademoiselle. I am certain you must have other questions," he added with great sobriety.

I *almost* asked why the picture of Marguerite was missing from his desk, but stopped myself. I didn't want him to get any sort of idea that I cared about that . . . even if I did. And then I almost asked about what he'd done during the Occupation, but I squashed that topic as well. I still wasn't certain I wanted to know.

"No," I replied, and then I heaved a little sigh. "It's only that I feel . . . well, conflicted, I suppose, about Monsieur Block."

"What is this? You have developed the soft heart for a killer, have you, mademoiselle?" But his voice was mild, and I suspected perhaps he might too feel the same conflict.

"Monsieur Block is not a killer . . . not really. Not any more than a man is a killer when he is sent to war," I said, thinking of all of the young men I knew back home who were now killers . . . but who really *weren't*. "What happened—I mean, what he learned about would be enough to drive anyone mad. I can't imagine how it was with his wife during the war, with the Nazis here, and the police rounding up the Jews and never knowing when . . ." My voice trailed off as I remembered I was speaking to a policeman who might very well have been here during the Occupation. "And then finding out that a neighbor, a colleague, had actively worked with the Germans . . . I can sort of understand it. Do you think . . ." I glanced up and found his eyes dark and steady on me, and it made my stomach drop a little.

"Do I think they will go easy on him? The courts, the judge? The people of Paris?" he said. "That I do not know. He did, after all, take a life. With his own hands. And it did not, in the end, change anything, did it? What he did to Lannet? The horrors still happened, and we cannot deny them. They have affected us all. But . . . do I think they might take into account the full story, the reason for his actions? Perhaps. I think there is still a taste for the settling of the score with those who collaborated, and though we might wish to move on, it is still here." He touched his forehead, and then his chest, where his heart was. "For many."

Just then I heard the sounds of Grand-père coming back from the greenhouse and Oncle Rafe coming up the steps. The creaking of the dumbwaiter told me that Julia would be right behind him . . . almost as if the three of them had somehow coordinated their returns.

I didn't know how they might have done so, although I did know that the greenhouse on the portico overlooked the courtyard, where Oncle Rafe had taken Oscar Wilde. I sighed inwardly, glad that they were returning but annoyed that those machinations were probably just as obvious to the very observant Merveille as it was to me.

"And here we are," sang Julia, bounding up the stairs just as my messieurs were taking their seats—after refilling their drinks, of course. It was not lost on me that the herbs Grand-père had been supposed to gather from his garden had not been used on the cassoulet.

As if reading my mind, Grand-père said, "And here are your herbs, Madame Child."

"Oh, yes, thank you. I'll take them home with me—I need them for the veal *ballotine* I'm making," she said with an arch glance in my direction.

It didn't take long for each of us to be settled with a shallow bowl of rich, savory, dark cassoulet and a glass of red wine.

"It looks *magnifique*, Madame Child!" cried Grand-père as he sniffed his bowl. "What a treat, as usual, *non*, Rafe?"

"I'm only grateful you were willing to eat it right away," Julia said, settling into her seat now that the servings had been dished up.

I was just scooping up my second spoonful—it was *so delicious!*—when Merveille made a little sound meant to gather everyone's attention. "If you please, I must confess an error on my part," he said.

My heart gave a little lurch. Was he about to admit that I'd figured out something with the murders he hadn't?

"Ah, is it so?" said Oncle Rafe, hardly pausing from tasting his own stew.

"And what is it, then, Merveille?" said Grand-père, also uninterested in slowing down from enjoying his dinner.

"*Oui.* You see, I told Mademoiselle Knight the other evening that we were eating the best cassoulet in the city," Merveille said, holding up a spoon that had obviously been used. "But I was very wrong. *This*, Madame Child, is the best cassoulet in the city. *Merci beaucoup!*"

Julia laughed in delight. "And thank you too, Inspecteur Merveille. Now everyone, let's enjoy! Bon appétit!"

AUTHOR'S NOTE

I had the most delightful time writing and researching the third An American in Paris Mystery, immersing myself in the world of haute couture.

Sadly, I am not a French speaker, and although I have had resources who've helped me with some of the French and I've done my very best, any errors are most definitely my own. I must give a big shout-out to Marty Lewis for answering questions and helping me to keep any French errors to a minimum. Miriam Miller painstakingly reviewed the entire manuscript (warts and all!) and her feedback, corrections, and suggestions were *invaluable* and very on the mark.

I am also indebted to my friend, designer, and fashion academic Jennifer Smith of Donna Jason Designs, who reviewed my book for any errors that might cause the "fashion police" consternation.

Most of all, I'd like to thank the entire amazing team at Kensington Books for all the love and effort they've put behind the An American in Paris Mystery series.

On a daily basis, I am blown away by the attention to detail, the creativity, the enthusiasm, and the sheer energy that has been invested in these books. *Thank you* from the bottom of my heart, especially to my unflagging agent, Maura Kye-Casella, along with my brilliant and patient editor, Wendy McCurdy, and her on-top-of-everything assistant Sarah Selim. Larissa Ackerman, Matt Johnson, Vida Engstrand, and the entire publicity, marketing, and social media team are consistently hitting things out of the park. Big kudos to Susanna Gruninger and Jackie Dinas for subrights management for these and all of my titles at Kensington. You all blow my mind, and I'm very grateful to you for your support for this series. A heartfelt shout-out also to Seth Lerner, who has created three of the most stunning and appropriate covers (so far) for the Tabitha and Julia books. . . . I couldn't have imagined anything more perfect for them. Thank you.

I want to extend special gratitude to the Julia Child Foundation, and Todd Schulkin in particular, for their steadfast commitment to honoring Julia Child's legacy and advancing the culinary arts. I very much appreciate your collective work in all forms of media (television shows, museum exhibits, etc.) to that end, as well as the time you've taken to personally share your stories and knowledge of Julia with me.

I am additionally thankful for Kate Miller Spencer, Kate Leder, and Donna Yen from *Cherry Bombe* for embracing "The American in Paris Mysteries" and sharing the inaugural volume, *Mastering the Art of French Murder*, with your wonderful community.

I fully enjoyed my research for *A Fashionably French Murder*, and found it both fascinating and heartrending to learn about Christian Dior and his sister Catherine and their respective actions during the Occupation. In particular, I was blown away by Mademoiselle Dior's bravery and commitment to her cause. She is truly a hero and one I hope will gain even more recognition and respect—both through this book and the television series, *The New Look*.

Much of the details about what it was like being a mannequin for an haute couture atelier came from a self-published memoir called *Another Me* by Ann Montgomery. It was a gold mine of information and I devoured it. I found other interesting details in Christian Dior's autobiography, as well as numerous books about his fashion house and interior designers. The tidbit about the special formula for the signature Dior-gray was one of my favorites.

Dear Reader, thank you for picking up *A Fashionably French Murder*. I hope you enjoyed the read and perhaps learned something in the process.

I love to hear from readers and can be reached at my website, colleencambridge.com.

—Colleen Cambridge, May 2025